PROMISE ME

PROMISE ME

Barbie Bohrman

Montlake
Romance

Printed in the United States of America.

Published by Montlake Romance, Seattle
www.apub.com

ISBN-13: 9781477849576
ISBN-10: 1477849572
Library of Congress Catalog Number: 2013913098

To my beautiful daughter, Belinda.
You'll never be too old to chase your dreams…
…but you're still not old enough to
read this book.
I love you,
Mommy

PROLOGUE

It's him.

If you had told me it was him and I hadn't seen him with my own eyes, I would have called you a liar. Somewhere in the back of my mind, where I can barely process what is going on around me, I tell myself that I shouldn't be here watching this. I should walk away, or better yet, run as fast as I can, to nowhere in particular. But I don't. I stand there frozen in the shadows watching him through the window. Him.

He's my first love and my life . . . and he's kissing my best friend.

My anger is boiling just beneath the surface, making my skin feel like it's about to burst. My eyes probably look like they are going to fall out of my head at any moment. Yet I cannot stop staring as Chris and Lisa hold, caress, whisper, and kiss each other over and over as if each of their lives depend on it. Exactly the same way I'd felt when he did those things with me.

With each subtle change in their embrace, I remember the many times he has held me, touched me, loved me. . . . Memories flash in my head, like a catalog of moving pictures on a big screen: The first time he held my hand, our first kiss, the first time we made love just a few shorts weeks ago. Each memory feels like a stake through my heart, and then my body begins to tremble.

The overwhelming feelings of betrayal and heartbreak are building their way up to my throat, threatening to break the dam of emotions I'm just barely able to keep in check as it is. My eyes have closed of their own accord, and the tears slowly begin to fall. I vaguely remember that no one even knows that I'm at this party, so I decide to make a quick getaway in the hope that no one will notice I was here. I just want to go back home, crawl back into my bed, and sleep away what could only be described as a nightmare. Unfortunately, I know that when I wake up that won't be the case. I will never forget the scene playing out in front of me.

I take a few cautionary steps backward, away from the window and bump into something hard. I let out a loud gasp and instinctively cover my mouth to stifle any noise. I feel movement behind me and catch a glimpse of a hand as it is lightly placed on my right hip. I stare down at the mysterious hand and know at once who it belongs to. A tattoo peeks out from the pulled up sleeve of a white thermal shirt, twisting itself around the defined forearm of its owner. The black ink is in such stark contrast to the color of his shirt that for a second or two I'm lost in its intricate design. As I slowly begin to get my bearings and I'm able to say anything in protest, I sense movement again. I feel his breath on my left ear and his raspy voice whisper, "Be careful, Sabrina. You don't want them to know you've caught them."

I whimper when I hear this and look up again through the window as my boyfriend's hands begin to wander down my best friend's body, and what little control I had left is gone.

I start sobbing. The hand that was covering my mouth has dropped, and I automatically place it over my heart in the hopes that it will keep it from spilling out of my chest. Luckily, the music inside has been playing fairly loud and since I'm hiding on the side of the house in the dark, no one else can hear or see me while I cry uncontrollably.

"Don't cry," he says in my ear, "they're not worth it."

I freeze at his words. His hand rubs my hip slowly as if he's trying to calm a frightened animal, which keeps me from making any attempt to turn around and face him or to run away. With just his hand he keeps me locked in place, my back to his front.

"This isn't the first time. They've been doing this for a while," he says.

When these words escape his mouth, I'm left to wonder exactly just how long this has been going on. My mind is now working in overdrive, trying to quickly piece together every missed call and every late practice Chris may have claimed to have. Again, I try to run away. Using both hands now, he quickly pulls me back to him and holds me in a tight grip. Through tears, and after what seems like an eternity, I finally am able to speak.

"How long?" I ask him.

His body stiffens behind me and his hands are now clutching my hips to the point of discomfort.

"How long, Tyler," I plead, "please...tell me."

"A few months," he says simply.

"Why? How could they do this to me?"

He slowly turns me around to face him. I can barely make out his features under the soft glow of the full moon. I lift my head up to look at him, and I'm not sure what is behind his hard expression. His jaw is set tight, as if he's clenching his teeth, and his chocolate brown eyes lock with mine.

As he studies my face, I feel the intensity behind his gaze. His face is a mask of emotion that I cannot decipher since I'm too busy trying to keep my composure. I momentarily consider the fact that he might just be trying to be nice to me, which is at complete odds with his reputation. Tyler is particularly known in our high school and hometown as a "bad boy."

I've known Tyler almost my entire life, having been in the same classes since kindergarten, but we have never been friends. Right now, I'm confused by his demeanor and I take a couple of quick steps back. He doesn't let me go anywhere. Instead, he pulls me closer and puts his arms around me. At first, I'm hesitant, but I am no match for his strong arms. I reluctantly give in, letting him pull me even closer until my head is tucked firmly under his chin. I take in the scent of him while I try to calm down. I faintly register his hand rubbing small circles on my back, and I begin to feel the smallest sense of being safe in his embrace.

Even though I know rationally I should stay away from him, I am comforted by his touch and the warmth of his body all around me. He shifts me just so, and I find myself curled up in his side as he begins to walk forward with me still wrapped in his arms and away from the window where my heart has just been obliterated. He walks me back toward the street where lines of cars are tightly parked from all the partygoers. When we're standing in front of my car, I slip out of his arms and he looks at me intently for a split second until he speaks again. "Give me your keys," he says quietly but with enough authority so that there is not a doubt of whether I should consider it for a moment. I hand him the keys and he opens my door, carefully guiding me into the passenger seat. I watch him while he closes my door and walks around the front of the car. Without saying a word he slides in, starts the engine, and begins to drive. As I stare out the window, I can't help but think of what I had witnessed. The scene just repeats itself over and over in my head.

Just today I had told my boyfriend Chris that my parents weren't letting me go to the party, having been grounded for something that I can't even remember right now. He was disappointed, or at least I thought he was. But when Lisa sidled up to our conversation and joked that she would keep an eye on him for me, we all laughed, knowing full well that Lisa was more apt to get herself into some harmless trouble than Chris. Lisa walked away to her next class, but Chris stayed behind. He grabbed my hand and told me how sorry he was that I couldn't make it and that maybe he shouldn't go either. I instantly brushed the idea way, insisting that he go ahead and have fun.

After dinner, I had tried calling him but got his voicemail. Instead of leaving a message, I had decided to have some fun and be a little defiant. My heart raced as I'd impatiently waited in my bedroom for my parents to go to bed. I had never snuck out of my house before. It's not like I had to go to the party, but I couldn't get the disappointed look on Chris's face earlier in the day out of my head when he found out I wouldn't be able to go. So, at around 11 o'clock, I had tiptoed out of my room, down the hallway, until I reached the back door of the house. I was having second thoughts about sneaking out so late when I turned the handle to leave, but I quickly threw them aside as I'd thought of Chris being surprised and happy to see me.

Arriving at the party, I'd decided to go around the house and enter through the back door so that he wouldn't notice me right away. Walking along the side of the house, I had glanced to my left and looked through the windows. I'd seen plenty of people I knew dancing, drinking, and having a great time. As I'd approached the last window, I'd smiled when I looked up and saw Lisa's small frame being hoisted up by a guy until her legs were wrapped around his waist. It was then that I'd frozen with the realization that she was with Chris. They'd been locked in a passionate kiss, breaking away from each other for a second to get some air until they started right where they had left off. At first, I'd had a fleeting notion of confronting them. Then, as the initial shock and anger had settled into my thoughts, an immeasurable amount of hurt had rolled through me. The pain had kept me tethered to that spot by the window, forcing me to look on silently while my boyfriend had started tugging at my best friend's shirt. *My* best friend. I can't believe she could have done this to me, her "sister," as she would sometimes call me. I thought I knew her. Now, I'm sure I never did.

"He doesn't deserve you."

Tyler's voice is quiet, but loud enough to snap me out of my reverie. I look over in his direction to see him staring blankly at the road before him. My eyes trail down to his hands to see he is gripping the steering wheel tightly. His forearms are flexed and the veins are visible in the faint light of the dashboard.

I don't answer him, instead I return to staring out my window in a daze until my street comes into view. Before I can tell him where to park my car, he pulls it deftly into a space across the street from my house and kills the engine.

I can't move. I'm glued to my seat and staring at the floorboards. The silence is unsettling; making it worse is the fact that I can feel him staring at me. He turns slightly in his seat and from the corner of my eye I see his hand cautiously approaching my face. He places his hand lightly under my chin, slowly tilting it up and turning it toward him. Whatever thoughts he's having, he's hiding them behind his intense stare. I feel embarrassed, remembering that he has now seen me at my lowest. He senses that I'm about to turn away, so he holds me firmly by applying more pressure to my chin.

"He doesn't deserve you, Sabrina."

I gather up the courage to look straight in his eyes and tell him, "You keep saying that."

He hesitates before he answers me, but not before a sigh escapes his lips. "You're special. You're the most beautiful girl I've ever seen."

Did he just say that he thinks I'm beautiful? My expression must mirror the surprise I'm feeling because the corners of his mouth twitch slightly as if to stifle a grin.

My voice drops so low that I barely hear myself ask, "You think I'm beautiful?"

"Yeah, I do," he says just as quietly. "Not only are you beautiful, but you're really smart and too good to be with an asshole like Chris Lyons."

My brain is not absorbing what he just said. This night couldn't get any worse or crazier if I was in an episode of *The X-Files*. Tyler Anderson, probably the hottest and most dangerous guy in town, is telling me all of this on the same night I caught my best friend since grade school and boyfriend of three years going at it like there was no tomorrow.

"But you don't know me at all, Tyler," I tell him as I feel the tears break free again. And really, he doesn't. I've seen him here and there, but can't say that I know anything real about him other than what I've heard through the grapevine. He inclines slightly forward so that he's just a few inches from my face. He takes the opportunity to tenderly wipe away some of the tears that are trickling down my cheeks. I feel like a moth to a flame, drawn into his chocolate gaze, and I begin to mentally chastise myself for feeling nervous—the good kind—when I'm still reeling from the night's revelations.

"I know you and I see you," he whispers softly, "the real you."

He leans closer and I tense up thinking that he's going to kiss me. Instead, he unlatches my seatbelt and pushes up the manual lock on the passenger door. He pulls back, unlocks his door, and walks around the front of the car to open my door, holding out his hand to help me. He hands me my keys, but not before scanning my face as if he's looking for something specific. With a slight grin that causes his lips to curl up just enough to look ridiculously sexy, he says, "You're going to be fine, trust me."

Before I walk across the street to my house, it dawns on me that he drove my car here and that he has no way to get back to the party. "Tyler, let me give you a ride home, at least?"

He shakes his head and says, "No thanks."

In the back of my mind, I'm considering whether I actually want him to leave me at all. The thought terrifies and thrills me all at the same time.

"I'm walking. Don't worry about me, I'm good. Thanks anyway," his response comes out clipped as he shoves his hands into the pockets of his jeans.

"I feel terrible that you'll have to walk," I counter and try to maneuver around his large frame to make it to the driver's side of my car. He grabs me by the arm, pulling me close so that we are pressed together. His hand comes up to tuck a lock of my auburn hair that has fallen out of my pony tail behind my ear. He bends down to place a chaste kiss on my cheek, his face lingering a second or two longer than necessary before he pulls away for good.

"Go to bed, Sabrina," he says to me. "And promise me that tomorrow you'll dump his sorry ass, cut that bitch out of your life, and try to hold on as best you can until you're out of this shit-hole town in a couple of months."

I don't even know what to say to him. I still can't think clearly. My brain is in a haze of painful visions of Chris and Lisa all over each other, intermingled with Tyler being sweet and gentle and taking care of me.

"Promise me," he says in a slightly more demanding tone, but his voice still soft enough that I know he's sincere.

"I promise."

He nods, as if he's content with my response and turns to walk away from me. When I step off the curb to cross the street, I hesitate and call out to him. "Tyler!" He stops and turns around, but I can still see his face clearly. "Thank you…for everything."

He smiles at me one last time then turns around and walks into the night, disappearing completely from my sight.

CHAPTER ONE

The graduating class of 2001 invites you to our 10-year class reunion!
June 25th, 2011, Skippack Golf Club
Five-thirty for cocktails
Followed by dinner and dancing at six-thirty

The invitation arrived yesterday, and all I could think was, how the hell did they find out where I live? I mean, I don't really stay in touch with many people from my hometown except for my parents. I definitely wouldn't put it past them to give out my address in the hopes of getting me to come home for a visit, though. Being an only child, they make sure to check up on me at least twice a week, three times even, if I don't take the initiative to call them on my own at least one of those times. Every call is filled with the usual questions about my job, my life, and so on. They keep me up to date about what's going on back home. All the calls end the same way, wanting to know when I'll be coming back home for a visit. My answer? "We'll see."

"So, are you going?" My roommate and best friend Julia asks as she sits across from me at our kitchen table, about to pour an obscene amount of creamer into her coffee. Over the years, it never ceases to amaze me how much crap this girl can put in her body and still look like she belongs on a runway in Milan.

"Jesus, Julia," wondering at what point would be enough cream for her, "how about some coffee with that cream?"

Julia looks at me with big blue eyes from under her blonde veil of bangs, giving me the look she usually reserves for someone annoying the hell out of her. She puts down the creamer, leans forward, puts on a sickly sweet smile, and says, "Answer the question."

"Seriously, do I even have to answer that question?"

"Hell yes, you do!"

My non-answer is the answer, and she knows it. She knows I don't want to go back there and face the past. Even after all this time, it's hard to move on after heartbreak, especially when your best friend and your boyfriend hooked up behind your back. Adding insult to injury, they ended up getting married and are presently living happily ever after. Meanwhile, I ran away to college hoping to forget all about the embarrassment I went through, spending the first couple of years away from home as a recluse.

During my junior year at The University of Miami, I met Julia. She was funny and outgoing from the start. She showed me that I could again have a sincere connection with someone after my unfortunate situation with Lisa. She was my polar opposite, personality wise—and I loved it. She coaxed me into living my life a little bit more every day, and always has my best interests at heart. I like to think that our mutual adoration of *Felicity* and all things J.J. Abrams helped bring us closer together though. To this day, we have a standing appointment every few months for a *Felicity* "best of" marathon, which is always followed up spending an inordinate amount of time debating the age-old question: Ben or Noel?

It was Julia that convinced me to take the opportunity of a lifetime and enroll in an art history internship program in Florence, Italy, after graduating from college. Living there was beyond my wildest dreams. I pretty much lived and breathed art before then, but being in the epicenter of it all was invigorating. It gave me a sense of purpose and only helped to solidify my chosen career path. I stayed there for a couple of years until the internship ended and it was time to go back home to Miami and find a job.

It took awhile after what happened with Chris, but I did eventually start dating again. No one has ever really been special enough to last more than a few months though. There was one exception, a guy whom Julia dubbed "Romeo." We met while I was in Italy. He was an art student, like me, so it was easy to open up to him and eventually let him be just a little more to me than other guys had been. I'm sure that the romantic Italian backdrop surrounding us helped as well. However, staying in Italy for only an abbreviated time, we eventually stopped seeing each other right before I moved back to the States.

Upon my return stateside, I immediately moved in with Julia, much to the displeasure of my parents who thought I'd be returning to my hometown. They couldn't grasp that becoming a head curator for a famous art museum one day would never happen, living in a small town like Skippack, Pennsylvania. So, Miami it is, for now. We live in a cozy two-bedroom house in Coral Gables that Julia's parents bought for her as a gift right after college. Since she had plenty of room, it was kind of a no-brainer. We're just a few short blocks from the world-famous Venetian Pool, where Julia and I can be seen any weekend, lying by the pool, perfecting our tans.

Glancing back to the invite between us on the kitchen table, the memories start to flood my mind. Ugh, just the thought of the two of them, even all these years later, makes me uncomfortable. I'm hoping that Julia will drop the subject. Her glare tells me otherwise, so I take the easy out and stand up to replenish my coffee. She starts tapping her nails on her coffee mug like she's playing the piano. I can feel her eyes boring holes into the back of my head until I can't take it a second longer, so I turn around to face the music. "What?"

"You know what, Sabrina…come on, you know you've thought about it…about him," she says with a sly grin.

I have. I've often thought about Tyler Anderson over the years. I've wondered what happened to him and what he's doing with his life. My parents have never once mentioned his name in any of their calls and I don't dare ask, since I know it would only lead to more questions. They don't need to know that he took care of me the night I found Chris and Lisa together, or that I made him a promise. A promise that I've kept every day since I made it.

The very next day, I confronted them and moved on. I didn't have much of a social life after that, but it was by choice. I focused primarily on my last two months of high school, setting my sights on college and getting out of my hometown, trying my hardest to never look back. Over the years, that's been difficult to do. My parents never knew the full extent of Chris and Lisa's betrayal, so they tend to think it was my ambition to do well in my career and get to college with no attachments that drove them together. My mom never lets an opportunity go by to inform me just how well Chris is doing or how Lisa's the doting wife and mother to their two children. I'm probably imagining it, but every time my mom tells me these kinds of things I hear a perverse kind of glee in her voice, like she actually enjoys twisting the knife a bit more and reminding me how I made a mistake in choosing my career over Chris.

It's not worth fighting at this point. Instead, I let her ramble on for the obligatory five minutes, hoping she'll eventually stop. Apparently, the statutory limit on how much time can go by according to her standard has yet to come to fruition. The only bright spot in letting her wax poetic about them is the memory it brings me of Tyler.

Tyler Anderson was the town's rebel. He was always in some sort of trouble since we were in grade school. He wasn't a person that you casually said hello to; he either talked to you or you didn't exist. By the time we were in high school, all the girls would drool whenever his name was mentioned. Yes, he was that gorgeous. The quintessential tall, dark, and handsome type who would probably break your heart in a million pieces while making sure you had the time of your life in the process.

He was also my savior that horrible night years ago. He helped me when I needed it most and for that I'm forever grateful. But that sure as hell doesn't mean I would bite the bullet and go back home for our ten-year reunion just to satisfy my curiosity about him.

"Bringing up Tyler isn't helping your case, Julia," I tell her, but I can already see the wheels turning in her head. "I seriously regret ever telling you about him in the first place."

"Girl, I don't regret it. I've even fantasized about those...what did you call those eyes of his again? Oh right! Willy Wonka Chocolate River eyes."

I grab a dishtowel and throw it at Julia, who is doubled over laughing. She catches it easily and gets herself together before pleading her case. "Come on, Sabrina, I know you're dying to see him. What would it hurt? And please don't give me that 'I don't want to see Chris and what's-her-face' excuse. You have a couple of months to prep yourself mentally to see them. Get yourself together and get your ass back up there and show them that you don't give a damn about them...and then...throw in a little dirty, filthy, hot sex with your dream man while you're at it. Because girlie, you seriously need to get laid."

That last bit, she says as serious as a heart attack. Worst part about it is that I don't even have an answer. She's right. I do need to do something about my sex life—or I should say, lack thereof. I'm not a virgin and not a prude either. Cautious might be the better word to describe my self-imposed celibacy. I think after finally losing your virginity to your boyfriend of three years, then two weeks later finding out he's been cheating on you with your best friend would do a number on anyone. "Romeo" was my last sexual escapade, and that was a little over four years ago. It's not so much that I don't want to have a sexual relationship with a man; I just can't seem to muster enough trust in any potential candidate to take the relationship to the next level.

"Technically, they were more deep chocolate than Willy Wonka Chocolate River chocolate," I correct her, trying to keep a straight face. I can't stay mad at Julia for long. She's always been there for me when I needed a shoulder to cry on, and I know she means well. "I don't know, Julia, I need to really think about it. He probably won't even show up anyway. Tyler Anderson isn't the type of guy who would be into this kind of thing. It would be stupid to think he'll even be there. Plus, he could be married with kids by now."

Julia puts down her coffee mug and looks at me as if she's the cat who ate the canary. "From everything you've ever told me about him, he doesn't strike me as the marrying type. He's definitely still single and he'll be there. No doubt in my mind about that. I'd say he's probably been fantasizing about you for ten years. As a matter of fact, I'm willing to bet you the price of your airline ticket that he'll show up and make it more than worth your while."

"You're nuts, you know that, right," I tell her between sips of my ignored coffee that I might as well throw out. I turn slightly and toss out the dregs into the sink before I hop onto the countertop and take a seat. "And what makes you think he'll even remember me?"

Standing up from the kitchen table, she glides across to the sink, puts her coffee mug down, and turns around to face me while putting her hand on her right hip. *Uh-oh, I know this look. She's about to give me the business.* "This ought to be good," I mutter between a giggle at her stance.

"Pffft, that's simple. You said so yourself, he said you were the most beautiful girl he had ever seen and that he saw the 'real you'...this guy wanted you. He might have never said anything or shown even the slightest bit of interest before that one time he swept in like Prince Charming and saved the day. But Sabrina, trust me on this one, no guy goes around telling girls stuff like that unless they're into them. This guy was really into you and for whatever reason he never said jack shit to you before that night. This is your chance to do something about it."

I have to admit it, she's right. Who says things like that? God knows Chris never did when we were together. Sure, he said he loved me, blah, blah, blah, but he never said any of the things Tyler did that night. Things that to this day make my insides feel like mush and my knees go wobbly. The thought of him saying those things again or, better yet, doing things to me, makes me blush instantly. I turn my face to look down at the tiles on the floor while I fiddle with the hem of my tank top before I respond. "OK, so let's assume you're right about Tyler's feelings toward me back then. What if he doesn't show up to the reunion? I'll be stuck there having to deal with *them*."

"Not a problem," she says, "you'll be looking so hot that Chris will regret the day he ever decided to fuck you over with your best friend. As for that bitch, well, she'll be so jealous by the way Chris is looking at you that she'll be dying to get out of there quicker than she can say 'I'm a slut.'"

"Damn, Julia, remind me never to get on your bad side," I say as I eye her up and down like she's about to start kicking my ass in our own kitchen.

"Listen, it really sucks to have a guy cheat on you, trust me, I know, we've all been there. It's like some messed-up rite of passage into the Ya-Ya Sisterhood of the Traveling Pants. I get it. He's a piece of shit and deserves to have his dick shrivel up and fall off. But, there is a whole other level of bottom feeders, and that's where your girl Lisa is for what she did to you. There's definitely a special place in Hell for chicks like her." She backs away from the sink and starts walking backwards out of the kitchen. Hesitating for a moment, she freezes in mid-step as if she's just had an epiphany and says, "It's like *Fight Club*. The number one unspoken rule of best friends is that you don't steal your best friend's boyfriend right from under her nose."

After imparting that last piece of wisdom, she turns on her heel and struts out of the kitchen and down the hall until I hear her bedroom door close behind her. I turn my head just enough to catch a glimpse of the invitation still sitting on the kitchen table mocking me. Maybe she's right. Maybe I should go and get it over with, I think to myself.

"STOP THINKING ABOUT IT! JUST GO!" I hear her yell from her room.

My head snaps quickly to the hallway. "Fuck me," I say under my breath; she knows me too well.

As if on cue, she yells again, "AND STOP CURSING. IT DOESN'T SUIT YOU!"

Shaking my head, I jump off the counter and snatch up the invite, laughing to myself that Julia, of all people, is telling me that I shouldn't swear. She's right, I rarely do. So, when the occasion does present itself, she's the first person to point out that something major must be going on for me to bring out the "big guns," as she puts it.

Walking back to my room, I beeline to my closet. I open the door and look up toward the row of shelves on the back wall. On the top shelf is a box marked "old stuff." Shoving things aside, I grab the corner of the box and jerk it toward the edge of the shelf until I can easily manage to get a good grip on it and take it down.

I walk the box back to my bed and then plop down and stare at it for a second as if the contents might jump out at me like a jack-in-a-box. Finally, I open the lid to reveal what little items I kept from high school. At the very bottom of the box, I see what I'm looking for. I pull out the yearbook and start flipping through the pages until I get to the picture of Tyler. I remember as if it was yesterday how his strong arms felt around me. How it felt to have his breath fan my cheek as he pressed his lips against it and how he tenderly wiped my tears away. Clutching the yearbook to my chest, I fall back onto my pillows and close my eyes. I can picture him standing in front of me, pulling me into his arms and holding me so close that I don't know where I end and he begins. When my eyes flutter open, I pull the yearbook off my chest and spare one more glance at Tyler's picture. Julia's right. If I don't go, I'll always wonder about him and I'll regret it. I already do.

"Damn it," I gripe out loud, "I can't believe I'm actually going to do this."

Hastily, I sit up and close the yearbook with a loud clap then toss it back into the box. I grab my cell phone from my night stand and scroll through the recent calls until I see the number I'm looking for. Answering on the second ring, she says, "Good morning, sweetheart."

Before I can chicken out, I tell her what she has been waiting to hear from me for the past ten years. "So, looks like I'm coming home for a visit, Mom."

CHAPTER TWO

I love Miami. I love everything about it except one thing: the heat. It's ridiculously hot almost year round. Whenever my parents visit, they spend almost half the time complaining about it. Thank God it's late May, since I don't think I can handle the 99-degree days just yet. If it had been one of those days, I would be drowning in a pool of sweat during the ten-second walk from my front door to the car.

The one thing I do miss about my hometown, Skippack, which is about forty-five minutes outside of Philadelphia, are the winters. Even when we didn't get much snow, it still had that winter wonderland feel to it. Now, I have palm trees with Christmas lights to look forward to every year. It's a small price to pay for being able to go to the beach in the middle of January with all the other "snow-birds." I like to think that I'm making out on the deal.

I pull out of my parking spot and in a few short turns, I'm at my usual morning pit stop, Sergio's. Most people nowadays are Starbucks devotees. Not me. After the very first time I took a sip of what the locals here call *café con leche*, I've been drinking it ever since.

"Hola, Sabrina, the usual?" Maribel, the waitress behind the outside counter asks as I walk up to order.

I smile and put my sunglasses on top of my head, "Si, muchas gracias, Maribel." Thirty seconds later, she's handing me a to-go cup of heaven and rings me up.

"Have a good day," she says.

"Igualmente," I answer and start to make my way back to the parking lot.

"Your Spanish is getting better," I hear her say while opening my car door. You would think after living here for about eight years I would speak fluent Spanish by now. No such luck. I only know a few words and phrases, but they do come in handy. Before ducking back into my car, I say, "Gracias, Maribel. Te veo mañana."

I plug my iPhone into the audio jack in my car and command Siri to put my music on shuffle as I start my commute. I work at The Art Center on Lincoln Road in the heart of Miami Beach. I've been there for the past four years, at first as a receptionist and all-around gopher, slowly making my way up to gallery assistant about a year ago. After my internship in Italy I somehow managed my way into this place, and I'm probably one of the few people I know who loves her job. It's always been my dream to work somewhere like The Museum of Modern Art in New York City, but for now, I'm happy where I am and I love the people with whom I work.

In the distance I can make out the now familiar art deco building that is my home away from home. The white curved concrete is surrounded by large glass windows to allow a passerby slight glimpses inside. I purposely drive a little further from the front entrance of the gallery until I find a spot that is partially shaded by a palm tree. This is a must in Miami. If not, your car may go up in flames by the end of the day from the sun's glare.

Walking in the front door, I'm immediately greeted by Sarah, our receptionist. She's a 20-year-old stereotypically bubbly "Barbie" blonde, who, from the looks of it, has never experienced a bad hair day in her entire life.

"Good morning, Sabrina, how was your weekend?"

I can tell she's dying to tell me how hers was so I shrug my shoulders, smile and ask her the same question. "Oh my God, I met the hottest guy at that new club on Washington I told you about. We're meeting up after work tonight. I can't wait!" She proceeds to animatedly tell me all about this new guy, who, according to her, is more into her than her last guy, or even the guy before that one.

"Just be careful, Sarah," I tell her and start to head toward my office.

Before I can make it down the hall she calls me back, "I totally forgot to give you your messages. Your mom called a couple of times already this morning."

I look at the phone messages then up at Sarah. "Did she say something was wrong?"

She looks at me nervously and says, "No, but I guess she really wants to talk to you. Gosh, I hope everything's OK, Sabrina."

I roll my eyes and give her a tight smile, "I'm sure everything's fine. She probably just wants to go over my flight information for the millionth time."

I still can't believe Julia talked me into going to that damn reunion. As soon as I told my mom I was coming home for the event, she squealed so loudly on the phone I thought my ear drum would explode. Needless to say, almost every other day since then she's been calling to make sure I haven't changed my mind. I think I'm more afraid of what Julia would do to me at this point if I didn't go. She's been bringing it up pretty consistently since I bought the non-refundable airline ticket. Yes, non-refundable. That one was all her idea. She thought it would make it next to impossible for me to back out if I couldn't get a refund on my air fare. Although, according to her predictions, she'll be paying me for my ticket after I have "hot, dirty sex" with Tyler. Yeah, right.

Sitting down at my desk, I pick up the phone and start dialing. "Hi Mom," I say as soon as she picks up.

"Oh thank God. I've been trying to call you all morning."

"I know, I just got your messages. Why didn't you call me on my cell? Is everything OK?"

"Sweetie, everything's fine…but…" she trails off and I start thinking the worst.

"Mom, is Dad OK? You're freaking me out."

"No, no, no, don't be silly, your father is fine." She hesitates a moment then she takes a big breath before hitting me with the real reason she's been calling. "I ran into Lisa at the Village Shopping Center in town yesterday. She asked about you and brought up the reunion. I told you were coming and then she…she asked me for your phone number."

"Please, Mom, tell me that you didn't give it to her."

"Well, that's the other reason I'm calling you so early, I wanted to make sure I caught you before she called you so I can give you fair warning."

Through clenched teeth, I just barely get out, "Mom, I don't want to talk to her."

"I figured you'd say that, but I thought it would be a good idea to talk to her a bit now so that when you get here in a few weeks you'll have already cleared the air with her."

I don't even know how that conversation could possibly go well or how my mom would even think I'd be OK with her giving Lisa my phone number when she knows we aren't friends anymore. "Mom, I have to get back to work. I'll call you later in the week." "Please don't be mad at me, Sabrina. I did it for your own good. You need to make amends with Lisa. The sooner the better," she says, like I'm the one at fault for ruining our friendship. "Mom, I can't think about this right now. I've got to go. Love you, bye."

Putting the phone back on the receiver at my desk, my eyes veer to the left and see the calendar that shows a big red circle around "D-Day," June 25th, and I let out a breath that I didn't even know I was holding. Just a few weeks away now and I still don't have any clue of how I'm going to get through this. I need reinforcements so I pull my cell phone out of my purse and shoot a quick text to Julia.

Lunch? 12:30 ... Burger & Beer Joint?

A light knock on my door makes me pop my head up as if I've been caught sleeping in class. My boss, and owner of the gallery, Alex Holt, is leaning in the doorframe with his arms crossed over his chest, smiling at me.

To say Alex is good looking would be putting it mildly. He is beautiful. I take a quick inventory of him today and he doesn't disappoint. His dirty blonde hair is just a tad too long but tamed with some hair product that probably cost him a fortune. He's wearing a top-of-the-line black suit, tailored in all the right places, and a crisp white button-down shirt. He's forgone the tie today, so the top button is undone, allowing me to catch the tiniest hint of his perfectly tanned skin. His sky-blue eyes are dancing with mischief when he makes his way into my office to take a seat across from me.

"Good morning, Sabrina," he says as I hear my phone vibrate on my desk. "Do you need to answer that?"

"Um, no, it can wait," I say sheepishly.

This man makes me nervous. He bought the gallery a couple of years ago and has always made me feel like a complete jackass. Not because I don't know my job or what I'm doing; it's more the sexual vibe that oozes off of him everywhere he goes. Sometimes, I could swear that he's flirting, but I promptly toss out the thought since that would be ridiculous. I mean, he is my boss, right?

"OK, well, I just wanted us to go over some of the details of that new exhibit you've been working on," he pauses a second to unbutton his suit jacket, crosses his legs and slowly leans back in the chair.

"Well, everything seems to be in place. The final artist has signed on and has agreed to show at least five to six pieces," I say while reaching for the nearest thing I can get my hands on from my desk to grab. I find that if I have something in my hands keeping me busy, my mind will keep from straying to impure thoughts.

"Great," he says as his eyes are now focusing on the pen that I'm currently bobbing back and forth in between my fingers.

"Yes, I'm really excited about it," feeling more confident all of a sudden, thanks to a pen? Seriously, what the hell? "I think we really needed some balance in the exhibit and this artist's work really provides that. He'll be in later today to discuss it further." I hesitate a moment before asking my next question. "Would you like to be in on the meeting?"

"No need, I trust you," he says then stands up and winks at me before leaving my office. My phone buzzes again, breaking me out of my thoughts of Alex and all his gorgeousness.

You had me at burger... see you at 12:30.

Smiling now and a bit more at ease, I turn on my computer and spend the remainder of my morning going through emails, dealing with potential sponsors for the gallery's upcoming exhibit, and trying to complete as much work as humanly possible so I can make it to lunch on time.

As twelve o'clock approaches, I'm on my way out the door when Alex catches up to me. "In a hurry?" he asks smiling down at me.

I can't form a coherent response since the cologne and general "Alex" scent is flooding my senses. It's a mixture of sandalwood and the beach. Just lovely, perfect really. *He's my boss, he's my boss, he's my boss,* is the mantra on repeat in my head.

"Not really," trying to sound as casual as possible. "Just wanted to beat the lunchtime traffic. I'm meeting my friend for lunch."

"Julia?" he asks while trying to not look as if he's hiding his amusement at my obvious discomfort. While I nod in the affirmative, he steps back and puts his hands in his pant pockets. "I was hoping to take you out to lunch today," he pauses before adding, "to discuss some work-related matters. But seeing as you already have plans, maybe tomorrow."

"Sounds good, it's a date then."

Why on God's good green earth did that just come out of my mouth? Chuckling at my verbal slip-up, Alex takes his hands out of his pockets and props the front door open for me. As I go to pass him and take my first couple of steps out the door, I could swear I hear him say, "Not yet," under his breath. My head couldn't have snapped back quicker if I tried, but the door was already swinging closed behind me. Repeating the *he's my boss* mantra about another hundred times in my head, I get into my car and set out for lunch.

CHAPTER THREE

"So let me get this straight," Julia says while she reaches over to grab a French fry that is slathered in chili and cheese. "Since you left the house this morning, your mom called to give you shit about Lisa, or the whore, whichever works for you. And for the record, I prefer 'the whore.' Anyway, the aforementioned whore has your phone number now, thanks to your mom. And finally, for the trifecta, Alex, your crazy-hot boss, wants to get into your pants."

"Actually, all of it except the Alex wanting to get into my pants part is right."

Almost choking on her food, she takes a quick sip of her diet soda before saying, "He so does want to get into your pants." I shake my head and tell her she's bonkers before she starts to break all the facts down as if she was Nancy Drew.

"Number one, he winked at you. I've seen you two at gallery events before and have caught him once or twice winking at you. Now, you could chalk that up to harmless flirting, but with the way that guy looks at you as if you were his next meal, not even a possibility. Two, he asked you to lunch. You can argue that he's your boss and it's normal to do that sort of thing. But you have never, ever gone out to lunch, just the two of you, to discuss anything. There's always been a buffer present. That tells me he wants you all to himself. Finally, number three, he's hot and you're hot, and everyone knows that hot attracts hot."

She's quite proud of herself, going back to her chili cheese fries and sliders as if she's just solved the world's greatest mystery. I, for one, am not sold. There is no way that my boss could be interested in me in anything other than a working relationship. As if she can read my mind, she says in between bites of her slider, "Please don't make me repeat all of that."

"What are you talking about?" I ask.

"The whole Alex thing. You're not blind, right?" I must look hopelessly lost since she sighs at my confusion and says, "Sabrina, you're super hot."

I've been told I'm good looking, beautiful even, and not to toot my own horn, I do know that I'm not hard on the eyes, but hot? Correction...super hot? I don't think so.

"Seriously," pausing for emphasis, "have you looked in the mirror today? All you need is a pair of glasses and you'd be every 15-year-old boy's wet dream. You look like that chick in the 'Hot for Teacher' video, except for the hair color."

I look down at myself, a bit uncomfortable now thanks to Julia's vivid description of 15-year-old boys masturbating. I'm wearing a black pencil skirt that reaches just above my knee with a capped sleeve, white pin-tuck shirt that is tucked and kept in place with a black patent leather belt. My toes are slightly peeking out of my favorite matching black patent leather pumps. I've never been a big jewelry person, so I've decided for the bare minimum today, diamond studs, a gift from my parents after graduating from high school. My auburn hair is in a low pony tail at the nape of my neck with side swept bangs. "Are you kidding me? And by the way, thanks so much for the mental image, I've lost my appetite now."

"Nope, and that right there is yet another reason I'm sure Alex is dying to get into your pants. He knows that you have no idea how hot you are. It's a turn on for a guy like him. A conquest, if you will," she says between sips. "Look at yourself, for crying out loud, with those curves, that hair, and your green eyes. I've said it before and I'll say it again, your mom must have fucked a gypsy to get you."

This rant is annoyingly familiar. Julia swears that I'm of gypsy blood. I've tried countless times to explain how I take after my mother's side of the family, which is mostly of Greek origin, but she likes to tease me about my "gypsy" blood, convinced that either, a) I was left on my parents doorstep by a group of gypsies, or b) my mother bedded an actual gypsy to conceive me. Instead of encouraging her any further on this issue, which would undoubtedly lead to her singing a few bars of "Gypsies, Tramps, and Thieves," I just roll my eyes and change the subject.

"Enough with the Alex talk; there are more pressing matters at hand. Case in point: Lisa. What should I say if she actually calls me?"

"Yeah, that kind of sucks that she got the jump on you," she says as she wipes her mouth with her napkin and then proceeds to throw it on top of her plate. She signals to the waiter for the check before continuing.

"You have two options. One, you can talk to her and find out once and for all why she did what she did and then tell her off. Or two, you don't answer her and just show up at the reunion, where obviously she's going to want to talk to you, and then you can tell her off in person."

If I decide to answer her call, she's going to want to rehash the past and explain everything. If I don't answer her call, then I'm going to be forced to deal with her at the reunion with a lot of witnesses. I'm not big on confrontation, so I'm not exactly fond of either option. The last time I had a confrontation was with the dry cleaner, and that ended up with me paying for the bill even though they shrunk my favorite pair of black slacks. Julia thinks I'm a pushover, but I think it's just easier to move on and forget about it.

"How about I just cross that bridge, when and if she actually calls me?"

"Whatever, it's your reunion, not mine," she says and hands the waiter her credit card. After signing the receipt, she walks me to my car parked on the street before walking back to her office just a few doors down from the restaurant.

Julia runs a small event planning company that was previously managed by her father. Since his retirement a couple of years ago, he handed over the reins to his only daughter, only to see the company flourish under her leadership. She's really good at what she does and it shows. Her clientele list is growing, and her events have been heralded in the local paper. She's also been spotlighted on one of the local TV stations as an up-and-coming "Miamian to watch." I've actually been able to get Alex to use her services to promote exhibits at the gallery a few times, including the latest one we are working on.

Returning to the gallery, the rest of my day is pretty uneventful. I meet with the new artist for the next exhibit and finish up some other miscellaneous tasks. After lunch

I had turned off my cell phone just in case Lisa decided to call me. Pulling the phone out of my purse, I turn it back on and notice the time, almost six-thirty; more important, there are no messages. Turning off my monitor, I throw the phone back into my purse and grab my keys. I walk out my office door and right into Alex, knocking my purse to the floor and spilling its contents every which way.

"Oh my God, I'm so sorry. I didn't see you there."

"Not your fault. I was just checking to see if you were still here, actually," he says as he bends down to retrieve my belongings.

"You don't have to do that," I say then bend down to start picking up items and chuck them back into my purse as quickly as possible. I look up at him when he hands me the last item, of all things, a tampon. I'm beyond mortified. If the ground could possibly open up at this moment and swallow me, I'd welcome it. I yank it out of his hand and shove it in my purse as if it were a stick of dynamite. Standing up, I try to smooth out the wrinkles in my skirt with my hands while I tell him good night and walk around him.

"Sabrina, wait. I was just coming by to see if you'd like to have a drink with me tonight?"

This is where Julia would come in handy. Her overabundance of confidence would help in this kind of situation. I, on the other hand, am a bumbling idiot. "A drink?" God, if she was here she'd probably smack me on the back of the head. As if it had a mind of its own, my hand dives into my purse and grabs my keys to keep them occupied.

"Yes, a drink. Turns out I'm going to be out on a business matter all day tomorrow, so I was hoping to discuss some things with you now," he says and his eyes pick up on the keys I'm nervously twirling around my finger. When he looks back up at me he smiles, then points in the direction of the gallery's front door. "Shall we?"

We walk out the front doors of the gallery, and while he's locking up, his phone begins to vibrate. Excusing himself for a moment to answer the call, I take the opportunity to text Julia.

Going for a drink with Alex. See u later.

If there was a world speed record for return texts, Julia broke it.

Hells yeah!

I shake my head, giggling at her response, and put my cell phone back into my purse just as Alex reaches me. "Is everything OK?" he asks.

"Oh, yeah, I just wanted to let Julia know that I'd be later than usual getting home." Satisfied with my response, he leads us toward the bar a couple of doors down from the gallery.

Rio Station is one of my favorite after-work spots. Formerly known as Zeke's, it's most popular for its beer menu. From the most exotic to the most common brands, it's guaranteed to be there. Aside from the few tourists that frequent the place, it still has that "regulars" kind of feel to it. For being located in one of the trendiest areas in South Beach, the inside is more simple than most. With its plain old long oak bar and weathered bar stools, to the few flat screen televisions, it's definitely cozier than the usual fare around here. A few of us from the gallery end up going there every couple of weeks to people watch while seated on the outdoor patio because you never know who or what you might see. As we make our way through the crowd seated outside, Alex puts his hand lightly on the small of my back to lead me inside. It's not like he's never done this before but for some reason, tonight…it feels different. If I'm being honest with myself, I don't know if I like it or not. Before I can begin psychoanalyzing the hell out of it, he pulls his hand away and motions toward the bar. Grabbing two seats at the far end, I notice that the jukebox is playing one of my favorite bands.

"Do you like Pink Floyd?" I ask him while he's trying to get the bartender's attention. "I do," he answers without looking at me. When the bartender finally reaches our end of the bar, he orders me a glass of pinot grigio and a foreign beer that I've never heard of for himself.

"How did you know that's what I wanted to drink?"

He turns slightly in his chair, locking eyes with me. "I pay attention."

Holy shit! With just that one little statement, I'm starting to question if this was a good idea to begin with. I am so out of my league here it's not even funny. The jukebox is ironically playing "Comfortably Numb," perfectly capturing how I feel at this moment since I can't come up with anything to say back to him.

"So tell me about this new artist who's signed on for the exhibit," he says when our drinks arrive. I take a sip of my wine and proceed to tell him about the meeting I had with the artist earlier in the day. He makes comments every so often, but for the most part he lets me talk and seems genuinely interested in what I have to say. Just as I'm finishing up my glass of wine, he's already motioning for the bartender again. I hear my cell phone vibrate in my purse and his one eyebrow rises in amusement.

"Julia checking up on you again?" I laugh at his comment, digging my cell phone out of my purse, knowing he's probably right. Instead, I freeze when I see a phone number I'm not familiar with one with the 610 area code of my hometown.

"Sabrina, are you OK? You look like you've seen a ghost," he says. My mind scrambles through a variety of ways to tackle this. I can answer the call and just get it over with. The thought of talking to Lisa here, right now, doesn't particularly appeal to me. Like, at all. I can excuse myself, but that idea doesn't win me over either. Somehow I know I'm just not ready to deal with her. Especially here with Alex just a few inches away from me. Whatever happens during this call will undoubtedly affect me. I mean, ten years is a long time not to talk to the very person who betrayed you without a second thought. As I decide to ignore the call for now and strategize my next move, my phone stops ringing. A few seconds later it vibrates again, alerting me to a new voicemail.

"Sabrina?"

"Yes," I say with an obvious shakiness in my voice and turn to face him, "I'm fine, just…I should really be going home." I stand up and go to grab my purse. "Thank you for the drink."

He takes my hand, effectively stopping me in my tracks and says, "You don't look alright to me and I'll be damned if I'm going to let you leave me like this. Please just sit and tell me what that was about." He motions to the now empty bar stool next to him and lets go of my hand. Nervously, I take my seat again and instinctively grab my glass of wine for some liquid courage. Finishing its contents, I put the glass back down on the bar. It didn't help. I'm still in a tailspin over the call and whatever it is she may have left for me to hear. Glancing to my left I see Alex in rapt attention, waiting for me to continue.

"Do you need more," he says pointing to the empty glass in front of me.

"Yes, no, I mean no. No, I don't. I'm really OK, Alex. I'll be fine," I say, slightly flustered now since he's already alerting the bartender for another round.

Before I can say another word, the bartender puts another glass of wine in front of me. Alex takes a sip of his beer, all the while keeping his eyes on me. It's really disconcerting at this point; he is my boss, why would he want to know so much about me? Unless, of course, Julia is right and there is more to his flirting than I had previously given credit. Either way, I can't tell him about this. He'll think I'm certifiable. I need to put an end to this right now before the alcohol gives me the mental green light.

"I'd really rather not get into it right now," I say to him. "I appreciate your concern, I really do, but I'll be fine."

"Sabrina," he pauses, putting his bottle on the bar and turning completely around in his seat to face me again, "you've worked for me for the past two years, right?" I nod, trying to avert his eyes, but he doesn't let me. He takes my hand again and squeezes it softly. "I know I'm your boss, but I hope that I'm not being too forward by saying that I'm really interested in knowing more about you."

My stomach is in knots. Scratch that. I feel like a twisted-up pretzel in a contortionist's dream. My pulse is racing and my mouth has dropped open. With his free hand, he taps lightly once on my chin, forcing me to close my mouth as his lips curl up in a smile.

"Alex, I'm flattered, but...."

I let go of his hand and try to regain my composure. I push my seat away from the bar and abruptly stand up to leave. "Good night, and thank you for the drink."

I'm suffocating; I need to get out of here as quickly as possible. Rushing through the people in the bar, I'm also hoping he doesn't follow me. The panic flowing through my veins is at an all-time high as a couple of people step aside and I see the front door like a beacon ahead of me. The air outside hits my lungs, and I'm finally able to breathe. Taking in quick breaths of the salty air around me, I look right, then left before setting off down the block toward my car. If I'm being honest with myself, I'm not sure whether it was Lisa's phone call or Alex's disclosure that has me reeling. Once I'm sitting in my car, I pull my cell phone out of my purse and stare at it as if it's going to explode in my hands. I can't bring myself to listen to the message just yet. Throwing it carelessly on my passenger seat, I start my car and head home.

Walking through the front door, I see a pajama-clad Julia sprawled out on the couch with her feet propped up on the coffee table, watching a rerun of *Seinfeld*. In a flash, she reaches for the remote, shuts off the television and says, "Tell me everything. I mean it, Sabrina. I want to hear everything about your date with Sawyer."

Quizzically, I look up at her as I'm flinging my purse to the ground and plunk down beside her on the couch. "Sawyer? What exactly have you been doing while I've been gone? You're really starting to worry me, Julia."

"Hardy har har," she says through a fake smile. "I just realized tonight who Alex looks like. He totally could be

Sawyer's twin from *Lost*. Now, tell me how he called you Freckles and how he wants to take you to an island somewhere to live and have lots and lots of sex."

"Ha! If only that was what actually happened," I say to her while I shake my head and take a moment to pull my hair out of its clip so it falls just below my shoulders. Putting my feet on the coffee table, mimicking Julia's position, I give her the blow by blow.

"Lisa called while I was at the bar with him." Holding up my hand to keep her from interrupting me, I keep right on talking. "No, I didn't answer. She left me a voicemail that I still haven't listened to. Then, I had what can only be described as a mini-freak-out in front of Alex, who proceeded to tell me that he's definitely interested in me being more than his employee. My panic drove me to abandon him at the bar. I literally ran off and hid in my car before driving myself home."

For the first time in all the time I've known Julia, she's speechless. "Give me a minute to process this," she says as she takes her feet off the coffee table and begins rubbing the heels of her hands on her eyes.

"OK," she says when she pulls her hands away from her face, "first, let me just say, I told you so about Alex. Now that we know for sure he definitely wants in your pants, what are you going to do about it?"

Thinking over the night's events and everything that has led me to this point in my life, I already know my answer. As much as I am obviously attracted to Alex, I can't put aside the fact that he is my boss, and mixing business with pleasure is not something that I'm interested in pursuing. It kind of sucks. I can tell he's actually a good guy.

"Nothing," I respond to Julia.

"Are you fucking kidding me? Please tell me you're joking." She picks up her left hand to count off all the reasons I've lost my mind. "One, he's hot. Two, he's successful. Three, he's smart. And four, he's hot."

Before I can say anything in my defense, she beats me to the punch, "I know I said he's hot twice, but it most definitely bears repeating."

Feeling defeated, I bring my knees up from the coffee table and encircle my arms around them. I don't know how to tell her that I'm putting all my hopes in a basket with a big bow on it called "Tyler." His memory alone, I think, has ruined me for other men. Every time someone has ever been potentially interested in me, something always keeps me from giving in completely. It wasn't until tonight—when my past and present collided at the bar—I realized it's because of him.

Just above a whisper, I say, "It's because of Tyler."

"What do you mean, 'it's because of Tyler'?"

"I don't know how to say it without sounding like I'm crazy, Julia. I need to go home in a few weeks and see him. I need it so much that it scares me to death."

The great thing about Julia is that she knows exactly how to deal with my brand of crazy. She sweetly takes the hair that has fallen in front of my face and sweeps it over my shoulder and says, "Sabrina, what if he doesn't show up? I know, I know, trust me, no one wants him to show up more than me. But, what if he doesn't?"

"Honestly, as much as I'm hoping he'll be there too, I know that I need to deal with all of my past, not just him."

She smiles, sweeping me up in a big hug before she says, "I know you do, sweetie, and I'm so proud of you for having the guts to go through with it. I know having to see them again is not going to be easy for you. Speaking of which, let's listen to the voicemail that whore left you."

I nod nervously and retrieve my phone from my purse. I slide the "unlock" feature and bring up my voicemail. Before I press play, I hand the phone over to Julia. "You do it."

"With pleasure," she says eagerly. We're both now huddled together listening to Lisa's voice, which after ten years, still makes me shudder.

"Sabrina, it's Lisa. I heard from your mom that you're coming to the reunion. What I want to know is why? What could you possibly gain by showing your face around here? I doubt you'll call me back, so I just hope you get this message loud and clear... nobody wants you here!"

It's so quiet that you could hear a pin drop. We're staring at each other, and then staring at the phone until Julia can't take it anymore, "Oh, it's on like Donkey Kong! That bitch is going down!"

CHAPTER FOUR

It's been about three weeks since my "date" with Alex. Being the gentleman that he is, he has since apologized for coming on too strong. Thankfully, he's hasn't brought up that night again and our working relationship has not suffered. Lisa has not called me again, nor have I made any attempt to call her back. My mother, on the other hand, has moved on to what Julia calls Defcon Level 5. My mom has been calling me every day for the past week, since my flight is scheduled to leave in a couple of days. She's asked if Lisa ever called me, but I've decided to keep that tidbit of information to myself.

That call changed something in me. Ever since I heard her voice, all these years later, I've been feeling surprisingly resolved to confront my past. I've had little time to dwell on it since I've been quite busy working on the latest exhibit for the gallery. The opening is tonight, and the theme perfectly ties in with how I've been feeling: Hope. For the first time in a long time, I have the overwhelming feeling of hope that whatever comes my way, I'll get through it. I've even come to terms with my mini-obsession with Tyler. Whether or not I see him—and yes, I'm still hoping for the latter—I know I'll be alright.

Putting the finishing touches on my outfit for the opening, I take a quick perusal of myself in my dressing mirror. Plum, stretchy, just above the knee dress with kimono sleeves. The right sleeve is a little longer, so it hangs off my shoulder to show just the right amount of skin. I've worn my hair in a low, side-swept ponytail, matched with my silver chandelier earrings. Slipping on my black strappy heels, I hear Julia in the other room yelling at some poor soul from her staff. From what I can make out, someone did not get the caterers the memo that they were supposed to be at the gallery at least two hours before the opening. I cringe at every obscenity that flies out of her mouth. I have no idea how anyone in their right mind would want to work for her. Shaking my head, I turn the corner into our living room, catching her as she's flipping her phone shut and I get my first full look at her ensemble for the night. Wow. Her eyebrows rise up and she looks down at herself before she asks, "What? Is there something on my face?"

Her black, sleeveless, fit-and-flare cocktail dress is cut slightly higher on the thigh, showcasing her beautifully long, toned, and tanned legs.

"You look incredible."

"Thanks, sweetie, you don't look so bad yourself," she says, winking at me. "You ready?"

"Yep, I'll follow you in my car," I tell her and then head out the front door.

Arriving at the gallery a short while later, it's a whirlwind of commotion. Catering crew, event staff, and my co-workers are bustling in every direction. Sarah grabs me as soon as I walk in to tell me that the caterers arrived late, to which

I laugh out loud since I know they must have gotten an earful already from Julia or from someone in her staff. From the corner of my eye, I see Julia talking to Alex, probably about the same exact issue. Darting through several bodies dressed in white tuxedo shirts and black slacks, I take a last walk through of all the pieces that I selected for the exhibit. This is my favorite part of an opening—being able to see all the pieces in the right lighting before the guests arrive and I'm too busy to get a quiet moment to appreciate them for myself.

When I reach the last painting, which is furthest away from the hustle and bustle that is currently going on within the gallery, I hear footsteps approaching me from behind.

"You've done an amazing job, Sabrina…as usual, of course."

I keep my back to him, staring at the painting in front of me for a moment longer. "Thank you, Alex."

Finally turning around to face him, I find myself still in awe of how handsome he is. The man is simply breathtaking. Smiling now, he comes up a bit closer to me and asks, "You're going on vacation in a couple of days, yes?"

"Yes, I am."

"Well, I hope you have a good time, wherever you're going," he says and inches even closer to me. Putting my hands up to keep some space between us, they come in contact with his stomach, and *oh my God*, he must be carved out of stone.

"Alex, I thought I made it clear that I'm not interested in—" I'm cut off when he bends down and lightly presses his lips against mine. I'm too startled to move. Suddenly, his hands cup my face as he gently coaxes my lips open until

I'm kissing him back on my own. My hands, that were trying to keep him at a safe distance, are now around his waist, holding him close to me. Coming to my senses, I break off the kiss. I'm sure my cheeks are flush with not only embarrassment, but desire too. He's looking at me until he breaks the uncomfortable silence between us. "Sabrina, you can't tell me that you don't feel something between us."

"Alex, I can't."

Pulling his hands reluctantly away from my face, he backs up a step before saying, "You're seeing someone else, aren't you? I didn't think so at first, but from the look on your face, I'm thinking I might be right."

I can't answer him because how can I possibly begin to explain that there technically isn't someone else, as much as the *idea* of someone else. Before I can attempt to talk my way out of this, Sarah calls out for me from the other side of the gallery. Stepping aside to try to move around him, he grabs my hand and says, "I hope he knows how special you are," then lets me go and stalks away.

The rest of the night goes by rather quickly. The showcased artists speak with prospective buyers, while I spend my time between guests and the event staff. I keep my distance from Alex but I catch him staring at me at one point and quickly avert my eyes. I see Julia a couple of times, but neither of us have any time to stop and talk. Quite a few pieces sell, and from all indications, the event is a success. As the evening draws to a close, all that's left are some of Julia's staff, a few co-workers, and Alex. I finally get Julia cornered long enough to tell her most of what happened with him earlier.

"You're killing me."

"How exactly am I killing you?" I ask her, throwing my hands up in the air in defeat.

"Look at him over there, Sabrina."

We both turn to look over in Alex's direction as nonchalantly as possible without attracting attention to ourselves. He's in a deep conversation with Sarah, who is busily taking notes without having to look up at him.

"Are you sure you want to pass that up? Maybe you can just take him for a test drive," she says and licks her lips at the sight of him.

"Test drive?"

"Girl, you need to tap that."

I lightly take her by the elbow and pull her away until we are in an alcove in the gallery so that she can no longer drool at the sight of him.

"Julia, I can't 'tap' that as you so beautifully put it. He is my boss, or did you forget?"

"Nope, didn't forget at all. That makes it even hotter, actually. Just imagine yourself being summoned to his office. He grabs you and pushes you face down on his desk, pulls up your skirt and starts to spank you with a ruler. Then he starts to stroke your—"

Before she goes any further, I hiss between clenched teeth, "Stop! Seriously, what the hell is wrong with you? Is this what you daydream about?"

She blankets herself with her arms, rubbing them as if she's trying to keep herself warm before she looks at me with apologetic eyes. "Sorry, I don't know what came over me. I watched *Secretary* recently and just got a little carried away in my head."

"I can't be with him like that. Not only because of the whole boss thing, but because of you-know-what, too," I say warily and look over my shoulder to make sure no one is within ear shot.

"I know, sorry. Listen, just keep it as professional as possible and most importantly, do not be alone with him."

"Alone with whom," I hear a familiar voice say.

Alex. Damn it all to hell! Just my luck. He walks up right at this moment. Julia looks at me like she's a deer caught in the headlights. She quickly recovers, turns to him and says, "Oh, no one in particular, just girl talk, you know."

"Julia, would you give us a moment please," he asks, keeping his eyes on me the entire time. Since I know she doesn't think I should be alone with him, I already know what her answer will be.

"Sure, no problem. See you at home, Sabrina."

Traitor. Benedict Arnold. I can't believe she just did that. I'm staring at her in shock as she quickly marches out of view until I hear her far-off voice instructing her remaining staff to pack it up, or else. Coming back to the task at hand, I look at Alex who is trying to stifle a grin, but it's not working too well.

"Don't laugh, it's not funny," I say while I try to keep a straight face.

"I'm sorry. I shouldn't have snuck up on you both like that. That was very rude of me."

He starts to close the space between us, so I automatically put up both my hands to stop him before he gets any closer. "Alex, I can't do this. Please don't make this any more difficult than it is."

"Fine, understood," he stops and then quickly nods. "I didn't mean to make you feel uncomfortable, Sabrina. The last thing I want to do is lose you."

I look at him with a raised eyebrow in confusion before he clarifies further while grinning, "As a business colleague."

He starts walking toward me again, causing me to move backwards until I reach the wall. He stops just an inch or two away from me, never breaking eye contact. "I think I may have waited too long," he says. I open my mouth to say something back to him, but he puts up his hand to stop me before I even start. He's so close and for a split second I want to forget everything and just kiss him senseless. I lick my lips in anticipation, bringing his gaze to momentarily focus on them before he breaks the silence between us.

"Sabrina, it's no secret how I feel about you. I wanted to say something to you sooner, but it never seemed to be the right time. I'm sorry if I've made a mess of things between us, but I just couldn't wait any longer."

His eyes show a trace of defeat in them. It makes me want to tell him how I wish things were different between us. It makes me want to not get on that plane in a couple of days. It makes me close the gap between us and pull his lips to mine. His lips taste like the most decadent wine I've ever tasted. One of his hands frames my face, while the other has wrapped around the back of my neck to keep me in place. Unlike the kiss from earlier, which was soft and slow, this one is full of desperation. Taking one more step forward, he pins my back to the wall. He takes his hand from my face and runs it slowly down my neck, collarbone, and over my chest until it rests on my hip. All the while our tongues are dancing, finding a rhythm of their own.

Suddenly, he stops and pulls away. "As much as I want you right now, I think it's for the best if we stop," he says and dips his head so that his forehead is resting against mine.

"I'm sorry, Alex, I didn't mean to get so carried away."

Grinning at me, he puts his finger lightly on my lips. "I'm not sorry at all. I've wanted that to happen since the very first time I met you."

He takes his finger away and moves back a bit, putting some much needed space between us. "Alex, I think you deserve to know that I do feel something for you, but…."

What do I say? I don't want to really tell him about my trip or about the whole Tyler obsession, so I find myself right back at square one.

"You don't have to say anything to me. Go on your trip. How about we discuss it when you come back."

His smile never leaves his face, making it easier for me to take the temporary olive branch he offered and just nod at his request. He steps further away from me and tips his head slightly, motioning me to leave the alcove. Before leaving him, I turn and say, "Thank you, Alex." Pivoting back toward the hallway, I make my way back to my office, pick up my purse, and practically run out the door.

Driving home, my mind is racing at a mile a minute. I can't believe the disaster I have just created for myself. I slap the steering wheel with the palm of my hand, wanting to kick myself over everything with Chris and Lisa, Tyler, and now Alex.

What is wrong with me? I have the opportunity to pursue something with Alex but what do I do instead? I run like a scaredy-cat in the opposite direction like I do with every other potential relationship in my life before him. I feel a slight panic run through me at the thought of how my past has taken over my entire life, shaping a lot of my decisions. Something's got to give...soon.

I take a few calming breaths before I decide to turn the radio on. The opening bars of Van Morrison's "Into the Mystic" are just starting. I let the song's slow-building crescendo seep into me and feel more and more relaxed with every word. I pull into my driveway as the last few lyrics flow from my speakers and sit there for a few seconds before I turn the car off, letting the song wash over me like an antidote to what ails me. Walking inside the house, I head straight to my bedroom, ignoring Julia completely. Closing the door behind me, I fall face first on my bed and mentally replay the lyrics I just heard.

I let the words soothe me until I feel my eyelids grow heavy. I kick off my shoes and wrap the blanket around me, not bothering to even take off my dress. For once in my life, I wish that I could make a decision without feeling insecure or even slightly afraid of the consequences. I want more than anything to let go and...just live. Just as I'm about to fall asleep, my cell phone vibrates. I reach over to my night stand to grab it and look at the screen. It's a text message from Alex.

Thank you for giving me a chance...

I stare at it for a moment or two before throwing the phone back on my night stand in defeat. Fuck my life.

CHAPTER FIVE

The sound of Julia's light tapping on my door wakes me up. I don't want to move, so I just tell her to come in. She walks over to the bed and takes a seat beside me.

"That bad?" she asks.

"You have no idea."

She lifts up my blanket to take a peek and sees that I'm still wearing my dress from the night before. "What the hell happened?"

I give her the recap after she left me high and dry, before adding, "Thanks so much for throwing me under the bus." She flips her blonde hair and bats her lashes, giving me her best "who me?" look.

"How was I supposed to know you'd end up shoving your tongue down his throat all on your own? Which, by the way, nice job," she says and then lifts her hand to give me a fist bump. When I don't raise mine to meet hers, she looks disappointed. Not one to give up so easily, she reaches over to my arm and forces my hand into a fist to meet hers. "That's better."

"Julia, my head feels like it's going to explode. I'm leaving tomorrow for my ten-year reunion, which will bring me face to face with Chris and Lisa, and maybe

Tyler. If all that stress wasn't enough, now I have Alex to worry about."

I prop up on my elbows when it dawns on me that Julia is still in her pajamas and it's a weekday. She's usually up and about, if not already out the door by this time.

"Why are you still home, anyway?"

"I'm taking the day off, and so are you, missy."

Before I can argue my way out of whatever she has planned, she quickly dismisses me and says, "I don't want to hear it. My best friend needs me today. I've already called the gallery for you to let them know you'll be taking an extra day today. As for me, well, what good is being the boss if I can't take a mental day when I need to."

I'm relieved that I don't have to go anywhere today. I drop back down into my bed and curl myself up in a ball under the comforter.

"Um, what are you doing? Just because I said I called the gallery for you doesn't mean I intend to watch you sleep the day away. We have plans today."

"I'm going to sulk."

"No, you're not. Get your ass up and in the shower. We have a spa appointment at the Biltmore in about an hour, on me."

Right before she stands up, she slaps me on my behind and starts to run out of my room before I can retaliate. I stay put, going over in my mind everything from last night with Alex. It's like a twisted cosmic joke that in all the time I've known him, he decides now is the right time to make his move. If not for the fact that I am leaving tomorrow, I'm fairly certain I would throw aside my reservations about pursuing a relationship with my boss. I glance over at my cell phone and I feel tempted to text him back something flirtatious, but common sense holds me back. At this point, encouraging this situation further would not be wise on my part so I resist the urge. Instead, I reluctantly kick the comforter off, and then traipse out of my room and into the shower. Once I'm done and wrapped in my robe, I amble my way into the kitchen where Julia is waiting for me with a fresh mug of coffee.

"Thanks."

"You're welcome," she says as she leans against the counter.

"So, the Biltmore, huh?"

"Yup. Then, after a day of pampering, we're going to Frankie's for your favorite pizza. Then, we'll come home and watch as many *Felicity* episodes as it takes to cheer you up."

"I love you," I say while smiling at her and take a seat at the table to drink my coffee. She walks toward me, pinching my right cheek and says, "Ditto."

We sit in silence for a few minutes, until she gets up and makes her way back to her room to get dressed. Taking my last sip of coffee, I get up to grab a refill and catch a glimpse of the invitation for the reunion that is being held up by a magnet on our refrigerator. I peel it out from under the magnet carefully and put it on the counter in front of me. Just like all the times before, my heart starts to beat so quickly that I can almost feel the blood running through my own veins. My eyes scan over the embossed words slowly, thinking of what I would say to him all these years later.

"He's going to be there. I can feel it," Julia says when she makes her way back into the kitchen. She perches her chin on my shoulder so she can look at the invite that's lying on the counter in front of me. "Come on, go get yourself ready for the spa. No talking about dickhead, the whore, Sawyer, or Willy Wonka for the rest of the day. And that's an order," she demands as she reaches around me and snatches the invitation. My lord, she has nicknames for everyone. I shake my head and do as I'm told while she tacks it back to the refrigerator door.

Our morning at the spa was luxurious and relaxing. Julia and I both got an aromatherapy massage, followed by our favorite mango manicure and pedicure. When we settle back into her car a couple of hours later, I'm fairly certain I've never felt more relaxed in my life. So much so, that while she weaves in and out of traffic, it lulls me to sleep. A soft nudging from her alerts me that we've arrived at what I thought was going to be Frankie's, but as I open my eyes, we're actually in front of a boutique in Coconut Grove.

"What are we doing here?"

"Happy birthday and merry Christmas, roomie," she says and grabs her purse from the backseat.

"My birthday is not for another two months and Christmas is in December, in case you forgot."

"Oh, I didn't forget. But you're getting all your presents early. You need them today more than you will two months from now," she explains as she steps out of the car into the blazing Miami sun.

I'm still in the car staring at her as she rounds the hood and stops to look back at me. She puts both her hands on her hips and pouts, effectively making me roll my eyes and get out of the car as well.

"Julia, this is too much." The spa alone must have cost her a nice chunk of change.

"Sweetie," she says and takes both my hands in hers. "You need this. Please let me do this for you. I know that if the tables were turned, you would be doing the same thing. God knows, you've helped me through some crazy break ups in the past. Besides, what's the point of making money if you can't spend it while you're still able to enjoy it? Now, come inside and let me buy you a dress that will blow them away."

"I love you," I say to her as sincerely as possible. She is amazing. I don't know what I did in a past life to find her, but whatever it was, it had to have been really good.

She pulls her sunglasses off her eyes, puts them on her head, and smiles before pulling me into a hug and ushering me into the boutique. I try on at least a dozen dresses, one after the other, until we both agree on one that is "not too slutty." It's a black, soft satin, almost gauzy material, with no sleeves, that reaches to about mid-thigh. It has a boat neck cut, hugs my body in all the right places and from the front has a very classic and simple look to it. It's the back of the dress that is the show stopper. There is almost none to speak of. The material doesn't start again until about an inch from my waist, leaving almost my entire back on display. According to Julia, a bare back will drive a man wild. Whatever. I love the dress. And if I'm being honest, I do look pretty damn good in it.

"I already have the perfect shoes for it at home," I announce before she feels the need to spend more money on me.

"Ok, then let's go to Frankie's and pick up a pie so we can sit back and crush on Ben for awhile."

"You mean, crush on Noel," I correct her, throwing down the gauntlet yet again. She scoffs at the mere mention of Noel and gives me a sly smile before she says, "You're so lucky I love you too," and we head off to pick up dinner.

Four back-to-back episodes of *Felicity*, one large cheese pizza, and several glasses of red wine later, we're still lazing on the couch discussing the dynamics of our favorite show. It's almost midnight, my flight is just under ten hours away, and I have yet to pack one single thing. With that admission, we scramble to my room and start to go through my closet, trying to make the best selections possible given that we are both fairly tipsy at this point. Julia mumbles something under her breath about going to check on something in her room and that she'll be right back, leaving me alone in the eye of the storm, or of what's left of my closet.

Right where I had left it a few weeks ago, the box marked "old stuff" is sitting on its perch. Before switching off the light to my closet, I pull it off the shelf and hunker down right in the middle of a pile of rejected clothes. This time, I immediately open the box and dig out the yearbook. As I flip through the pages, Julia returns and slides down the wall to sit beside me, asking me questions about certain people. When we get to Tyler's picture, I stop and touch my fingers lightly over it.

"Hey," Julia says breaking me out of my trance, "no sulking, remember."

"I know. Just...." I trail off, not sure of exactly what I want to say.

"Just, nothing," she says. "It's all going to be fine, trust me. Now put that away, I have something for you."

She hands me a box that's been wrapped beautifully with a big red bow. I carefully tear off the paper and gasp out loud at the sight of the designer's name. I look up at her and see she's sporting a smile from ear to ear.

"Julia, it's too much, I can't take them," trying to hand the box back to her. She puts out her hands to shove them back in my direction.

"Every woman deserves a pair of Louboutins. Didn't you know that one pair of shoes can change your life, Sabrina?"

No, I didn't know that, but I do know that they cost a fortune. I look up at her again, and she raises her eyebrow to warn me that there is no way in hell she's going to take no for an answer. I gingerly lift one of the shoes and hold it in my hands as if it were a semi-precious stone. They're black satin, peep-toe pumps with an ankle strap that is adorned with a bow...and, of course, the trademark red sole.

"Thank you so much, for everything. They are the most beautiful shoes I've ever seen and they're going to look amazing with the dress I'll be wearing. You've made me feel like I'm Cinderella today."

I pull the shoes out and clutch them to my chest, causing the box to fall from my lap, and about a dozen condoms spill onto the floor. Laughing at the ridiculousness of it all, I grab one and throw it at Julia.

"Yeah, figured you might need those too," she says, winking at me.

After we quickly clean up the mess in my closet, Julia gives me a hug and calls it a night. I crawl into bed, catching a glimpse of the clock on my night stand: 2:15 a.m. Staring at my packed suitcase, I sigh out loud and roll over. I eventually fall asleep and dream about Cinderella running after her pumpkin carriage in the most kick-ass pair of Louboutins I've ever seen.

CHAPTER SIX

I hate travelling. Period. But with a hangover, it's excruciating. I'm cursing myself for drinking so much last night when the plane finally arrives in Philadelphia. At least I was able to squeeze in a power nap for much of the flight, but I'm still dragging.

Navigating my way through the terminal to get to my rental car, I stop at a stand full of tourist brochures. I grab the flyer for the Philadelphia Museum of Art and stuff it in my purse, making a mental note to check out some of the exhibits while I'm visiting for the next week. Why I let Julia talk me into booking my flight an extra couple of days before the actual reunion is beyond me. Not only that, but she somehow talked me into staying for an entire week. God, I'm such a pushover sometimes. I swear that girl will be the death of me. Shaking my head, I think about her departing words when she dropped me off at the airport earlier today. "Don't let dickhead and the whore ruin this for you. You go and get your man, girl."

Getting into my rental, I turn on the GPS to get to I-476. It's been ten years since I've been back here so I need all the help I can get. Finally, after a couple of "turn right" and "turn left" prompts, I'm on the open road and heading home. The rest of the way I can probably do in my sleep since I use to spend a lot of weekends at the museum, usually by myself. At first, Chris would come with me, but after the fifth time he confessed that it really wasn't his thing. I turn on the radio and settle on the classic rock station. As Stevie Nicks's "Edge of Seventeen" comes on, I try to get as comfortable as possible for the rest of the drive.

My exit becomes visible in the distance, and my palms begin to sweat as I grip the steering wheel a little tighter. Ten years is a long time to be away from home. I say home, but it doesn't really feel that way to me. It hasn't felt that way since I left for college. This place feels tainted to me somehow. On any given street, a memory can come crawling back out of nowhere from my time with Chris and Lisa. Back then everything was so simple and innocent, and I was completely in the dark of what was really going on, right under my nose.

Taking a breath and then exhaling loudly, I calmly try to tell myself that I'll be fine when I take the final turn onto my old street and see my parents' house come into view. My mom must have her dog ears on today since I can already see her pushing open the screen door, waving like a lunatic. Laughing at the sight of her, I pull into the driveway and barely get my car parked before she's squealing with delight.

"My baby's finally come home!"

My mom, for all of her fifty-two years of age, doesn't look a day past thirty. The woman must drink from the fountain of youth. She's petite, curvy, and as beautiful as ever. Her auburn hair that I was lucky enough to inherit is chin-length and falls softly across her cheek as she starts walking down the front steps. And from where I'm standing, I can already see that her green eyes are glistening with happy tears. I give her a big hug and remind her that we see each other once, sometimes twice a year, when they come to Miami to visit me.

Then the screen door props open again, and I look up to see my dad coming toward me. His large frame lumbers across the front yard briskly. My dad is usually very soft spoken and lets my mom's vibrant personality take the spotlight quite often. Today is no different. His grey eyes light up at the sight of me through the veil of my mom's hair while she's still hugging me. That is, until he wants to cut in and she finally steps aside.

"Let the girl breathe," he says to my mom before he picks me up into a bear hug. "Welcome home, baby girl."

"Daddy, I can't breathe," I try to say but it's muffled since he has me pinned in his arms like the Crocodile Hunter.

"Sorry," he says with the biggest grin I've ever seen on his face, "we're just so happy to have you home, is all."

Before I can protest, my dad grabs all of my bags from the trunk and carries them directly into the house. My mom ushers me in right behind him, and when I cross the threshold I feel like I've been transported back in time. Not one single thing has changed. The furniture, the paint color, everything…it's exactly the same. If this is any indication, I'm afraid to check out my old room. I say as much to my mom, but she ignores it and continues talking a mile a minute. Stopping long enough for me to get a word in, I ask her about our dinner plans for tonight.

"We made reservations at The Roadhouse, your old favorite, at 7:30."

"Thanks, Mom." I kiss her on the cheek, letting her know that I'm going to take my bags to my room. I glance at the clock on top of the fireplace and hope that I might be able to get another nap in before we head out, since the one I took on the plane isn't quite cutting it.

Opening the door to my old bedroom and dropping the bags on my bed, I look around. The corkboard over my desk still has all my concert tickets tacked on it along with several famous artist postcards that I used to collect, including my favorite that I used to keep taped in my locker, *Blue Nude* by Pablo Picasso. I've since bought the print in a larger size and it sits in my office at the gallery. I smile at all the other items that are still on my desk, as if they've been waiting for me to come home too. "I can do this," I say to myself and walk back over to my luggage to begin unpacking.

A quick power nap and I feel rejuvenated as I start to get ready for dinner. After I blowdry my hair straight, I decide on a pair of black linen shorts, white tank top, and a red short-sleeved cardigan. I slip on my black wedge sandals and a pair of silver hoop earrings then grab my clutch to head out to dinner with my parents.

The drive to the Roadhouse takes all of ten minutes and since we have reservations, we're seated quickly. Our table is dead center of the restaurant, easily allowing me a full view of every other diner in the place. I recognize a few people, and they wave politely and nod their heads in acknowledgment. I smile and find that I'm surprised by my reaction to being home. I honestly thought I would hate it already, but it's actually…nice. A wave of relief washes over me so I sit back and start to peruse the menu in front of me.

As the waiter finishes writing down our dinner order, I hear a loud gasp and then in an almost-shrieking voice, "Sabrina Chandler, is that you? Oh my God, it is!"

I tilt my head toward the hostess stand and see Lauren Callahan, a fellow 2001 Skippack High School graduate and, from what I remember, self-proclaimed gossip hound, pointing at me in disbelief.

She rushes over, completely ignoring the stares that have now been garnered by every single person in here. Even the kids who were absentmindedly playing on their electronic devices have put them down in an effort to see what is going on. "I can't believe it, you're actually here for the reunion!"

My parents look so uncomfortable by the attention, so I nod at her question and put a finger to my lips to motion to her to keep it down. "Yes, I'm here for the reunion."

As if the heavens parted for just a moment, the waiter arrives with our drinks. Just this morning I had sworn off alcohol, but instantly make a grab for my Cosmopolitan and take a huge gulp, almost downing it completely. "Well, Lisa told me that she talked to you, and you told her you weren't going to be able to make it."

My mother gives me a confused look then asks, "Sweetie, when did you talk to Lisa?"

"I didn't," and before my mom can start the questions, I turn my attention back to Lauren. "Obviously, you were misinformed, because here I am, in the flesh."

She's chomping at the bit, dying to ask me more questions, but I effectively put an end to it before the inquisition can begin. "Lauren, I'm so glad I got to see you, but as you can imagine, I don't get to see my parents that often," I say motioning over to my mom and dad.

She puts her hand over her chest, feigning innocence, "Oh, of course! I'm so sorry to have interrupted. Enjoy your dinner and I'll see you on Saturday at the reunion, OK?"

"Sure thing, see you then."

And away we go…in the next hour the gossip phone chain will be ringing off the hook. Alerting everyone within a 20-mile radius that the long-lost Sabrina Chandler is actually in Skippack. Awesome. So much for flying under the radar. Might as well just keep the tab open and the drinks flowing. I motion for the waiter to bring me another drink, and my mom makes a big show of clearing her throat to try and get my attention. "What's wrong, Mom?"

"What is going on, Sabrina?"

I sigh and lean over the table slightly to keep the conversation as contained as possible. "Mom, it's complicated."

The last thing I want to do is get into a discussion about Lisa, and everything that it entails, right here and now. "Can't we just enjoy dinner and not discuss Lisa for a change?"

"Yes," my dad, finally speaking up, says and winks at me.

"I guess so," she concedes, but not before she adds, "I just want you to be happy."

I ignore the jibe when the waiter finally arrives with our meals. The steak I had ordered melts in my mouth, making all the drama from just a short while ago almost worth it. It's really the little things sometimes that make it all OK. I decline dessert and excuse myself from the table to go to the ladies room while my father is requesting the waiter for the check.

When we arrived for dinner, the bar portion of the restaurant was fairly crowded, and still is as I make my way through it to get to the restroom. A couple of patrons are cheering on the Phillies on the huge flat-screen TV above the bar. When I reach the door to the ladies room, a voice that I haven't heard in ten years quietly says, "It's really you."

All of a sudden, everything around me stops and I feel like I've entered *The Matrix*. The only thing I can make out is my own heartbeat that is pounding in my ears. I take a breath and then quickly exhale, *I can do this*, I think to myself as I turn around and come face to face with the boy who broke my heart.

His sandy blonde hair is a little shorter than what I remember and he's put on a few pounds, but they don't look bad on him...the bastard. He still possesses that all-American, boy-next-door look, but it's his baby-blue eyes that still send me reeling while I stand here frozen. They were always his best feature. He had this way of command-ing me with his eyes to persuade me to do things, like he was my own personal hypnotist. Even though the intensity behind them is the same, they look sad at the moment.

"I can't believe you're really here," he says breaking the silence between us. "I can't tell you how many times I've wanted to call you."

"To tell me what, exactly," I snap back. He winces slightly at my response, but I stand my ground.

He puts both his hands in his pocket and tilts his head downward. As he lifts his eyes back up to me he says, "Sorry. That I'm sorry for everything. I was young and stupid and I believed everything Lisa told me back then." He takes a quick breath before continuing. "Sabrina, if I could, I would take it all back. I wouldn't have ever listened to her and I would have never hurt you."

What. The. Fuck.

What exactly does "listened to her" even mean? In the back of my mind an image forms of them together at that party years ago. Him, picking her up and kissing her passionately.

Lisa breaking off the kiss and throwing her head back while he continued kissing her exposed throat. Yet, here he stands, trying to tell me that it's not what it seemed.

"You're so full of shit, Chris," and I go to walk past him to get away from him. He grabs me by the elbow and nudges me back further into the hallway that leads to the restrooms.

"Please, let me explain."

"No," I breathe out and jerking my elbow from his grip. "It's too late for explanations."

I turn to walk away from him but his words stop me in my tracks.

"Lisa," he says through clenched teeth, "told me that you were planning on dumping me before you left for college. She convinced me that you didn't really care about me, about us. She said that you were going to leave us both behind and that we only had each other. She—"

"*Stop!*"

He tries to continue, but I say it again, this time with more venom behind it. I feel sick to my stomach. How dare he try to pin this all on Lisa. I saw him with my own eyes. He sure as hell didn't look like he was being forced into anything back then. Not to mention that he's been married to her for almost ten years.

I take a step or two toward him until we are inches apart. He looks defeated, almost pathetic, and I surprise myself by letting out a quick laugh before shaking my head in disbelief.

"Go home to your *wife*, Chris."

I leave him standing there and make my way back through the bar to my parents so that I can get the hell out of here. So much for a quiet arrival.

CHAPTER SEVEN

The drive home is awkward, to say the least. I haven't said more than two words to my parents after leaving Chris and his bullshit excuses behind. Those two words being, "Let's go." A part of me wants to just get back on a plane and head home. But another part of me, the one that's been slowly building herself up to face all of this, doesn't want to walk away just yet. It's that part of me that's keeping me focused and not losing it while I sit in the back seat of my parents' car and stare out the window.

How dare he do this to me? How could he think that approaching me after ten years in a crowded bar to lay his sad story on me after everything would be even remotely OK? And the story, in of itself, is beyond infuriating. What kind of cryptic crap did all of that mean? Lisa, being the svengali behind it all. Like she was The Great and Powerful Oz. Hiding behind the curtain, pulling on secret levers, in the hopes she could get Chris to do her evil bidding. I guess he conveniently forgot that I actually saw them together. And that it takes two to tango.

Finally arriving back at my parents' house, I get out of the car, slamming the door in the process. All I want to do is go in my room and shut everything out. Reaching for my doorknob, I hear my mother at the end of the hallway. "Sabrina, what in *the* hell is going on?"

I open the door to my room and turn my head toward her before going in, "Mom, you don't want to know."

"Yes, I do. What is all of this about you and Lisa talking on the phone? Why did you lie to me about that?" She starts walking down the hallway toward me as she continues, "Lisa really wanted to talk to you, the poor girl. She looked so upset when I told her you were coming to the reunion. She couldn't wait to get your phone number so she could call you herself."

That's it, the proverbial straw that breaks the camel's back. That *whore* (Julia would be so proud) has made my own mother believe that I'm the one to blame for their mistakes.

"You want to know what happened?" I ask her.

She nods and says, "Yes, I most certainly do."

"Fine," I bite out, "Lisa and Chris were seeing each other during high school."

"I know that," she says and hesitates before going on. "you told us they got together after you broke up with him."

"I lied."

"What did you lie about?"

"Everything. I found them together, one night at a party right before we graduated. I snuck out of the house and went to the party to surprise Chris. But guess who was really surprised? Me!"

She puts her hand over her mouth to cover the low gasp that escapes her throat. "Oh my God. I'm so sorry, I never knew. Why didn't you tell me?"

"What good would it have done? I was leaving in a couple of months for college and I just wanted to get out of here."

I instantly feel terrible for all the years I've allowed her to believe in a lie. I've had fleeting thoughts about just spilling my guts before this very moment, but somehow it just never seemed to be the right time. The guilt I feel is overwhelming at the sight of her standing before me open-mouthed and speechless. What kind of person am I that I would let this go on for so long? What does this say about me? I curse myself at the thought of how much I've let those two run my life without them even knowing how much of a strain it has put on my relationship with my own parents…and for what?

"You must think I'm awful," she says to me as tears begin to fall slowly from her eyes. "All these years, you've heard me talk about them and you never said anything. Why?"

"I don't know anymore, Mom. I just wanted it all to go away. I thought that if I just let you believe whatever it was you believed, you would leave it alone. I don't think you're awful at all. I'm the awful one for making a mess of this all on my own."

I sit down on my bed, feeling like a weight has been lifted off my shoulders. The first few tears that had been threatening just below the surface start to escape. My mom comes to sit beside me and gently takes my hand.

"Sweetie, please forgive me, I'm so sorry."

Her pleading eyes are full of tears now, causing mine to completely spill over. Although I'm relieved that I finally was able to tell her everything, the pain that I've caused her and myself for no reason other than shame and embarrassment is too much to bear. My hands shakily go to wipe the tears off my cheeks that are coming at an uncontrollable rate. She gathers me into a comforting hug and rocks me in her arms until the tears finally stop. She pulls me back to look at my face giving me the slightest hint of a smile cracking her lips before she says, "So, you snuck out, huh?"

With that, we're both laughing until we notice my dad leaning in my doorframe, arms crossed, looking more than pissed off. He looks downright deadly.

"I never liked that boy. Next time I see him I'm going to kick his ass and make him wish he was never born."

Between more giggling and sniffling, my mom pats my hand to reassure me and then turns to my dad, giving him a stern look. "You will do no such thing because after I'm finished with him he'll already be dead."

Giving me a light kiss on my cheek, she leaves the room and shoves my dad out of the way so she can close the door behind her but not before saying, "I love you, sweetie."

"Love you too, Mom."

Feeling a little better about the situation and the mess that is my life, I change into my tank top and pajama bottoms, crawl under the blankets of my old bed, and fall asleep fairly quickly.

The next morning, I wake up to the smell of bacon wafting down the hall. Slowly peeling the comforter off of my body, I do a quick stretch before I pull on my fleece robe and make my way down to the kitchen where my mom is making breakfast.

She puts down her spatula and pulls me into a hug and asks if I slept well. I tell her that it was probably one of the best night's sleep I've had in a long time. She gives me a light kiss on my forehead, letting me know that breakfast will be ready in a few minutes. While I'm waiting, I check my cell phone for any messages and see that Alex has sent me a text just this morning. At first, I think it must be work related but quickly realize that's not the case at all.

Thinking about you. Hope you're having a great time.

I'm flustered and excited by his text and am at a loss as to what to say back to him. My mind, apparently in self-preservation mode, runs through a quote from one of my favorite movies: "*I can't think about that right now. If I do, I'll go crazy. I'll think about that tomorrow.*" God bless Scarlett O'Hara, that little strategy is the way to go for now. So, instead of responding, I sit on the stool at the kitchen island and let my mom pile up the food on my plate.

"Why do you have that look on your face?" she asks.

"What look do I have on my face, exactly?"

"Like you're a deer caught in the headlights," she explains as she leans against the counter and wipes her hands with a dishtowel.

"It's nothing," I say dismissively with a shrug, but she's not buying it.

Maybe it's the fact that it has been ten years, or the bonding time we had after what happened last night, that I feel compelled to share with her more about my personal life than ever before. Well, except for the whole Tyler thing, which I'm not about to explain just because the woman made me some bacon.

"OK, OK," I mumble then take a bite from a piece of bacon and keep my eyes on my plate. "Right before I left to come up here, my boss made it obvious that he's interested in me. He just sent me a text, but I haven't answered it because I haven't decided what I'm going to do about him just yet."

I sneak a glance at her before ducking my head to grab my glass of orange juice. Her one eyebrow is raised and her hands are neatly folded in front of her. She clears her throat before she says anything.

"Well, isn't that what they consider sexual harassment in the workplace? Can't you complain to someone about that? You know, dear, there are laws in place for situations like this nowadays. You remember Anita Hill, right?"

Great, she's rambling. Now she's saying something about a woman's right to choose and how I can say no at any time. Why did I ever think this would go over smoothly? I stop her as she starts on the topic of women's suffrage and how "we've come a long way baby." Did she really just even say that?

"Mom, stop. Take a breather."

"Sweetie, I'm just trying to help you," she says quickly.

"Mom, it's not as sinister as all that. Alex is a really nice guy. Trust me, I've got it under control."

She opens her mouth to say something, but I stop her. "Mom, I swear it's not like you think. I know what I'm doing."

I really don't have a clue, but I'll say whatever it takes to appease her and get her to change the subject since anything else is better than "truth time with Mom" at this point.

We go back to an uncomfortable silence, interspersed with the occasional question about my job and what I'll be wearing to the reunion. It's not until my dad comes strolling in a few minutes later to eat his breakfast in his golf clothes that I'm able to relax again.

After breakfast, my dad kisses us both goodbye and heads out to meet a couple of his buddies for a round of golf. My mom and I then try to decide on our plans for the day. "What about coming with me to the museum in Philly?" I ask her.

"I was thinking more along the lines of doing some shopping at the Village, and then maybe grabbing a late lunch at the Back Porch Café. It is Friday, so it might be a bit crowded, but I think you'll have a good time."

"Sounds good," I agree, resigning myself to the fact that my visit to the museum is not looking too good at this point. Oh well, maybe one day next week, since my flight isn't until Thursday morning, *all thanks to Julia,* I say to myself then step into the bathroom to start getting ready for my day of shopping.

A few hours later I find myself in yet another specialty shop. This time it's cookware and baking needs. I guess if I was a chef or enjoyed cooking even in the slightest I'd be pretty psyched right about now. At least it's a step up from the previous store that specialized in dreamcatchers, nothing but.

"Mom, aren't you getting tired of shopping?" I ask as I eyeball a retro diner-style salt and pepper shaker.

"Not really," she says and continues to search for that ever-elusive item that must be bought before she realizes that she really doesn't need it. "Are you getting hungry?"

My stomach answers with a growl before I can actually respond. My mom laughs out loud and puts down a pair of ridiculous-looking oven mitts that have a picture of all the stars of the Food Network on them. She hooks her arm in mine and leads me toward the front door and we step outside. The café where we planned on having lunch is just a block of stores ahead.

About halfway through our trek, my mom stops suddenly. Since our arms are hooked together, her stopping causes me to falter a bit when I try to keep on walking without her moving.

"Mom, what's the matter? I thought the café was further down this way," I say, pointing directly ahead of us.

She slowly pulls her arm out of mine and points with vigor to the left at two women who are browsing and giggling at items in a storefront window. One of them is easily recognizable since I just ran into her the night before, Lauren, a.k.a. gossip hound. The other woman, I can't easily determine the identity of, so I roll my eyes and turn my attention back to my mother who is still standing there staring, and from the looks of it getting—dare I say—pissed off.

"Mom, just ignore her, I can handle Lauren. Let's go, I'm starving." As I attempt one more time at moving my mom the other woman turns around and I see for the first time in ten years my arch nemesis, Lisa.

For the most part she looks the same, except that she's put on some weight, I assume from the two pregnancies. She's changed the color of her hair from mousy brown to mousy brown with highlights. She's dressed rather nicely, upscale even, causing me to think that Chris must be doing well enough for her to afford the clothes and accessories she's wearing. When she starts her casual approach toward us, I can tell that she's wearing a bit too much makeup for a casual Friday stroll in a shopping mall. Lauren is almost ready to combust with excitement as she follows Lisa over like a dog on a leash. I have to laugh, remembering how much Lisa used to hate Lauren and all her gossiping. Yet, right here in front of me, they are like two peas in a pod. My, how things change.

I'm not nervous, anxious, or scared of this moment that I've been dreading for so long. I'm ready as I'll ever be. Momentarily forgetting that she now knows everything, I glance to my left and see my mom is ready to pounce. One thing about my mom is that you shouldn't cross her; she will never forget or forgive. A big grin comes across my face, and I cross my arms over my chest as I wait to watch the sparks fly. This is going to be good.

"Hi Sabrina, Mrs. Chandler, how nice to run into you today," she says and pulls her mouth into the most artificial smile I've ever seen. It turns my stomach and I have to bite my lip to keep my emotions in check because surprisingly, I feel the need to spit in her face, so out of character for me. Lauren is watching me closely, waiting for me to say something, anything.

I plaster a smile on my face and quite cheerfully respond, "Hi Lisa, it's been a long time, hasn't it?"

"Yes, it has. I got your number from your mom and just kept forgetting to call you. But, now that you're here…," and she stops, but I can tell she's thinking about something clever to say, but my mom starts her attack.

"Lisa, would you just shut up!"

I knew my mom would go for the jugular, but I'm still shocked. My head turns to Lisa and then back to my mom. Lauren is doing the same thing. It's like we're in the front row at a tennis match at the U.S. Open.

"How dare you talk to me like that?"

My mom laughs and then steps in closer, takes her index finger and waves it in Lisa's face before she can say another lie.

"Just stop lying already. We all know you're trying to save face in front of your *friend* here, and you did call Sabrina in Miami and told her to stay away."

"Well, *I* didn't know all that," Lauren says out of nowhere. My mom promptly gives Lauren a dismissive look before turning her attention back to Lisa.

"For years, I've been making my daughter feel guilty because of you. All this time I've been trying to get her to make amends with you. And all this time, it's been nothing but a lie." She pauses, takes my hand in hers and continues, "Lisa, you should be ashamed of yourself. Prancing around here like your shit doesn't stink. Well guess what, it stinks to high heaven! Do yourself a favor and don't you dare show your face around me again. If you see me coming, turn in the other direction because you make me sick." With that, my mom pulls me to the left, sidestepping Lisa and Lauren. "I'm starving, let's go."

While she pulls me along for a few steps, I turn my head around to take one last look at the shocked expression on Lisa's face and the devilish grin on Lauren's. I wave at them both, smile and say, "See you tomorrow night at the reunion." I turn back to my mom who is on a mission to make it to our original destination before we were thwarted by Tweedledee and Tweedledum.

"Mom, that was awesome."

"It was, wasn't it?"

We both start giggling like school girls and eventually make our way to the café where we eat a late lunch and then head home for the night.

CHAPTER EIGHT

I'm not even the slightest bit nervous. How is that possible? I've stressed over this moment for months now. What I would do? What I would say? Now, facing myself in the mirror, dressed for the reunion, I'm not worried. The only thing left to conquer is whether I'll see Tyler there, and I can't think too much over that since the trip so far has been a success. I mean, it would be like gravy if he were to show up, but really, I'm OK with it if he doesn't. Having been able to confront not only Chris but Lisa as well has been, as cliché as it sounds, cathartic.

Wow, Julia was so right; the shoes are amazing and go perfectly with my dress, which looks like it was made for me. I'm going to take that girl out for a night on the town for convincing me to pick this one. After putting the finishing touches on my hair, which I've decided to wear in a low, loose bun with side swept bangs, I put in my diamond studs. I take one last look at myself, more than satisfied with the reflection smiling back at me, and head out for the reunion.

The drive there takes all of fifteen minutes. Probably would have taken me ten if it wasn't so difficult trying to maneuver the gas and brake pedals with the Louboutins.

Pulling into the parking lot of the Skippack Golf Club at approximately 6:15 p.m., I pat myself on the back for arriving fashionably late, as per my mom's advice. I walk through the front doors of the building and see a sign that leads me toward the correct ballroom. The music and chatter gets closer and closer until I finally cross the threshold and take a moment to canvas the entire room.

Our school colors were purple and white and it seems like someone got the memo. Purple and white helium balloons are floating on the ceiling, purple and white streamers cascading the walls, and finally, purple and white table cloths grace the tables. There are two bars strategically placed on the far corners of the room, flanking the barely filled hardwood dance floor. On the stage area, with his turntable, sits a DJ, who is already being harassed by guests for requests.

It takes about ten seconds for me to spot Chris and Lisa, holding court at a table. Chris is smiling but it looks forced, while Lisa is speaking to a few of the other guests enthusiastically. I start to walk slowly into the room and try to make my way to the bar. At the same time I'm looking for Tyler. So far he's not here, but that doesn't surprise me. I remember my conversation with Julia the day she convinced me to come. I'd told her that he didn't seem like the kind of guy that would come to these kinds of things. I should have made a monetary wager on it. I smile at the thought and finally make it to the bar. While waiting on my glass of wine, a few people I know stop to say hello and engage me in conversation.

It's funny how people can change over the course of ten years. Other people, not so much. I continue to sip on my drink and talk casually to fellow 2001 graduates until

I notice that I'm in need of a refill. Excusing myself, I get to the bar to order another glass of wine when Chris appears next to me. Actually, so close to me that I don't have enough room to pull a dollar bill out of my clutch to tip the bartender. I ask him as politely as possible if he can back off, to which he responds, "I need to talk to you, please, Sabrina."

I can smell the alcohol all over him. He's hammered. He takes a step back and goes to grab my hand to pull me toward him. I yank it back forcefully.

"Chris, we have nothing to say to each other. Please just leave me alone."

He hangs his head and starts to loosen the tie he's wearing. "I need to tell you how sorry I am. My God, Sabrina, I wish I could take it all back. I don't love her, I've never loved her."

I stare at him for a second because honestly, I'm so over him and his apology that is ten years too late that I want to make sure I get the next thing I say completely right so he can just leave. Before I can open my mouth, I barely make out that he's saying something else. It doesn't help that his words are starting to sound slurred at this point either. So, I lean in closer to hear him say, "She tricked me. I was trying to get away from her, but then she told me she was pregnant. Then there was a baby coming and I was stuck. I tried to leave her but she tricked me."

I really don't care. I have to admit that I'm surprised at this revelation; I've come to terms with all of this, and it feels so good. There honestly isn't anything else they can tell me or do to me that would make one iota of difference. I'll be leaving for Miami, while they will be stuck with each other in their "relationship." This seems to be penance enough from all indications. I sigh and tell him this in not so many words, "I really don't care anymore, Chris."

"You don't get it. I tried to leave her to go back to you. I loved you, I still do."

With that, I've had enough of his drunken ramblings. I look him in the eyes and tell him he's pathetic before I grab my wine glass and bump into a few bodies on my way outside to get some fresh air.

There are a few other people out here, smokers mostly. Since I don't smoke, I just meander my way toward a gazebo about thirty feet away that looks to be unoccupied at the moment. I just want some peace and quiet before I go back in there.

I pace around the confines of the gazebo for a while, sipping my wine, when my cell phone vibrates in my clutch. Now what? I see that it's Julia calling.

"Hey girlie," she says, "I was hoping to call you earlier to wish you luck, but I was stuck in a last-minute meeting."

"Thanks. I'm actually already here."

"*And?*" she says, drawing the word out. "Come on, the suspense is killing me."

I'm in no rush to get back inside and I can feel the effects of the alcohol by now, so I walk her through the events of the last couple of days. Every so often she interrupts me with the following commentary: "Holy shit! You've got be kidding me! What a piece of garbage! I can't believe that whore tried to pretend nothing was up!" Finally ending with, "Your mom is my new hero!"

"Yeah, mine too. It was pretty awesome, you would have loved it," I say to her while glancing up at the building to see some more people milling about the entrance.

She stays silent for a moment before she asks, "So, he's not there, huh?"

"Doesn't look that way, no."

"I'm sorry. Are you OK, sweetie?"

I ponder her question for a second, really thinking about it. Yes, I'm OK with it. I say as much to her, and she's doubtful of my response. I try to explain that even though this originally started out as a way to see Tyler again, it turned out to be something more. Something that I should have done years ago. I needed to see Chris and Lisa. I needed to have closure to move on with my life. Although it would have been even more closure, so to speak, seeing him after all these years. Regardless, I feel like, for the first time in my life, I can stop doubting myself.

"Wow, I'm impressed, Sabrina. Who would have thought that going to a ten-year reunion would be like going through a lifetime of therapy sessions."

"Ha ha," I say sarcastically while looking down at my red-painted toes peeking out of my shoes. "In all seriousness, I'm good. I'm going to go back in a few minutes and have a bite to eat. Plus, my wine glass is looking for a refill." I pause, ask her how she's doing, and then drink the last vestiges of my glass.

I'm still looking down at my toes and wiggling them when I hear footsteps coming my way. Julia's going on in my ear about some new client and her ridiculous demands as a pair of men's black dress shoes comes into my view.

"Sabrina."

His smooth voice wraps around me like a silk blanket, causing every nerve ending on my body to stand up and take attention. Somewhere in the back of my mind I'm aware that Julia's still talking, but I can't be sure. Quite frankly, I have no idea if she's asking me a question or waiting for me to say something. Either way, I couldn't string a sentence together right now if I tried. My heart is in my throat as my eyes start a lazy trail from his feet up his body.

Not only do I notice the black tailored dress pants that fall perfectly on his hips, but I can also make out the muscular legs shifting underneath the fabric of those pants. His black button-down shirt is tucked in and held in place with a black leather belt with a simple, yet effective, silver square buckle. The shirt sleeves are rolled up, revealing the elusive tattoo on his right forearm that I've dreamt about for years. His right hand is holding a beer bottle, and I follow it to its destination when he brings it up to his mouth.

Finally reaching his face, those eyes, chocolate as ever, have a hint of mischief behind them. His dark brown hair is not too short, with a few strands hitting his brow. It has that "I'm trying to look like I don't care about my hair so I just run my hands through it" look. It works...well, since all I want to do is run my fingers through it. As he licks his lips after taking a swig of his beer, he grins.

I'm robbed of the ability to speak, but somehow, of all the things I could possibly say at this momentous occasion, I manage to say under my breath, "Holy fucking shit."

He actually laughs out loud at the fact that the first thing out of my mouth to him after ten years is a string of curse words. Great.

"Sabrina! What the hell is going on?" Julia says in my ear in a panic. Quickly pointing out that I don't curse normally and breaking me out of my spell, I remember that she's still on the phone.

"Gotta go, Julia."

"Wait, are you OK?"

"Yes, totally OK, gotta run."

"Oh my God, he's there," she screams in my ear so loud and I'm sure Tyler can hear her since he's chuckling at the scene playing out before him.

"Seriously, gotta run. I'll call you tomorrow."

"Don't you dare hang up on me. Please tell me two things," she pleads.

I'm already making an ass of myself, might as well prolong it. "Make it quick," I tell her.

She asks the next two questions so quietly that I'm barely able to hear her ask, "How hot and is there a wedding ring?"

I look at Tyler's left ring finger, and quickly answer her, "Super, and no."

She's squealing like a little girl when I hang up on her and see Tyler taking another sip of his beer. This time when he pulls it back from his lips, he takes a step forward while I pull my clutch from under my arm and shove the phone back inside, but not before I turn off the ringer completely. He tilts his head to the left slightly, making a stray lock of hair fall into his eyes, which are making a trail from mine to my feet and back up again. I swear that I can almost feel his hands on me as this happens, and it causes me to squirm. He chuckles at my reaction before he finally says, "I was hoping I'd see you here."

Did he really just say that out loud or was it possibly my imagination? I want to pinch myself to make sure this is all real, or better yet, reach out and touch him to make sure this isn't all in my head. I take a deep breath and try to regain my composure, thinking for a second before I say something else that will make me look more like a moron than I already do.

"Hi, Tyler," I breathe as smoothly as I can muster, dragging some loose hair behind my ear.

His lips curl up on one side into that sexy smile that looks exactly the same as I remember it. "Would you like to come back inside with me?" he asks, then glances down at the empty wine glass between us before he looks back into my eyes. "You need another drink."

"Yes."

I start to walk out of the gazebo as he falls in step next to me and places his left hand lightly on my back. It startles me since I can feel his fingers touching my bare skin. I turn my head slightly to look up at him; I find him grinning and I smile as I adjust the hair behind my ear again. He opens the door for me and when I make my way through it, he grabs hold of my hand. I stop and look from our interlaced fingers to his face as he leans down and whispers, "Don't be nervous." He pauses then adds, "I won't bite, I promise."

CHAPTER NINE

I don't think I've ever felt so many eyes on me at one time. I should say, on us. As Tyler and I walk back into the ballroom with our hands still locked together, I see necks craning and conversations come to an abrupt halt to stare at us like something out of a movie. I turn my head to check behind me to make sure there's no one of extreme importance there before Tyler squeezes my hand to bring my attention back to him. He smiles at my misunderstanding before he starts to pull me forward. For not having seen him after all this time, and in fact only really spending all of one hour with him in my entire life, there is no question in my mind that I am more than comfortable as he leads me back into the reunion.

He lets go of my hand when we reach the bar, and I immediately miss the feeling. Not just the physical touch of him, but the warmth behind it as well. Being this close to him again after all this time is intoxicating, and I find myself wanting to curl up into him like a cat. And as foreign as this feeling is to me, it actually feels comforting, like coming home. I take a brief moment to enjoy it, this feeling that I've been longing for, by noticing how absolutely beautiful he is—just as I remember, only better. Even in my four-inch heels he's much taller than me when I look up at his face again and he locks his eyes onto mine. He bends slightly and asks, "What were you drinking?"

"Pinot grigio, thank you."

While he leans on the bar with his right arm and orders our drinks, I stare at the tattoo that's been in my mind's eye for what feels like an eternity. I try to follow the familiar black swirls, but they disappear under his sleeve. I wonder to myself how far up the swirls go exactly and, if at all possible, how I could go about finding this out. He twists slightly to hand me my wine glass and catches me staring at the design. I try darting my eyes back up to his quickly but I know I'm busted. Instead of calling me out on it, he motions to my left to a table that is currently unoccupied in the far corner of the ballroom.

On our walk over to the table, I notice a few women openly gawking at him, husband or no husband, date or no date, but he doesn't seem to notice. If he does, he doesn't let it show as his attention is completely focused on me. He pulls out my chair and I thank him before I carefully attempt to cross my legs in my dress without giving him a free show. We sit in silence for a moment, taking each other in while we take sips of our drinks. After taking a pull off his beer, he places it on the table and turns his chair so that we are more directly facing each other. Finally, I lean forward and say what's been in the back of my mind since he appeared in the gazebo.

"I didn't think you'd be coming tonight."

Curse you, alcohol. I make a mental note to slow it down on the truth serum and try to regain control of the situation before I start telling him all kinds of things. My hand nervously goes up to tuck a stray hair behind my ear, but he beats me to it. The motion takes all of a second or two, but it feels like time is standing still when he takes the hair and carefully tucks it behind my ear for me. He pulls his hand back, smiles, and says, "You always used to do that when you were nervous."

I'm trying my best to keep it together and look cool, calm, and collected after he tells me this. Miraculously, my other hand is still holding the wine glass gracefully. How I manage to do that, I have no idea since my nerves have just ratcheted up a notch by his admission. I tip back the glass to my lips and try to keep up the appearance without downing it in one gulp, which is exactly what I really want to do right now. I mean, how does he even know that? Julia calls me out on it all the time, but I live with her. I've been with him all of fifteen minutes and he has to go and say something to throw me totally off guard. I can tell he's enjoying himself, but it's not in a malicious way since I'm not put off by it. I'm honestly more intrigued. So, instead of backing down, I attempt to steer the conversation toward the now.

"So...what have you been doing the past ten years?"

"Well, as soon as we finished school I left town and moved to Philadelphia. I had a few jobs here and there but they were just enough to make ends meet." He pauses and takes another sip of his beer while I put my drink down for good, patting myself on the back for remembering to bag the drinking around him for a bit.

"A buddy I met in Philly eventually hooked me up with a job cooking in a restaurant."

"Cooking," I say more than ask. "That was the last thing I expected you to say."

He chuckles casually and asks, "What did you expect to hear?"

"I don't know, to be honest," I confess, now slightly embarrassed. I have thought about him so many times but the actual thought of what he could possibly be doing was more along the lines of "bad ass extraordinaire," not cooking in a restaurant.

He puts down his beer and leans toward me more so that his elbows are resting on his knees before he continues. "To be fair, I didn't really know I had it in me either. Turns out, I love it."

"That's great," I say, genuinely happy for him. "Cooking has never been one of my strong suits. Maybe you can give me a few pointers."

"I'd be more than happy to," he answers with a hint of flirtation in his voice as he leans back in his chair. He takes another sip of beer before he asks, "And what have you been doing for the last ten years?"

"Kind of like you, I left right after graduation and went away to college in Miami."

"Is it really as hot as they say it is down there?" he asks.

I have to laugh a little at his question before I answer. "Let me put it to you this way, when I boarded my plane a few days ago, it was a pleasant 95 degrees in the shade."

He laughs at my answer before he says, "I take it you loved it enough that you decided to stay there after college."

"Yeah," I say with a smile, "I do kind of love it, heat and humidity included."

"I've never been there … now I have a reason to visit." We both let that hang in the air between us until he prompts me to tell him what I do for a living.

"Well, right after college I was accepted into an art internship program in Italy. I stayed there just shy of a couple of years and then got my foot in the door at an art gallery in South Beach. I've been there for a few years now and I was recently promoted to gallery assistant and…."

PROMISE ME

"And what," he asks, pulling the beer bottle an inch from his waiting, full lips that I can't seem to tear my eyes away from.

"Oh, nothing, really," I muster trying to recover from being caught staring again. "I was just going to say that I love working there."

Wanting to know more about him, I ask, "So, do you still live in Philadelphia?"

"I do." He hesitates and looks down at my toes that are peeking out of my shoes then grins before bringing his eyes back to mine. "I own a restaurant there."

He owns a restaurant? I'm processing this information in my head and all I can come up with is not only how incredibly sexy that is but it's super impressive too. Now I have a million more questions to ask him at the same time I detect that the DJ is saying something about slowing things up. The music goes from upbeat Top 40 variety to the opening bars of Lady Antebellum's "Just a Kiss."

Tyler stands up slowly then holds out his hand to me and says, "Dance with me." It's not a question. My eyes dart from his face to his outstretched hand and back up again. Whatever questions I had are forgotten since the look of longing in his eyes is all the push I need to make me put my hand lightly in his again, stand up, and let him lead me onto the dance floor.

He wraps his right arm around my waist possessively as my left hand rests atop his shoulder. He takes his free hand to pull my other hand in it so it's resting on his upper chest and begins to lead me into a slow seductive sway to the music. His thumb makes lazy circles on the exposed skin on my back and I smile at the intimacy of the gesture. When he smiles back this time, I feel more at ease and relax into him completely. My forehead rests just below his jaw line, and I feel his lips just barely making contact with it. I close my eyes as we continue to move together, mentally savoring every second of this moment: His strong arms around me. His delicious cologne. His ability to make me feel comforted. All of it.

When the song begins its descent, I pull my head back an inch to look up at him again and he tilts his head to kiss me softly on my cheek. Before he pulls away he lightly drags his lips to my ear and says, "I don't want to let you go just yet."

I quiver at his words and want so badly for him to drag his lips back so that they're finally touching mine. I can feel his heart racing under my palm, which is still on his chest letting me know that he's having the exact thoughts as I am when the DJ decides to switch back to an up-tempo beat.

"Well, don't you two look cozy?"

Hell no! This crazy Stepford wannabe is not going to ruin this night for me. I try to step back from Tyler's embrace, but he keeps one arm on the small of my back. I see that he has a smirk on his face while he turns his head to look at Lisa.

"Sabrina, who would have thought you'd go slumming tonight," she says and waves her hand that is holding a drink in his direction, spilling some on the dance floor in the process. Fantastic. Two drunks for the price of one. This can only get worse when I feel Tyler's body tense up against mine, and other people on the dance floor start to stare at the scene unfolding before them.

"Lisa, don't you have anything better to do than harass me and embarrass yourself," I say in a matter-of-fact tone that catches her completely off guard. She mumbles something about me always thinking I was better than her before she puts on her fake smile again and asks if she can speak to me in private.

"I don't have anything else to say to you," I calmly say. I drop my hand from Tyler's chest and leave the dance floor, making my way back to our table.

He's following close behind but doesn't say anything when we both sit down again. I can feel his anger radiating off of him at what just happened. I turn my head to look at him and see that his jaw is clenched. I manage to smile at the memory it invokes when I had tried to decipher what it had meant that night years ago and knowing the cause of it right now. I reach out my right hand to touch his jaw, but chicken out at the last second and pull it back to my lap instead.

"I'm sorry," I say to him.

"Why are you sorry?"

I should be honest with him; rather, I feel like I can be completely honest with him and he wouldn't judge me. It's a hunch I've had about him from that very first night and the little time I've spent with him here, now, which I know doesn't seem rational but it makes total sense to me. I take a deep breath, exhale, and let the chips fall where they may.

"I'm pretty sure we were having a moment there and she ruined it." I turn my face down toward the floor, afraid of what he could be thinking, hoping I wasn't wrong about him.

He doesn't say anything for what feels like a lifetime. From the corner of my eye, I see his hand come into view to grab hold of my chin and turn it back slowly toward him. "Hey, look at me," he says and I finally bring my eyes to his.

"If you think for one second that I would let anything or anyone ruin my time with you after all these years, you're crazy." He pauses and then adds, "And for the record, it was definitely a moment."

I nod when he lets go of my chin, and I can tell that he is visibly more relaxed. He asks if I'm alright and if I'd like another drink, to which I say yes. I watch him walk away and find myself grinning at the trail of ogling eyes from every female as he passes them. I'm still staring off in his direction when the chair he had been occupying a short while ago scrapes against the hardwood floor.

I don't need to look to know who it is. She's relentless, this one. I sigh and turn my head back slowly to see Lisa sitting in Tyler's seat. Drink in her hand, check. Phony smile plastered on her face, check.

"Jesus Christ, Lisa, what didn't you understand when I said I had nothing else to say to you."

She crosses her legs and leans back in the chair as if she's planning on staying for a spell and visit with an old friend. Somehow she's forgetting that this old friend is the one she stabbed in the back and doesn't want anything to do with her. The phony smile smoothes over to reveal sadness in her demeanor while she contemplates what to say next. Before she can say whatever she's thinking of, I see a new wine glass being placed in front of me on the table.

"Get up and walk away…now," Tyler says from behind me in a slightly menacing tone.

Now, if I was her, and someone spoke to me like that, I'd like to think I could take the hint. But she doesn't move. Instead she keeps her eyes on me and says one more time, "Sabrina, I really would like to talk to you, in private."

I don't know if it's the inflection of sadness in her voice or if I just don't want this scene to play out any further in front of every other fellow 2001 Skippack High School graduate.

"Fine," I bite out.

I reluctantly stand up and as I'm about to pick up my wine glass to bring with me, Tyler says, "You don't owe her anything, Sabrina."

"I'll be fine," I say to him and tuck my hair behind my ear.

He grins knowingly and looks over my shoulder at Lisa. "Are you sure?"

I nod, hoping I'm right, then turn on my heel and see Lisa impatiently waiting for me a few steps away. When I reach her, I gesture with my free hand toward the front door of the ballroom and say, "By all means, lead the way."

CHAPTER TEN

I follow Lisa down the long corridor that leads to the front door of the building, passing quite a few people on the way. She's having trouble walking in a straight line, making a spectacle of herself in the process. When we get outside, she turns right and heads toward the far end of the building, away from any possible onlookers that may be lurking around at the moment. Realizing that we are more than well enough away, I stop. "This is as far as I go."

She turns around and just stares at me for a minute. I take the opportunity to casually sip my wine. This seems to bother her since I can tell she has a look of disdain on her face. Now, I'm just plain pissed off. This girl, woman, whore, whatever the hell she is, has the nerve to be upset with me? I mean, really, she has got to be joking!

"Say what you have to say, so I can go back inside and enjoy the rest of my evening," I say as nicely as possible to her in the hopes that she'll finally get on with it.

"To who? Tyler?" She laughs as his name escapes her lips. "Really, you couldn't do any better than that, Sabrina?"

I choke on a small giggle at her attempt at an insult, but inside my head I'm thinking back to all those times when we would sit on my bed like lovesick teenagers and fantasize about him. She used to go on and on about him, so to hear her say this is kind of humorous since I know it's eating her up to see him here with me. Not that I planned it, but she certainly doesn't need to know that.

"You don't show your face for ten years, and then all of a sudden you show up here when I told you to stay away," she says with pure hatred in her voice. She takes a second to run her hands through her hair that looks completely disheveled at this point before she continues, "You always thought you were better than, me, better than everyone, better than this town. You just couldn't wait to get out of here!"

"What the hell are you talking about, Lisa?"

She smiles at me, then says, "You know Chris always wanted me, not you, the *perfect* Sabrina Chandler. He just never had the balls to tell you. That's why we had to sneak around for so long."

She keeps going but not before her smile morphs into a devious grin, "You have no idea how happy I was that you found out the way you did. I bet you cried like a little bitch."

I've heard enough. My blood is boiling and if I let her speak one more second, I cannot be held liable for my actions. I take a step toward her and she takes a step back. I'm not a menacing figure at 5'5", about 5'9" in the heels, but I must look that way to her right now from the flash of fear—or is that doubt—in her eyes?

"First off, your beloved Chris just told me a few hours ago that he's never loved you, that he still loves me," I say to her and let it in sink in before I go on. "Not that I give a shit, but just thought you'd like to know."

"That's a lie," she says quickly.

I can tell by her tone that she knows this to be true. Hell, anyone within a three-mile radius can pick up on the vibe that there is something seriously wrong in that relationship.

"Secondly, who the hell do you think you are to tell me where I can and can't go?" I ask her but don't intend to let her answer. "And what kind of person are you that you would trick a guy into staying with you by getting pregnant?" She gasps out loud not expecting me to have known that piece of information. Her eyes are beginning to water, but I don't care; I keep right on going.

"That's right," I say to her and take a step even closer so that we are inches away from each other, "your husband told me all about that one. Bravo, you must be so proud of yourself."

Ten years of pent-up hatred finally out of my system. I thought the weight lifted off of me after telling my parents the truth last night was invigorating, but this...this is so much better. In the back of my mind I think that maybe I should have taken it easy on her, but I instantly throw the idea away. Instead, I think of all these years that she has taken away from me. All these years that I've been lying to my parents. All these years that I couldn't come home to face her, or Chris for that matter. They are nothing to me. If anything, I'm mad at myself for having let it get this far. I *am* better than her. God knows, I would never stoop to her level to do any of the things she has done to me, herself, or Chris.

"I think we're done here," I say to her evenly, and take a step back to leave as she begins to sob openly.

"You don't understand," she starts to try and explain, but I'm not having it this time. I take a step toward her and cut her off before she can go on with her sob story.

"Lisa, quit with the whole 'woe is me' act, it insults my intelligence," I say to her as she wipes her eyes on the sleeve of her dress.

She looks at me through her tears and mascara-smeared face, and I can tell she is thinking of a way to regain control of the situation. I smile at her, copying her fake smile from earlier. "Now, I'm going to go back inside and enjoy the rest of my night. If you should so much as try to talk to me one more time, I promise it won't be as pleasant for you."

I turn to leave but hear her say in a tortured voice, "God, I wish you would have never come back here."

I stop and look back at her face to see that her mask is temporarily gone. In its place is a sad, defeated woman that is a small reminder of the girl I use to call my "sister" when we were such close friends.

"My parents used to always tell me that I should be more like you," she says frustrated between her sobs. She takes a deep breath before she elaborates further, "Nothing I ever did was good enough for them. So...I tried to be *you* instead. The good grades, the loving parents, and the perfect boyfriend."

For a brief second I actually feel sorry for her. I don't know how that is possible given all that she's said and done, but I do. I immediately put the lapse in judgment aside and look at her, really look at her, remembering every emotion I had been put through that night and since then. There is no way on earth that I'm letting her off the hook this easy.

"That's it? That's why you did all of this," I say calmly to her.

And she's back. The vindictive glint is back in her eyes as she wipes her face with her sleeve and juts out her chin at me. "Why couldn't you just stay away?"

"Didn't we already cover that," I almost shout, getting more exasperated by the minute at this conversation.

"All he's been talking about since you came back into town is how much he wishes that he never hooked up with me. That I'm a bitch. That you're 'the one' that got away," she says while using air quotes to emphasize "the one."

"Let me make this perfectly clear for you…you did me a favor. I wouldn't want Chris if you paid me. After everything I've seen so far, you two deserve each other."

"What the fuck does that mean?" She questions and then askes just as quickly, "You still think you're better than me? Well, let me tell you something, Sabrina Chandler, you're still that same stupid little bitch."

She smiles and folds her arms across her chest, basking in the glory of her last statement. I smile back, throwing her off her game. "Is that all of it, Sybil? This is what was so important that you had to drag me out of there?"

She nods.

"Good, because I want to make sure you're totally done talking out of your ass before I tell you to go fuck yourself!" I then proceed to throw the contents of my wine glass all over her face.

I turn on my heel as she's wiping her shocked face and run right into Tyler's chest.

She's close to shouting when she says, "How dare you?"

I glance up at Tyler, who's grinning from ear to ear, before I turn my head to look at Lisa one last time. I almost can hear the imaginary door being closed for good on our past. I'm feeling beyond exhilarated when Tyler's hand comes to rest on the small of my back and nudge me so that I start walking back to the entrance of the building.

At about the halfway point he stops and turns to face me. He puts his hands in his pockets and is searching my face for any sign of distress.

"Are you OK?" he asks, full of concern.

"I'm fine; I should have done that a long time ago," I say through a smile. "Thank you for looking out for me…again."

"Anytime," he chuckles and then pulls one of his hands out of pockets. He takes my chin in between his fingers until my face is tilted up toward his and says, "Didn't look like you needed any help though."

"No, I guess not."

I ask if we can go back inside, and he responds by dropping his right hand away from my chin and steering us back toward the reunion.

"Since you wasted that glass of wine," he says with a small smile, "would you like a refill?"

"Absolutely," I respond quickly while the adrenaline is still coursing through me from the altercation with Lisa.

Tyler starts veering us toward our table, but I don't feel like sitting anymore. "Do you mind if we stand by the bar for a little bit?"

"Not at all."

While he's leading me there, it dawns on me that he hasn't really socialized with anyone else the entire time he's been here. He hasn't left my side, except for when I went to talk with Lisa. I look at him curiously when he secures a spot at the far end of the bar. Raising an eyebrow at my expression, he bends his head and speaks quietly.

"Is something wrong?"

"Nothing is wrong," I quickly say. "It's just that you haven't spoken to anyone else since you've gotten here. I'm sure you want to catch up with some people in here tonight."

One side of his mouth curls up as he notices me fidgeting my hands. I swear if I was ever brought in for questioning, my nervous quirks would give me away and I would have to sing like a canary. I have no idea what he could be thinking or what is about to come out of his mouth when he leans in and says, "I've waited a long time to be this close to you again so I'm not going to waste my time catching up with a bunch of people who didn't give a shit about me ten years ago."

Oh. My. God.

I only caught the first part of what he just said. The rest sounds like Charlie Brown's teacher to me. Now, call me crazy, but that would mean that he's been thinking about me. I almost want to give him a high five and say *"you too?"* but I'm pretty sure that's not the way to play this. Instead, I let the information absorb into my subconscious and save it for a rainy day.

"What about you?" he asks, pulling me out of my thoughts.

The million-dollar question. Do I defy all rules of the sisterhood and spill my guts by telling him that he is essentially *the* reason I came home after ten years? To be fair to myself, I did pretty much have a life-changing event occur not ten minutes ago that had nothing to do with him, so...here goes nothing.

"I came to see you," I say apprehensively, still hoping that honesty is the best policy.

I wouldn't be surprised if he could hear my heart beating loudly in my chest like a bass drum. Tyler brings his hand up to brush the backs of his fingers against my cheek lightly. His eyes drop to my mouth for a second, and he licks his lips quickly before bringing his piercing gaze back to mine.

"You're more beautiful than I remember, do you know that?"

I can't say anything back to him. I don't even shake my head. I'm sure I have that deer-in-the-headlights look my mom was telling me about yesterday. The same pull that I felt ten years ago is still there, if not stronger. He has an innate ability to make me feel safe and comfortable in my own skin. How he can do that after all this time, I have no idea, but it also scares the living crap out of me.

"I would pay good money to know what's going on in that pretty little head of yours right now," he says and takes a step closer.

When he pulls his hand back from my cheek, I grab it and lock my fingers in between his, needing to feel his warmth for a moment longer.

"I was just thinking that you make me feel safe...you always have," I say quietly.

His beautiful, full-wattage smile makes my belly flutter with anticipation and melts away some of my nervousness. I manage to smile back when I feel his thumb trace circles on the back of my hand that he's still holding.

"Let's get out of here," he proposes out of nowhere, catching me by surprise. "Come back to my hotel with me for a drink. We have a lot more catching up to do."

Anyone else, it wouldn't be a question; I'd say no and probably run for the hills. Tyler Anderson, hot-as-hell bad boy who I've been wanting all these years and has grown into an even better version than what I've dreamt about...yes.

"Is that a yes?" he asks, slightly amused at my dazed expression.

It takes a second or two, but I finally am able to bring myself to say out loud that one little word that has so much meaning and possibilities behind it.

"Yes."

CHAPTER ELEVEN

I'm so relieved I decided to drive my own car over to Tyler's hotel. I'm spending the short three-or four-mile drive having an internal debate with a devil on one shoulder and an angel on the other. *"Don't sleep with him,"* the angel says innocently, while the devil screams, *"Do him twenty ways to Sunday!"*

Before I know it, I'm pulling into the parking lot of his hotel. Tyler parks his car, which by the looks of it, tells me he must be doing very well in the restaurant business. He steps out of his black Audi A5 Coupe while I sit in my parked car frozen, trying to figure out whether the angel or the devil won.

If I sleep with him, he'll probably think I'm a slut or easy. If I don't sleep with him, he'll think I'm a goody-goody. Which isn't a bad thing, it's just not who I am really. The fact that I haven't had sex in almost four years isn't helping the decision-making process in the slightest. My body wants to say yes so badly and throw caution to the wind, while I'm not sure my heart can take it. I am leaving for Miami in five days so that adds yet another element to the equation.

In the midst of my struggle, Tyler's light tapping on my driver's side window snaps me back to the here and now.

Shit. How long have I been sitting here? I'm slow to turn my head to look out my window, afraid that he might think I'm crazy. Instead, I find him leaning against his car door with his hands in his pants pockets and a huge grin plastered on his face. He's so gorgeous and it's so not helping my situation. I take in a breath, blow it out, and turn off the car. Reaching over the center console to grab my clutch on the passenger seat, he opens my car door for me and extends his hand to help me out.

"Thank you," I manage to say to him.

With his mischievous grin still in place, he lets go of my hand and steps back to lean against his car again.

"Would it help if I told you I was a little nervous too?" He brings his thumb and index finger within an inch of each other indicating to me just how "little" nervous he is. The lightness in his voice helps to put me at ease as I mimic his stance and lean against my car.

It does help knowing that he's even just a little bit nervous, and I tell him as much by nodding my head. Although, why would he be nervous? He doesn't strike me as the kind of guy who gets turned down often, if not at all. While I'm thinking this over in my mind, a cell phone vibrates. At first, I think it's mine, but I remember that after hanging up on Julia earlier, I turned off my ringer. Tyler digs into his pants pocket and looks at his phone and quickly presses a button to ignore the call. He puts the phone back in his pocket then steps off his car and asks if I would like to go inside to the hotel bar.

Walking through the doors of the hotel, we head toward the bar which has all of two other patrons inside of it. There are several open booths that I automatically start walking to, thinking that if we have a table between us, I'll be able to get handle on my nerves without him being in such close proximity.

I slide into my side of the booth, never taking my eyes off of him as he leans on the bar and orders our drinks. He puts his hands in his pocket, I think to retrieve his wallet, but he pulls out his cell phone again. This time, his face looks momentarily agitated when he presses a button or two on his phone to dismiss the call he must be getting and shoves the phone back in his pocket hastily as the bartender returns with our drinks. He walks back and hands me my wine glass and sits down opposite me.

"Can I ask you a question," I say out of nowhere.

He nods as a light bulb goes off in my head, reminding me of something I need to know about him before asking him my original question. "Are you single?"

He chuckles when he says yes. Definitely relieved, I'm about to ask my original question when I stop and say, "Wait. How come you don't ask me the same question?"

"Because I know you wouldn't even be here to begin with if you weren't," he answers with complete confidence in his answer. He's right. I get the sense that maybe he's been on the wrong side of that answer maybe once or twice before, but I trust him enough to know in my heart that he's not lying to me right now.

"Was that the question you wanted to ask," he says with a raised eyebrow and grabs his beer off the table.

I'm uncertain if I want to ask, but I've been dying to know the answer for years. "That night…," and my voice falters for a second before I go on, "how did you know I was there?"

He's about to answer when the bartender comes up to our table to let us know that the bar will be closing earlier than usual due to the slow crowd tonight and then asks us if we'd like to order another round. Tyler looks to me first; I shake my head. He then tells the bartender we're fine and the bartender leaves us alone again.

"To answer your question, I didn't follow you there, if that's what you were worried about," and I laugh at his attempt to paint himself as a stalker. "I had been inside the party for a little while and decided to just call it a night. I remember walking outside and caught you pulling up in your car." He takes a break from talking to take a sip of his beer before he keeps retelling that night from his memory. "I saw you walk up and dart to the side of the house and I remember thinking that was kind of strange...so I followed you."

"But why did you follow me," I quickly interject.

"I was worried about you," he says just as quickly. "I'll never forget how upset you were. It took all of me not to go back into that party and kick the crap out of Chris, but I wanted to make sure you were OK...so that's what I did instead."

He wanted to make sure I was OK. I turn the thought over in my head and I'm sure there's more behind it than he's letting on but I don't push him to explain further.

"I still want to kick his ass after what he did to you. He's lucky I didn't go back to that party."

"Where did you go then? I offered you a ride but you wouldn't let me take you anywhere."

He grins and tilts his head slightly to the side. "Home."

"Oh."

"Where did you think I would go?" he asks before grabbing his beer off the table to take a sip.

I laugh shakily because I just assumed he would have gone out somewhere or back to that party, or met up with some random girl. Definitely not home. Back then, he was always with a different girl. To my knowledge, he never had a steady girlfriend, more like a steady stream of them. I hate that I feel a twinge of jealousy for all those girls in his past and for the countless others that I'm sure he's accumulated since then, but I do. I wanted to, or rather, I've wanted to be one of those girls ever since that night.

"I don't know, to be honest. Maybe…"

"Maybe, what?" His sexy grin is on full display now.

I take a sip of my wine before the next sentence comes out rushed. "Maybe you went to see another girl, or something."

It takes Tyler all of a second to fill in the blanks. "I didn't. I went straight home."

Smiling uncomfortably when I tuck some hair behind my ears, he eyes me carefully before he speaks again.

"No girl could have ever compared to you anyway. You were… and still are, way out of my league."

I have no smart retort or even a feeble response to that. Instead, I change the subject completely by asking him how long he's in town for. When he says he's planning on going back home tomorrow, my heart temporarily drops to my stomach and back up again.

He notices the change in me and reaches across the table to take my hand in his. The jolt to my system is immediate with just that one innocent touch. And he thinks I'm out of his league?

"When are you going back to Miami?"

"Thursday," I say to him just before the bartender comes over to let us know it's time to clear out.

When the bartender walks away, Tyler leans forward slightly and gently tugs me by my hand so that I'm forced to lean forward as well. His face is a mere inches from mine. So close that I can feel his breath fan across my cheek when he speaks in a low voice that makes me twist in my seat.

"Do you want to leave?"

"No."

"I don't want you to leave either and I'm a selfish bastard for saying this, but I need more time with you."

Tyler's chocolate eyes are so dilated that they look like black discs. He closes and opens them back up quickly as if he's struggling with something.

"Come up to my room with me," he says softly.

My breath hitches since it's not lost on me that he didn't ask. I guess I should be embarrassed by that but I'm not...not even a little. That might be because as much as he's aware that I would follow him anywhere right now, I feel like he would do the same for me. Tyler doesn't wait for my answer. He lets go of my hand and goes to stand. When I slide out of the booth, he places his hand on the small of my back and leads me into the lobby, toward the elevator. At first I'm thinking I should be more reluctant but when I look up at his eyes while we wait for the doors to open, they convey something more than the obvious want behind them. Whatever it is, it stamps down my trepidation and I step inside the elevator with him.

As the doors close behind us, I go to lean against the wall to face him and he leans on the opposite side. His eyes rake over me slowly, from my feet all the way back to my eyes, which makes me uncross my legs and pull myself away from the wall when we begin our ascent to his floor.

He tilts his head just a fraction and in a suggestive tone says, "Come here."

I take a step to him, wanting to finally give into the magnetic pull I feel when I'm around him. On my second step, he pulls my clutch from under my arm, drops it on the floor and grabs me by the waist. Turning me around, he pins me against the wall and his mouth finally devours mine.

My hands wrap around his back, pulling him in tighter to me, but it's not close enough. His left hand roams from my waist then up my chest and I moan into his mouth at the brush of his palm against my nipple straining under the fabric, causing a low growl to escape his chest. If there ever was a sound that would make me want to tear off my clothes and offer myself up to him like a virgin at the sacrificial altar, that was it.

He moves his hand further up until it's cupping the back of my neck while his other hand moves down my back, all the while consuming my mouth with the deft strokes of his tongue, taking possession of me from the inside out. Even while he is finally doing things to me that I've dreamt about for years, I want more...I *need* more. So I take my hands from around his waist and roughly grab onto his hair hoping that I get my silent message across. He responds instantly by pressing his body against me with slightly more pressure. My right leg automatically starts to rise up his calf, and I can feel his hand on the back of my neck tightening in its grip as a result. His other hand slides down the back of my thigh until he hooks it behind my knee to lift it and wrap it around him, causing the hem of my dress to shift higher.

My body tightens at the sensation of his full-on assault when he tears himself away from my lips. I pull his face back down to my mouth but instead of kissing me, he licks and sucks on my bottom lip as his fingers clench down onto my outer thigh. I feel like I'm about to combust when the ding of the elevator goes off, alerting us that we are about to reach his floor.

He helps me put my leg back down on the elevator floor and adjusts the hem of my dress swiftly so that I'm decent.

"Thank you," I say, completely flustered.

Tyler's index finger traces from my eyebrow down to my chin while his lust-filled eyes stay locked on mine.

"My pleasure," he says too seriously for my own sanity. "I've been wanting to do that for ten years."

When the door finally opens, he takes a step back and bends down to pick up my clutch from the floor while I run my hands quickly through my hair.

"After you," he says while clearing his throat and motions to the empty hallway before us.

I glance over at him to catch him smiling back at me. I tear my gaze away from him and try to steady my breathing as we get to his door. He holds it open for me and the first thing I see is the TV unit and a small desk with a chair against the left wall that I drop my clutch on. Inching in a little further, to my right is a large bed that is still made with an open duffel bag lying on top of it.

Being in a closed space with him again after what just happened is making me second guess myself, more than I thought it would, and when he brushes past me to throw his wallet and cell phone onto the desk, my heart starts to race. My body wants to finish what we started but my heart…I don't know if I can take it. My nervousness is getting the better of me now, and he notices right away when I take a few steps backwards. It only takes him a couple of strides before he's standing within inches of me again.

"Please, don't be nervous," he says softly, "I'd never hurt you."

"OK."

"I need to tell you something," he hesitates, and for the briefest moment I see a hint of the nervousness in his eyes that he was making light of earlier. It's in such complete odds to the man I just spent the hottest minute of my life with that I just nod when he goes on to say things that make my pulse race faster than I thought possible.

"That night, it wasn't the first time I noticed you…or the last. I can't begin to tell you how hard it was for me to walk away from you back then, but…"

"But what?"

I'm literally on the edge of my seat as to what else will tumble out of his beautiful mouth that I can't help but lick my lips in anticipation. His eyes follow the movement and stays on my lips before dragging his line of vision back up to mine.

"Sabrina, we both know at that point in our lives it wouldn't have been a very smart idea," he says reluctantly.

"Why not?"

His smile doesn't reach his eyes when he says, "Well, for starters, I wasn't a very good guy back then, in case you forgot. You were…you *are* different. I couldn't have given you what you needed and deserved."

I can't help myself, I have to know. "And what did I deserve exactly, Tyler?"

"Someone who would treat you right, take care of you...cherish you."

Does that mean he's ready now? I'm not sure I want to know the answer to that question so I mentally wave it away.

"When I got the invite for this, I only thought of you and swore to myself that if I saw you again I would do everything I could to make sure that this," he stops abruptly, takes a step and puts his hands on the door on each side of my face, trapping me in place. "Whatever this is between us would finally happen. So please, trust me, because I have no intention of disappearing on you."

He brings himself even closer so that there's barely any space between us. I can't keep from looking into his hooded eyes as he drops his hands and lightly runs his fingertips up my bare arms until he's cradling my face. His head bends down slowly and he brings his lips to place a feather light kiss on my forehead.

"You feel it too, don't you," he says easily.

Before I can respond, he kisses both my cheeks and pulls back an inch to look into my eyes. In a seductive voice that makes my head spin, he goes on, "You have no idea how much I wanted to kiss you that night."

I know the feeling all too well, since all these years later all I've ever obsessed about when I think about him is how much I wished he had. I try to catch my breath as it's becoming increasingly difficult with him being so close after the elevator ride and his confession, but somehow I manage to finally admit it, "I wanted you to."

He smiles while his thumbs are tenderly rubbing my cheeks, then he bends his head again and brushes his lips against mine. I can tell his heart is racing as fast as mine when I slowly run my hands up his chest and back down again until they wrap around his muscular broad back. He presses his body completely against mine and kisses me again until his tongue flicks lightly on my bottom lip. As my lips barely part to taste him again, he angles his mouth over mine and I give in to him completely.

While the elevator ride with him was frenzied, this is beyond anything I could have ever imagined. He's so perfect, and I find myself not being able to control a whimper that escapes my lips when he takes one of his hands and wraps it around my back while his other hand slides up the nape of my neck and into my hair. My hands, on a discovery mission of their own, make their way back up his chest and neck until they reach his thick beautiful hair again so I can run my fingers through it. All the while, we continue to kiss each other desperately as if our lives depended on it.

It's not until I feel his hand lightly tug my hair that he breaks the kiss and drags his lips down my jaw to start raining kisses on my neck and collarbone. I arch my back just so to give him better access as he takes his time tasting every inch of exposed flesh.

"Tyler," I say between my labored breathing and I feel his lips curl into a smile on my neck when he murmurs a yes against my skin. The vibration of his deep voice from just that one word on my neck almost makes me lose my balance. He drags his lips back up to mine at the same time my hands release his hair and rest atop his shoulders. He smoothly moves his hand down from the nape of my neck to caress my bare back, causing the goose bumps to return. He chuckles softly across my lips at my body's reaction to him before he pulls back to look at me.

Some of his hair has fallen onto his brow, and I brush it aside with my right hand. He captures my hand on its trip back to his shoulder and turns it over to place a kiss in my palm.

"Stay with me tonight," he says as he locks his fingers in mine.

My mouth drops open at his bluntness and before I can answer he places his finger on my lips to keep me from saying anything.

"It's not what you think," he explains. "I promise, I'll be a complete gentleman."

"After the elevator ride and this, I'm not sure I can be held to such a high standard," I say, partly in jest.

A wicked grin comes across his face at my attempt to lighten the mood. He bends slightly to nip at my neck again, working his way up to my earlobe. Capturing it between his teeth, he lets go and then whispers in my ear, "Well... I could make an exception for you... because there's nothing I'd rather do right now than throw you onto that bed, remove this beautiful dress and taste every inch of your body."

I gulp, as all I hear is Liz Lemon in my head saying, "*I want to go to there.*"

Still nibbling on my ear and making me lose my mind, he stops and slowly pulls back to see my dumbfounded expression. "Don't worry," he says, "I keep my promises. I'll be the perfect gentleman. Besides, I'd say it's about time we talk about you letting me take you on a proper date."

I smile at him while his chocolate eyes show a trace of amusement still and I'm mildly put back at ease. It makes my decision a little easier than I thought possible given my ability to over think a situation to death. Although, the mere thought of sharing a bed with him and doing nothing other than sleeping is shaping up to be an increasingly difficult task if he keeps up the ear nibbling like he's doing again.

"OK, I'll stay with you."

When he tears himself away this time, I drop my hands from his shoulders and try to get this situation back to normal, which isn't easy with the way he looks right now. His hair has that "I just had sex" look going on, and it doesn't help that those brown eyes of his are still full of craving.

I clear my throat before I ask, "Now, what about this date?"

He winks at me and asks if I have plans for tomorrow. I don't, other than maybe thinking I was going to catch an exhibit at the museum in Philadelphia. I tell him this while he grabs my hand and leads me toward the bed.

"Good," he says, "You can come to my place in Philly... and pack a bag."

I sit down on the edge and he goes down on his knees in front of me to untie the clasps on my left shoe while lightly rubbing my arch.

Oh dear God, he's killing me.

I practically purr as my head falls back on my shoulders, "That feels *soooo* good."

His hands stop moving so abruptly that my head pops back up to look down at him and find his face devoid of expression except for the slight tick of his jaw.

"What?"

"I'm glad that it feels good and all, Sabrina, but you can't say things like that if you expect me to keep being a gentleman tonight. Deal?"

I blush then nod as he laughs and goes back to rubbing my foot again. After he does the same to the other foot and is half way to standing up again, he places a quick kiss on my lips and asks if I'd like one of his shirts to sleep in instead of my dress. I say yes almost instantly, since there is no way I'll be able to sleep comfortably in this thing.

When he starts to untuck his dress shirt in front of me, I can't help but stare. The smooth ripples of his muscular chest are revealed with every button he pops open. Reaching the last button, his arms flex as he pulls the shirt off his shoulders to show off the "V" that leads to…well, to there. But what has captured my attention more than anything is the rest of the tattoo that is finally on full display. I'm enraptured by the black swirls that start on his right forearm and cover most of his shoulder and upper chest. Simply beautiful. He's truly like a work of art and way too sexy for his own good.

"Here. You can change in the bathroom. There should be a hanger in there for your dress too," he says and hands his shirt to me. I look at it for a second, still momentarily lost in his perfectly sculpted body before I grab it and make my way into the bathroom to change.

I hang my dress up carefully behind the bathroom door and go to put on Tyler's shirt that I don't think I'll ever want to give back since it smells of him. Turning to face the mirror I undo the hairpins that are just barely keeping some of my hair still in place thanks to his handiwork. I give myself a final once over in the mirror before opening the door to find him in only a pair of pajama bottoms as he's putting his duffel bag onto the floor.

When he looks up to see me nervously play with the rolled up sleeves of his shirt, he sits down on the bed and looks me over thoughtfully.

"I always thought you were the most beautiful girl I had ever seen when we were younger," he stops then stands up to walk toward me. He takes my hand and leads me toward the bed before he continues. "When I saw you tonight for the first time after all these years, I was blown away. But seeing you in my shirt is probably the sexiest thing I've ever seen in my life."

When I climb into bed, I don't know what comes over me, but I blurt it out anyway, "You're not so bad yourself." And that's probably the understatement of the year.

He keeps his eyes on me the entire time as he stalks back to his side and turns off the light. Finally, he stretches out next to me so that we're facing each other lying on our sides.

Even in the dark, there is just enough light through the window to make out his handsome features. I bring my hand up to stroke his cheek softly, and I feel his smile underneath my palm. I can't believe I'm actually here with him. I giggle as the thought of how absolutely crazy this whole situation is crosses my mind.

"What's so funny?" he asks, with a trace of playfulness in his voice.

"Nothing...well, not nothing, but this," I say and remove my hand from his face then motion at the small space between us. "I mean, this is crazy, right?"

He scoots closer to me, forcing me onto my back in the process. He takes his hand and removes all the stray hairs from my face then leans in and starts to kiss me again until I'm just shy of panting. When he pulls back, he easily maneuvers me so that I'm on my other side facing the wall and wraps his arms around me from behind.

"Does this feel crazy to you?" he asks quietly.

I shake my head and melt into him, eventually letting the cadence of his breathing lull me into a state of complete relaxation. Just when my eyelids are about to close for good I feel his lip place a soft kiss right below my ear. Melting into him further, I feel his lips hover above my ear before he whispers, "Sweet dreams, Sabrina."

CHAPTER TWELVE

"You're gonna have sex, you're gonna have sex," Julia says in a singsong voice. I go to lower the volume on the speakerphone even though there is no one else in my car to hear her.

"You know, I called you for support and encouragement, not to give you free reign to poke fun," I say to her like I'm the only adult out of the two of us, which sometimes I'm pretty sure is a fair assessment.

"Girlie, you've got more than my encouragement," she says in a completely serious tone.

"Well, then, help me. If you can't tell, I'm having an anxiety attack!"

"OK, OK," almost sounding exasperated at my desperate tone before she continues. "First things first...please tell me you waxed before you left."

Is she kidding? I look at the phone wishing I can see her face before I answer, "Yes, and how exactly does that help me right now?"

"Easy," she says, "that's half the battle. When he finally strips you down, you won't have to worry if it looks like you have Chewbacca trapped between your legs."

I stare at the phone for a second and then back to the road completely speechless. She picks up on the crickets coming from my end so she adds, "That means you can totally relax when you're finally naked in front of him later." When I still don't say anything back to her she continues to rationalize. "Listen, you haven't had sex in a long time so I'm just trying to help here."

"Gee, thanks. Those are some really encouraging words there, Julia. I'm so glad I decided to call you," I say, dripping with sarcasm.

She tries to contain her laughter before finally getting it under control and continues with her rant.

"Seriously, you need to just relax and stop overthinking this," she says and I can tell she's still trying to collect herself.

It definitely felt right last night. I think if Tyler hadn't stopped when he did, this conversation with Julia would be totally different right now. I'm blushing at the thought and we really haven't gotten much past first base. I take my hand off the steering wheel and lightly run my finger against my bottom lip as I relive the delectable moment from last night when he finally kissed me. It was like he allowed the past ten years of holding out control him.

"Did you just sigh out loud?" she asks, breaking me out of my day dream.

"Um…no," I say, not even aware that a sigh escaped my mouth that she obviously heard loud and clear over the speakerphone.

"Girl, you've got it bad," and she laughs. "Tell me about last night so I can live vicariously through you for a minute before I go back to watching reruns of *Buffy*."

"Oh, what episode are you on right now?" I ask, way too excited for the change in conversation.

Her irate tone snaps me back to reality. "Sabrina, focus! Fuck Buffy, Angel, and may God forgive me, Spike! Tell me what happened. And don't you dare hold out on me."

I tell her everything. The dance at the reunion, the confession, the kiss, sleeping, as in actual sleeping with him, and waking up in his arms. That last part was heavenly. At some point in the night we must have changed positions since I woke up to find my head on his bare chest and his right arm wrapped around me. My free arm was draped over his stomach and my right leg was hitched over both his legs like he was my own personal body pillow, and I loved it.

"Julia, what do I do? I mean, I'm leaving in two days."

"Hell, forget about you coming home in two days. I was going to ask about Alex," she says matter of fact.

Alex. Shit. What am I going to do about him? I can't deny that I'm attracted to him. He is right, there is something there, but do I really want to explore it at this point? I left him thinking that I was giving him a chance, and I did mean it at the time. But now, I don't know. I have yet to answer his text from the other day, and I can't bring myself to go there just yet. I'm thankful I have these few days of reprieve but then think that I now have another potential problem on my hands. Logistically, how is this thing with Tyler even going to work?

"Sabrina, stop driving yourself crazy. I shouldn't have brought it up," Julia says snapping me out of my inner turmoil. "I can hear the wheels turning in your head through the phone. You're not dating Alex so . . . no harm, no foul there."

"I know that, but it doesn't make it any easier."

"Alright then. I was hoping I wouldn't have to bring out the big guns, but you leave me no choice," she says. I quickly glimpse to the cell phone in its cradle, afraid of what's possibly going to come out of her mouth as I turn onto my parents' street.

"Here's the thing, this is Tyler we're talking about, right? Tyler 'Willy Wonka' Anderson! This is the guy you've been obsessing over for years! The same guy who apparently sounds like he has had it pretty bad for you all of this time too. You need to stop thinking so much about everything and just go with it…and by go with it, I mean fuck him senseless!"

"Wow, Julia," I say while pulling into my parents' driveway and parking the car, "don't hold back on my account."

"I'm just trying to help put everything in perspective for you, since I'm not there to actually give you a swift kick in the ass," she says.

"OK, OK," and I grab the phone, letting out a small giggle, "I just got to my parents' house so I gotta run. Wish me luck."

"You don't need it, I have faith in your gypsy charms," she says confidently.

I laugh and tell her I'll be in touch soon when I look down at myself and groan out loud at the fact that I'm wearing my dress from last night. I can't believe I'm about to make the walk of shame into my parents' house but what other choice do I have? I didn't plan on last night to happen like it did, but it felt so natural to stay with him. True to his word, he was a complete gentleman. If he had any notion of going back on his word, he didn't let it show. I, on the other hand, was really struggling, especially after he climbed out of bed and I got a better look at his naked torso in the light of day.

I hear the porch door swing open, breaking me out of my thoughts of Tyler's gorgeous body, and I remember that I'm going to have to deal with this sooner than later. My mom comes to stand on the porch as I'm just getting out of the car and make my way up to the front steps with a huge smile on my face. I waltz right by her to see my dad sitting in his favorite chair reading his Sunday paper. He pokes his head just above it and mumbles something close enough to decipher as "good morning" and goes right back to reading.

Walking down the hallway, my mom is right on my heels when I reach my room and open the door. She follows and closes the door behind her while I go straight for my old dresser drawer. Rifling through the clothes that I had unpacked just a couple of days ago, I feel my mom's stare boring holes into the back of my head. When I eventually turn around with a few selections in hand and go to make a grab for my carryon bag, she finally can't keep quiet.

"Where are you going? More importantly, where have you been?"

I let out a heavy breath, trying to keep from having to remind her that I'm twenty-eight years old and have been living on my own for the last ten of those before I explain anything.

"I was just catching up with an old friend...we were drinking so decided that it was probably safer just to stay put instead of driving home."

Not one to be fooled anymore by my pretty weak delivery of this half truth, she keeps on staring at me with that look that only a mother can give. You know the one that makes you feel like you've swallowed a bottle of sodium pentathol and can't wait to spill every little detail? Yeah, that one.

"Sabrina, what are you not telling me? And before you say anything else, you should know that I went down to the grocery store first thing this morning and the word around town is you were with *that* boy, Tyler Anderson."

I mentally plot out my next words so that they seem less confrontational than how I really want them to be. Because I need to defend Tyler, but I know I have to do so carefully.

"Mom, when I told you the other day about what really happened with Chris and Lisa, well, I left out the part in the story where Tyler stepped in and took care of me that night and made sure I got home safe," I say and go to sit on my bed.

She comes over to sit next to me and asks, "What do you mean, he took care of you? I know about that boy and the trouble he used to get into around here."

I shake my head and tell her I heard the same things all my life growing up but that he's not like that. I begin to recount exactly how Tyler comforted me that night and drove me home. How all of these years later I've wondered about him and as it turned out he's been wondering the same about me. I tell her about last night, the run in with Chris and the altercation with Lisa, and how Tyler was there again to make sure I was OK. I can't believe it, but before I can stop my mouth from running, I'm telling her a little about what happened in his hotel room. To which she tries to quickly hide the smirk on her face before I go on to add that nothing actually happened.

"He is and always has been a complete gentleman with me, Mom," I say to her finally. "He invited me to spend a couple of days with him in Philly, and I'm going to go. If I don't, I'll always wonder what it would have been like."

She takes my hands in hers and gives me a reassuring smile. "This is the first time in a long time I've seen or heard you this happy, Sabrina, so I want nothing more than for you to go and have a great time with this boy. But I want you to be careful and if you need anything, your father and I will be here to help you."

"Thanks, Mom."

She kisses me on the top of my head and goes to leave my room as I stand up and continue packing, eventually settling on a few different outfits since I have no idea what his plans are for the next couple of days. I take the quickest shower in the history of the world, or at least for me and start getting dressed. I briskly put on my makeup, which consists of just a little mascara and lip gloss, and then start blowdrying my hair. Ten minutes later, I'm zipping up my bag as I notice the time and realize that I'm ahead of schedule to meet back up with Tyler by noon at his place. I dole out goodbyes to my parents and plant a kiss on my mother's cheek before heading out the door.

The drive goes by rather fast and before I know it, the GPS is telling me that I'm "arriving at my destination." I recognize Tyler's car parked on the street while I'm looking for a spot. At the sight of it, a tingle rolls up and down my spine while thoughts of what could possibly happen tonight form in my mind. And now, instead of just trying to find a spot, I'm a ball of nerves.

Finally, and not a moment too soon before I hightailed it back to my parents house, I find a parking spot about a half a block up. With my legs feeling like two stalks made out of jello, I shakily get out of the car and grab my bag from the trunk to walk back toward his building. When I approach the door to his apartment building, one of the other tenants comes out and holds it open for me, saving me the trouble of having to buzz him to let me in. The closer I get to the second floor and to his door, I swallow the big lump that is now in my throat. As calmly as possible, given my anxious state, I stop in front of his door and give myself a quick pep talk, remembering my conversation with Julia from earlier today.

Just when I'm about to knock, the door opens to reveal a woman standing on the other side. She's a young brunette with a perfectly hour-glass-shaped body. Dressed in only a tight black tank top, low-slung hip-hugging jeans, and a pair of flip flops, she is beyond gorgeous. For a moment I think I must have knocked on the wrong door until I hear Tyler from somewhere inside say something about closing the door behind her. Her crystal-blue eyes look me up and down conspicuously as she plasters a halfhearted smile on her face and extends her hand to me.

"Hi, you must be Sabrina," she says and I take her hand, then see Tyler coming to the door behind her.

He props the door completely open and I know he can tell from my face that this was not what I was expecting. He goes to rub the back of his neck as he says, "Sabrina, this is Ava. She's a friend of mine."

She turns slightly to look up at Tyler behind her then puts her hand on his stomach and lets out a light laugh, a motion that is way too familiar for my liking. When she turns her attention back to me, she winks and says, "Well, I also work for him, but 'friend' works too."

"Ava, enough," is all Tyler says while he keeps his eyes on my face, which must look crestfallen.

"It was *so* nice to meet you." She saunters down the hall until she's completely out of view. I already hate this girl. Whoever or whatever the hell she is to him, I hate her.

"Aren't you going to come in?" he asks while still propping the door open.

"I thought you said you were single."

"I am, I wouldn't lie to you, ever. Please come in and I'll explain," he says.

When I don't budge, he lets go of the door and comes out to stand right in front of me in the hallway.

"Not sure if this was a good idea," I mumble while my eyes go down toward the floor. He takes my face in his hands, forcing me to look into his penetrating gaze. I swear his beautiful eyes will be the death of me since I can't think straight when he looks at me like this. It is all consuming, as if he can see right into my heart.

"Yes, she works for me at the restaurant. Yes, in the past year we've spent some time together, in more than a friend type of way. But, she is *not* my girlfriend." He stops for a brief second before he adds, "I'm not a choir boy, but I'm not lying to you about this."

"Why was she here?" I ask, unsure if I want to know, but if he's willing to share, why not.

"I don't know why she showed up here today. When she called me last night I didn't answer," he says with a slight shrug of his shoulders. "I didn't invite her over here, if that's what you're thinking," he adds quickly.

The calls from last night. That's who was calling him while we were at the hotel. I ask him as much and he nods.

"I don't like her," I blurt out.

Tyler laughs a little at my jealous outburst, but I promptly try to backpedal. I attempt to find the words to say something else to him when he grins and inches forward.

"I told you last night, I've waited a long time to see you again, nothing and no one is going to get in the way of that. Don't worry about her, OK?"

I manage an all-too-breathy "OK" back to him before he brings his lips to mine and places a tender kiss there.

"Are we good?" he asks softly. I nod before he says, "Good! Now would you please come inside?"

CHAPTER THIRTEEN

Whoa. That's the first word that comes to mind when I see his apartment. Everything is open and flows beautifully from one room to the next. I make my way into his living room, taking in the rich, masculine décor, when his cell phone rings.

I'd be a liar if I didn't admit to myself that I feel a slight panic at the sound of his phone ringing now. I would have to be naïve to think that he didn't already have someone or several someones in his life. He probably has women fawning over him everywhere he goes. Hell, *I* would fawn at him if I didn't know him. What could he possibly see or want with me? I mean, even *I* think Ava is off-the-charts hot in comparison.

"I have to take this call," he says hesitantly.

"Of course, go ahead," I say, trying my best to hide the fact that I'm hoping it's not Ava. I must not be doing a very good job of it when he answers the phone abruptly by telling the other person to hang on a second.

Striding toward me, he grabs me lightly by the nape of my neck and says, "It's not what you think."

"It doesn't matter," I answer while my eyes dart everywhere but his face.

"Of course it does. Why would you say that?"

Letting go of my neck he pulls my chin up with his thumb and forefinger so that I have to look at him. By the way his dark eyes are drilling holes into me right now I'd say he's upset about something. Ugh, I *knew* this was a bad idea from the moment she opened the door. I should have run when I had the chance.

"Look, you don't owe me anything, Tyler. Maybe I should just go home."

"Stop it." His authoritative tone catches me off guard.

"What?"

"You heard me."

My mouth opens but nothing comes out. He takes the opportunity to render me completely speechless by kissing me on the lips quickly, then turns on his heel to leave the room with a smirk on his face. I'm left standing there in a daze, wondering what just happened, when I hear him talking on the phone to someone named Jimmy...definitely not Ava.

God, I'm an idiot! What is wrong with me? Technically, I have no claim on him and it's just a couple of days, right? Then I'll be going back to Miami and will want to be able to look back at this time with him as drama free. *So...suck it up, Sabrina!*

Taking a long calming breath, I can still hear Tyler on the phone in the other room when I turn to look out the expansive set of floor-to-ceiling windows that overlook his street. In the distance I can see the famous William Penn statue resting atop City Hall. The view is really spectacular, I think to myself as I make my way to his kitchen, which is completely open and just as large as his living room. While

I'm eyeing his state-of-the-art Viking stove, Tyler sneaks up behind me and wraps his arms around my stomach. He kisses me just below my ear lobe causing me to giggle out loud.

"Are you ticklish?" he asks, amused at my reaction while continuing to kiss the hypersensitive spot just below my ear.

"No," as another giggle comes forth, "or at least I thought I wasn't."

He keeps kissing my neck and the funny part of it is all gone as my body starts to react to him on its own. I lean back into him and my right arm snakes up his neck so my fingers can grab onto his hair and keep him in place. He lifts his head and takes his index finger to move my chin closer to his face and starts to kiss me passionately.

When he breaks the kiss, he stares at me with such intensity in his eyes that it almost makes me forget about the Ava encounter... almost, but not quite. Turning me in his arms, he picks me up without any effort on his part and puts me down on the countertop. He steps in between my legs and purposely keeps his hands down on either side of me like he's being extra careful not to touch me.

Making a conscious effort to wipe away any memory of Ava the sex kitten from his mind, I start to run my hands up his arms then down his chest until I reach the hem of his black t-shirt. All the while, he looks on, his curiosity definitely been piqued by my roaming hands. I lean forward and start to kiss his neck at the same time my hands reach underneath his shirt to touch his bare skin.

Tyler's hands grip my hips and pull me toward him so hard that my upper body is flush against his. My legs wrap easily around his waist the moment my mouth finally reaches his. He groans into my mouth and his hand fists in my hair when he starts to grind into me. And I swear on everything that is holy, I think I could easily climax right here on his kitchen counter if this keeps up.

Spurred on by this turn of events, I go to take his shirt off but he yanks my hair roughly to stop the kiss that has been spiraling out of control. We're both out of breath and our chests are heaving while he looks at me with craving in his eyes.

"We need to stop," he says finally.

Is he seriously putting the brakes on this again? I'm so turned on that I can barely see straight and he wants to stop? Perhaps I'm not that good at this seducing thing.

"Fine. OK, we'll stop." The fake confidence in my voice betrays me, and I know he can tell I'm hurt by his rejection.

I unwind my legs from the death grip they have around his waist and drop my hands from his chest while trying to scoot back an inch on the counter. Tyler doesn't let me move backwards though. He lets go of my hair and puts both his hands on my hips to keep me right in place.

"Sabrina," he says quietly, causing a shiver to run down my spine.

I can't look at him. My eyes are now focused on his shoulder for fear that if I look into those chocolate eyes of his I'll officially lose it.

"It's fine, Tyler. I get it."

With that, he palms my cheek and forces me to look straight into his eyes.

"No you don't," he says gruffly. "Do you have any idea how much I want you right now? My self-control is hanging on by a fucking thread here."

"I thought—"

His voice goes flat when he cuts me off. "I know exactly what you thought, and it has nothing to do with anyone else."

I go to tug the hair behind my ear but he does it for me instead, just like he did last night at the reunion. I manage a tiny smile before I ask, "Why not, then?"

Grinning while his thumb makes lazy circles on my cheek, he kisses my forehead softly then moves his mouth to my ear.

"Do you really want me to fuck you right now, on this counter?" he whispers.

My insides clench and that climax I thought I might have had a minute ago could still happen, simply by the sound of his silky voice.

"When I finally am inside you, I want to be able to take my time and savor every single second. Because you deserve so much more than a hard, fast fuck on a kitchen counter."

He kisses the spot below my ear and then runs his nose along my jaw line before reaching my lips, lingering there when he asks, "Now, do you understand?"

I breathe my answer into his mouth. "Yes."

"Yes, you understand? Or yes, you want me to fuck you on this counter, right now?"

My eyes fly open. He's still within an inch of my lips when he chuckles lightly against my mouth. "I'll take that as a yes, you understand."

I nod. I have to hand it to him, the man has the skills to throw me for a loop and rob me of the ability to speak or string a coherent thought in only a few seconds.

"Good, now that we've come to an understanding, how about we get moving on this date that's only taken us ten years to get around to."

My legs still feel a little numb as they dangle from the counter, and his proximity isn't helping to alleviate the ache I still have for him. I feel a small sense of accomplishment at the visible effect I have on him. It's enough for me to temporarily set aside my earlier reservations about Ava's little visit and concentrate on spending more time with him. Although, if this torture keeps up I'm liable to explode before the date even begins.

His face is still a breath away. My eyes trace the rigid lines of his jaw, his full lush lips, until finally settling upon his warm chocolate eyes that I'm sure will kill me sooner than later. *I'm going to drown in those eyes,* I think to myself while I stare dreamily into them.

He chuckles again, "Thank you, I think."

"Did I say that out loud?" I ask completely embarrassed that my inner monologue has a mind of its own.

"Yup."

I put my hands to my face to cover my faux pas. "Ugh, I can't believe I just said that out loud." I pause, dropping my hands from my face to find him still grinning at me. "I mean, you do have beautiful eyes, but I didn't mean to say that to you. Now you think I'm crazy or something, right? I wouldn't blame you in the slightest if—"

His lips are on mine before I can finish that last sentence. It's a quick one but effective nonetheless. When he pulls back he says, "You're so adorable when you're nervous."

He gives me a quick kiss on the tip of my nose while still grinning before he backs away from me and leans against the opposite side of the counter and asks, "Are you ready to go or do you need to freshen up?"

"Well, it depends, since I don't know where we're going. Do I look OK? Am I dressed accordingly?" I ask him, looking down at my casual outfit of fitted jeans, peasant blouse, and wedged sandals.

"You could wear a potato sack and look perfect to me." He winks and puts his hand out to help me jump down from the counter.

I grab my purse and then he leads me toward the door to leave. As we're walking toward his car I ask, "Aren't they going to miss you at the restaurant today?"

He shakes his head and says happily, "Nope, the restaurant is closed on Sundays. You're stuck with me all day."

He opens the passenger door of his car and closes it as soon as I sit down. I watch him confidently stride around the hood of his car and put his aviator sunglasses on. He sinks into his seat with ease, starts the engine, and then we're off. To where exactly, I have no idea, but my heart is anxious.

CHAPTER FOURTEEN

The Kings of Leon are pumping through the speakers while he makes several turns down cobblestone streets until we reach Benjamin Franklin Parkway, and it dawns on me where we're going finally.

"You're taking me to the museum," I say barely able to keep the exuberance in my voice.

He smiles, a heart-stopping, kill-me-now kind of smile, as he turns his head slightly to look at me and says nothing. Of all the places he could have picked for our first date, he picks the one place that means so much to me. I knew that he could be sweet, but this just bumps him up to a whole other stratosphere. He proceeds to drive a little more until he eventually parks the car a short distance from the museum.

"Thank you for this," I say excitedly, and I lean over the console to place a kiss on his cheek.

"You're welcome," and he takes off his sunglasses then clips them onto the collar of his black t-shirt. Still smiling at me, he tells me stay put as he gets out of the car and turns the hood so that he can open my door for me and help me out.

We spend the next few hours walking through the museum, talking about anything and everything under the sun. There is a great exhibition going on called "Paris through the Window of Marc Chagall and His Circle" that I ask if we can save for last. The whole time together he's holding my hand and watching my every movement and expression as I look over pieces and explain some of them to him when he asks. He's so attentive to everything I do and say that I can't help but think back to when I would come here with Chris and how he was so bored that he eventually stopped coming altogether.

"Is something wrong?" he prods carefully while I pull myself from a Chagall painting called *In the Night*.

"Nothing's wrong. Actually, everything is perfect," I say and turn to face him.

He takes his hand and caresses my cheek tenderly. "Something is going on in that pretty little head of yours. Tell me, please."

I take a little gulp of air because the memory is still unpleasant. "Growing up, I use to come here a lot. I mean, it was kind of like my home away from home," I confess with a small laugh. "Anyway, when Chris and I started dating, I use to drag him here with me on the weekends…that is, until he made it known that he hated it, so he stopped coming."

I turn my head back to look at the Chagall painting I had been admiring a few moments ago. "I guess I should have known then that he wasn't the right guy for me."

His jaw flexes and tightens when he takes a step closer to me, taking my attention away from the painting again. "He didn't deserve you."

I feel a bit exposed that we're having this conversation here, of all places, but I push him further after he says exactly what he said to me that night so many years ago.

"Why did you wait so long to say those things to me?" I drop my eyes for a second to his jaw that is still clenched before I go on. "You know, sometimes I wish that I could go back and be with you then. I know that sounds crazy after just one night, but, I don't know, it just felt right between us."

He gives me a small smile that borders on sad and cradles my face in hands. "Sabrina, I wanted to . . . I was a mess back then," he says quietly. "I needed to get my shit together and get out of that town."

"I wish I would have known more about you, Tyler. Maybe we could have at least been friends."

"We couldn't have been just friends and you know it."

"You don't know that. We totally could have been friends."

The corner of his mouth twitches like he's trying to stifle a grin. "No, we most definitely could not have ever been *just friends*. I wanted you too much."

"Really?"

"Yes, really," he says with conviction.

And it clicks. I mean it all really clicks into place. Finding out all the things he's revealed up until now has been amazing, but for some reason I haven't been able to rationalize it all. Now, with him saying he wanted me too much . . . well, it just made everything real for me.

"I see that it's finally sinking in."

I know I sound a little more than pleased when I say yes to him. The grin he was trying to keep under wraps unfurls itself and he looks like a cat that ate the whole canary. We stand there for a few seconds, grinning like a couple of fools taking each other in until a nagging thought crosses my mind. What was it that made him stay away? After his confirmation that we both felt something strong between us that night, there has to be more behind his decision to purposely stay away then.

"Please tell me...I need to know why you stayed away from me."

"I want to tell you, but it's not the easiest thing for me to talk about," he says and places a brisk kiss against my lips. "How about we go someplace else and we'll talk."

I say OK and he drops his hands from my face then moves aside so that we can walk back toward the parking garage. The drive is quiet for the most part and I start to feel even worse over having pushed the issue to begin with, but I need to know more about him. I've built him up in my head for so long that the prospect of shattering the illusion is a bit terrifying, but I want to know everything.

We pull up a few minutes later on a busy, well-lit street with lots of storefronts and people walking around enjoying the unusually cool late-summer weather. He parks the car, and I look around to get an idea as to our exact whereabouts until he catches my confused expression. Before I can ask, he steps out of the car and comes around to open my door for me.

"Where are we?" I ask warily, taking in his mischievous grin.

He doesn't answer me. Instead he places his hand on the small of my back and nudges me to walk up the block until we approach a large distressed red brick building that from all accounts is a restaurant that is closed for the night. The outdoor has a black cloth awning that covers a gated outdoor patio area with a few intimate tables. Looking up at the sign that says Deep Blue, I hear Tyler fumbling with the locks on the door and realize we're at his restaurant.

"This is your restaurant," I say, more than ask.

He nods and holds the door open for me to walk in while he turns on a few of the overhead lights. It's beautiful. There's a long oak bar to my left that has private booths with dark brown leather upholstered seats opposite it. A narrow hallway separates the bar area from the dining room, which is on my right and has quite a few tables already prepared for customers to sit and enjoy their meals. Each table throughout the room has a crisp white tablecloth with folded, black linen napkins. The modern decor is impeccable with splashes of color throughout to give it a cozy yet elegant feel.

"Do you like it," he asks from behind me somewhere, as I'm roaming around the place, genuinely impressed.

"I love it," I say turning back to find him leaning against the doorframe of the dining room with his arms crossed on his chest, "It's beautiful, Tyler. I'm so happy for you."

"Thank you, I appreciate that."

"I'm kind of bummed it's closed though. I would have really loved to have tried it out while I was in town," I say disappointed while looking around the room again.

He comes up to me as his lips curl up in a half smile, "For you, I'll make an exception. Come on." And he guides me back through the bar and a set of double doors that lead into the largest kitchen I've ever seen.

He leaves me for a minute or two and returns with a comfortable bar stool that he places on one side of a large stainless steel countertop. On the other side of the counter-top is the cooking area with four stoves that are just like the one he has in his apartment.

"How does parmesan-crusted tilapia sound?" he asks.

"It sounds yummy. Perfect."

He moves with grace and ease while he preps our meal right in front of me. The whole time I'm in awe as I watch him move around the kitchen like it was a second home to him. Not to mention that it is beyond sexy to watch him cook.

"So tell me how all of this," I say, waving one hand around me, "came to be."

"Well, my good friend Jimmy," he says, then turns his head over his shoulder to wink at me. "Yeah, well he gave me my first job cooking when I moved to Philly. At the time, I could barely make mac and cheese out of a box, so when I say 'cooking,' it was really more like I was the kitchen bitch."

Tyler excuses himself while I'm still laughing at his description and returns with items to make a salad. He begins efficiently chopping some lettuce and starts the story back up at the same time.

"He took me under his wing and taught me everything he knew. A couple of years into being his apprentice, he recommended that I enroll in the culinary program at the Art Institute here in the city. I completed the program and eventually... the young Padawan surpassed the Jedi."

He smiles then turns back around to pick up a cast-iron skillet and put it in the oven. I can't take my eyes off of him when he stops to wipe his hands on a small dishtowel and leans across the counter to give me a quick kiss and instructs me to go back to the dining room.

I walk back through the doors and around the bar to the dining room to find all the lights have been turned off with the exception of a flickering flame from a candle on one table in the center of the room. As I take my seat, I look up to see Tyler making his way into the room with two plates of food. He sets the plates down on the table and leaves again but returns a moment later with an unopened chilled bottle of wine.

"Tyler, I don't know what to say," I manage while watching him open the bottle of wine. "All of this. It's amazing."

He coyly smiles. "I'm glad you like it. But you haven't even tasted the food yet; you might hate it."

I have to laugh and tell him I disagree since the aroma coming from my plate is mouthwatering. He pours the wine, and we do a small clink of our glasses before I dig in. It's delicious and the wine goes perfectly with the food.

"So, Deep Blue... how did you come up with that name?"

"It's kind of a stupid story, to be honest," he says sheepishly.

I'm in the middle of chewing so I give him the "oh please" look to let him know that I want to hear it anyway.

"Well, my partner, Jimmy who I told you about before, he's kind of a big Beatles fan."

"I love the Beatles," I chime in quickly.

"Yeah, well, Jimmy takes it to a whole other level," he says with a laugh. "Anyway, a couple of years after completing the culinary program, I knew that I wanted to open up my own place eventually. Since he'd been such a big help to me when I knew absolutely nothing or nobody here, I approached Jimmy about it and he convinced me to go for it. Then, with his help and connections, we found this little spot." Tyler waves his around him before taking a bite of his food. He takes a sip of his wine after chewing and then continues. "Which was perfect for me since not only is it in a great neighborhood, but it's fairly close to my apartment. So,

I bought it. We started fixing up the place but kept having trouble picking out a name that we both could agree on."

"Like what kind of names," I interject.

He rolls his eyes. "All kinds of crap. We were so desperate that one time we were just driving and looking at street signs to see if anything caught our eye."

"Then how did you pick something having to do with the Beatles?"

He smiles. "Well, there we all were in Atlantic City for the night: Jimmy, me, and a couple of our other buddies from a local poker game I play in. So, we're all at the Roulette table and Jimmy goes on a crazy streak. I mean, the guy was either picking the right number or color every single time the wheel spun. It got to the point that he had made me so much money I told him that if the next number he picks hits, he could name the restaurant anything he wanted."

I lean forward and rest my elbows on the table. "What was the number?"

"Eight," he says with a grin. "Like I said, he's a Beatles fanatic, so it took him all of a day to find some really obscure song of theirs called 'Deep Blue,' which fit perfectly with the seafood portion of the menu we were planning. To be honest, as soon as I heard it, I fell in love with it and I just knew it was the one."

I can tell he's more than proud by the way his eyes light up when he talks about his restaurant. You would have to be blind not to notice it. His whole body is relaxed and his eyes glint with enthusiasm the rest of our dinner as he explains some of the things that happened during the building process. Before I know it, I look down to an empty plate and he's refilling my glass again.

"That was delicious," I say to him and hold my glass steady for him to finish pouring. "Thank you."

"You're welcome."

While he takes a sip of his wine, I blurt out, "This place is incredible, Tyler. I have to hand it to you, you really know how to impress your dates."

The air in the room instantly grows thick. I cringe inwardly at the way what I just said sounded out loud rather than how innocently it played in my head.

"Is that what you think?" he asks with one eyebrow cocked and calmly puts down his glass.

"I'm sorry, I—"

"Let me make this perfectly clear for you, Sabrina," he says cutting me off and leaning back casually in his chair. "I have never done anything like this for anyone other than you."

"Never?"

I don't mean to sound like an idiot, but really, never? The guy has all of this at his disposal and he's never tried to use it to impress a woman before?

"Never."

"Haven't you. . . ." I clear my throat because not only am I ecstatic that he told me this was all for me but I'm kind of embarrassed to ask the next question. The hell with it! Here it goes anyway. "Haven't you been in a serious relationship or even just had a steady girlfriend? I mean, you are quite the catch."

He laughs and I smile as the vibe in the room has visibly returned to its previous light feeling before I had stuck my foot down my throat.

"I did date a girl a few years ago, but it didn't work out."

I can deal with this. It's just one girl, right?

"We were together, off and on, for about a year or so."

Oh.

"Since then, I've casually dated a few girls, but nothing too serious."

Uh-oh, he's not into relationships. Maybe he's a player?

"I guess what I'm trying to say is that I'm not used to this, Sabrina."

Snapping me out of picturing him with all these faceless "girls" from his past, I ask, "What do you mean, you're not used to *this?*"

"This. You and me. A relationship."

The way I see it, I have two choices. I can either 1) dissect what he just admitted to death and drive myself crazy over it. Or, 2) I can leave it alone for now and get back to enjoying my time with him. I go with what's behind curtain number two and change the subject.

"Your family must be so proud of you," I say and bring my wineglass to my lips.

He leans forward slightly in his chair as his eyes darken under the glow of the candlelight. Uh-oh, I think I put my foot in it again. I honestly didn't know much about his family other than the fact that his mom passed away when he was very young, so I assumed that it was a relatively safe topic of conversation.

"I'm sure my mom would have been proud," he says cryptically.

"I'm sorry. I didn't mean to bring up a sore subject."

I bring my hand across the table to hold his. He looks down at our fingers and rubs his thumb against the back of my hand before lacing our fingers together. Lifting only his eyes, he speaks softly. "It's OK. You didn't say anything wrong."

Then with a small shrug of his shoulders he starts to tell me about his past.

"My mom and I were very close, since I was an only child." He smiles, just barely, but enough that it reaches his eyes as if he's reliving a memory.

"She spoiled me rotten," he says with a laugh. "She use to take me everywhere with her. I remember when I was five and she signed me up for tee ball, she was so excited. She would tell all her friends how her son was going to be the greatest baseball player that ever lived." Then the light in his eyes extinguishes as quickly as it had appeared. "Then she got really sick, and just after my sixth birthday, she was gone."

"I'm so sorry, Tyler," I say, tightening my grip on his hand. "She sounds really lovely. I wish I could have met her."

His body visibly tenses when I ask him about his dad. Since he didn't mention him yet, I get the distinct feeling that whatever he's going to tell me next will not be good.

"After my mom died, my dad never recovered. He kind of dropped off the face of the Earth after that. He started drinking. A lot. He couldn't ever hold down a job because he was drunk all the time. And since I was the only one around, he took all his frustrations out on me. Like it was somehow my entire fault my mom died of cancer."

My heart constricts at the thought of him not only having to deal with the loss of his mother, who obviously meant the world to him, at such a young age, but the knowledge that his dad treated him so poorly as a result. He lets go of my hand and runs it through his hair before he exhales loudly. His fingers land on the edge of his wineglass and he starts to tap it nervously. I feel terrible that I've made him relive this, and I tell him as much, but he ignores my plea and continues anyway.

"As I got older and bigger, I learned to fend for myself, and he eventually stopped using me as his punching bag. Then he just stopped acknowledging me altogether. It was like I didn't exist…so I would just leave. I started hanging out with the wrong crowd and got into quite a bit of trouble back then. I was pretty stupid about some of the shit I did and some of the people I chose to hang out with, but it was all I knew. Graduation day could not come soon enough for me, because I knew that the moment I was done with high school, I was getting the hell out of that house for good and never looking back. I was out of there the next day and never heard from my dad again. It was maybe two or three years later that I got a call from a lawyer that had tracked me down to tell me that he had passed away from liver failure and that the house I had grown up in was left to me. I sold it and used some of that money to help me open this place up a couple of years ago."

You can tell that all of what he just told me affects him to this day. He's still noticeably tense when he brings his glass up to his lips, and I can't help my reaction as my eyes begin to water. He leans forward and smoothly reaches over to rub a tear off my cheek that has fallen while a small smile reaches his eyes.

"I didn't tell you all of that so that you'd go and cry on me," he says quietly. "I wanted you to understand why I never told you how I felt about you before that night. My life was a complete and utter mess, and I seriously needed to get my act together. If I had said anything to you, I would have only been dragging you down with me and you didn't deserve that. Plus, after what happened with Chris and Lisa, you needed to get as far away from there as possible too."

"You made me promise," I say just above a whisper to him.

"I remember."

He takes his hand away from my cheek, and we stay silent for a long moment. It's as if we don't require the unnecessary complication of words that couldn't come close to quantifying the emotion passing between us right now. If pressed to explain, I don't think I would be able to. I don't even know how long we end up just sitting there quietly, but it's a special moment I will always remember no matter what happens after tonight.

Tyler finally speaks up after emptying his glass of wine. "I'm gonna start cleaning up here. I'll be right back, OK?"

"I'll help," I say as he's already pushing out of his chair to stand up.

I go to get up but he immediately tells me to please stay put and that he'll take care of it. While he's gone, the memories from that night and everything he just told me fall into place like pieces of a puzzle, and any hesitation or trace of anxiety from earlier today is vanquished from my mind. He returns a few minutes later, and I blow out the candle on our table before he can reach me. The darkness that instantly surrounds us causes him to stop walking so I stand up and go toward his silhouette instead, reaching him in a couple quick strides.

"Thank you for telling me all of that," I say placing my palm on his cheek. "I know that couldn't have been easy for you."

He turns his face so that his lips can press a kiss into my palm that I feel *everywhere.* "Are you ready to go?" he asks with a smile in his voice that is unmistakable.

This time, I don't bother to check in with the sisterhood or doubt myself for even a tenth of a second before answering him with that same one little word that I know will change my life forever.

"Yes."

CHAPTER FIFTEEN

We reach Tyler's apartment twenty minutes later, and every part of my body is firing on all cylinders. It didn't help that on the drive over, he spent either caressing my knee or occasionally grabbing my hand to link it in his, sometimes bringing the back of my hand to his lips to place a soft kiss there. He's been slowly killing me, and it's been a good death…but my body can't take much more of it. When I would look over at him, he would just flash me a sexy grin that would almost make me blush on sight at what could be playing behind those chocolate eyes of his.

He opens the door for me, and I walk toward the living room while he says something about getting us a drink. Before I sit down, I ask him where the bathroom is so I can freshen up. Walking down the hallway, I poke my head in the first room on my left and see that it's a guest bedroom and sometimes office; directly across is the bathroom. Further down the hall is another opened door, which I assume would be his bedroom.

I close the door behind me and begin to rummage through my purse for the necessary items: lip gloss, mascara, and hair brush. I do all three in record time and wash my hands. I give myself a good once over before I walk out, thinking that the last thing I want him wondering is why I'm taking so long in the bathroom. When I open the door to the hallway, I can hear him moving around the living room and kitchen area as I let my curiosity get the better of me and dart down the hall further to take a peek at his bedroom.

Opposite me is yet another set of floor-to-ceiling windows, like the ones in his living room, that are partially covered with long flowing drapes and let in just enough light for me to see. Walking a bit further into his room, I look to my right to see a partially exposed brick wall that has a flat screen TV mounted above a dresser. Across from it is a large platform bed that has a few pillows and a dark goose down comforter thrown on top of it and nightstands on each side. Well, he's a minimalist, a very neat one at that, as not a single thing is out of place.

I turn to leave when something above his bed catches my eye. I take a couple of slow steps until I'm standing at the foot of his bed trying to get a better look at it in the near darkness. Luckily, a car drives by on the street below, illuminating the shadows on the wall with the halogen lights long enough for me to make it out. A gasp escapes my throat when I can clearly make out that it's a framed print of my favorite painting, *Blue Nude* by Picasso. The very same one I had a postcard of and kept in my locker all throughout high school. I'm frozen in place staring wide eyed with the realization that Tyler has this here, of all places.

"I use to see it when I would pass by you whenever you were at your locker," he says breaking me out of my wonderment.

I turn my head slowly from where his voice is coming from to find him leaning against the doorframe with his hands in his jean pockets. I can't bring myself to say anything just yet so I turn my head back to stare at it while I hear him start walking toward me. He comes to stand directly behind me as I try to negotiate the thoughts currently swirling in my head.

"It's my favorite," is all I'm able to finally say.

"I never knew the name of it until I found it a couple of years ago and had it framed. It reminded me of you," he says simply, as if what he just said didn't have so much weight behind it.

The things he is making me feel make me want to cry. That he would do something like this just because it reminded him of me is more than thoughtful and romantic. I can't pinpoint the feeling since it's something I've never felt before. Whatever it is, I'm positive I don't ever want it to go away.

My heart is racing when I turn around to face him, knowing that I've never wanted something or someone in my life as much as I do right now. His face is partially obscured in the darkness as I look up at him and take my hands to place them lightly on his stomach. I inch them up his chest, and his arms sweep around my back to pull me closer to him. He slides one hand up my back to the nape of my neck as he angles his head down and brings his lips to mine.

He takes his time licking and teasing my mouth until I feel almost desperate. My hands make their way to the hem of his shirt and pull it up until we have to break the kiss so that he can yank it over his head; he throws it aside. He grabs my hips and pushes me directly against him while my hands lightly trail the hot skin of his chest. I place a soft kiss in the center, and his hand on the back of my neck tightens as my mouth lingers there a moment, savoring the taste of him. His hand delves further into my hair; he gently pulls my head back, and then looks into my eyes with pure desire.

"Are you sure?" he asks, while intently scanning my face for any trace of hesitation or doubt.

I drag my hands up his neck until my fingers can weave themselves into his luscious hair, "I've never been more sure about anything in my life."

A wicked grin crosses his face when he pulls my head back a little more to kiss my throat and walks forward until the backs of my knees hit the bed. He takes his hand out of my hair and cradles one side of my face as his mouth makes its way up my jaw line to reach my lips again. I open my mouth to him, and he smoothly snakes a hand up the back of my blouse. Just the feel of his fingers on my bare skin is an accelerant, and I break away from his mouth long enough to take my blouse off for him.

Another car drives by below us, bringing a flash of light as his hands come back to my neck to bring my lips to his. They slide down my collarbone until he trails his fingertips across the edges of the lace covering my breasts. He teases me for an excruciating few seconds, then pulls down the cups of my bra. He tears his mouth away from my mine to suck smoothly on one nipple while his free hand manipulates the other, making my back arch in response and a low rumble escape his throat. I undo the bra clasp on my back and slide the straps down my arms. He pulls back to look at my naked torso with a heat that sets my skin on fire without him even touching me.

When his eyes reach mine again, my hands are undoing the buttons on his jeans. Before I reach the final one, he grabs hold of both my wrists and brings his lips to my ear. In a raspy voice that causes my body to tremble like a leaf, he says, "Not yet, baby. Lie down on the bed."

I obediently kick my shoes off and drag my body up the bed to lie down while he removes his pants to reveal snug black boxer briefs. My body is humming in anticipation when he places one knee on the bed and leans down to place a tender kiss on my stomach. He undoes the top button of my jeans and zipper, then stands at the foot of the bed again to peel them off my legs, leaving me only in my panties.

Tyler crawls back up my body slowly, kissing me everywhere, until I'm almost squirming underneath him. When he reaches my lips, he kisses me hungrily as my legs wrap around him to feel him press against me; I moan into his mouth at the feeling. My hands run up his strong arms and into his hair to keep his mouth on mine while his body moves against me in a sensual rhythm. I'm thinking about how badly I want to tear his boxer briefs off of him when he rolls off of me and moves to my side, propping up on one elbow. His hand runs down my chest and stops just above my panty line, where he traces the edges of the fabric with one finger. His hooded eyes looking like if he could eat me alive he would and it still wouldn't be enough for him.

I bring my hand up to brush some of his hair away from his brow but he captures it and kisses my wrist gingerly before putting it above my head. He runs his fingers down my other arm until he grabs it by the wrist and pins it above my head as well. He kisses me just below my ear and applies slightly more pressure on his hold of my wrists.

"Don't move."

I lick my lips and nod in answer to his demand since I have no capacity to speak right now. He nips and sucks on my bottom lip and starts to make his way back down to my breasts. He takes his time, laving and massaging them in his hands and with his mouth, and then he slithers further down my body. He stops just above the apex of my thighs to place a kiss over the thin lace when I feel his fingers hook into the sides of my panties. Sliding them off of me, my eyes squeeze shut at the realization that I am completely bare to him for the first time.

I open them when I feel his body weight leave the bed to find him standing at the foot of it, taking me in with a ravenous gaze.

"You're so beautiful…perfect," he says while gently wrapping his hands around my ankles. I feel a blush creep onto my face as his lips curl up in a devilish grin, and I almost pant out loud at the sight. His hands tug lightly on my ankles, dragging me until both my legs from the knees down hang limply off the foot of the bed. His eyes never leave mine when he bends his body over mine and takes a nipple into his mouth again. I clench my legs together as my body responds with an ache that I need him so desperately to fulfill. I feel his hand go to softly nudge my legs apart while he looks in my eyes, and I can see the passion I feel mirrored in them.

"Open your legs for me, baby."

I hesitate and I know he can tell I'm nervous. I don't want to stop but I feel so unsure of myself and what to do, having had only two lovers before him. Not to mention the last time I had sex was almost four years ago. Even though

I'm sure it's just like riding a bicycle, I'm not sure if riding with no hands is really the way to go after so much time since the last bicycle ride. I wish I wasn't as self-conscious as I am. Especially when I finally have the man that I've wanted for so long right next to me. Why can't I just relax and let him touch me?

"I'm not going to hurt you, Sabrina. Trust me."

I try to avert his penetrating gaze, but he pulls my chin back to look at him.

"Did someone hurt you?" he struggles to ask as his jaw clenches.

"Nothing like that. It's just...." I sigh and cover my face with my hands. "I'm not that experienced with this kind of stuff. I'm not a virgin but I might as well be, and now I can't believe I actually just said that out loud to you."

"Look at me," he says softly.

I unlock the fingers covering my face to look at him and find a sweet smile on his face that makes my heart skip a beat.

He exhales sharply before he says, "You have no idea how happy I am that you said that because for a second there, I thought I was going to have to kill whoever it was that had hurt you."

A shaky giggle escapes me when he takes my hands away from my face and starts to kiss me again, quickly making me forget about the nerves I had a minute ago. He drags his mouth across my cheek to my ear.

"I told you last night that I've waited a long time for you, and I'll keep waiting if that's what you want."

I feel like the air has left my lungs, and I can't articulate my thoughts. Instead I take a deep breath and try to remember to breathe when I take his hand to place it on top of my heart. Keeping my hand on top of his, I guide it slowly down my body until they are both just below my navel. I hear and feel his low groan against my neck and it spurs me on to slowly open my legs and move his hand further to where I want him to touch me.

I let go of him when his fingers begin to stroke me slowly. He lifts his head as I turn mine to kiss him with all I have, and my body is already throbbing for release. Wrenching himself away from my mouth to stand at the foot of the bed, he drops to his knees before me. His hands skim my thighs until reaching my hips where he grips into my skin and drags me further down to the edge of the bed. Just the feel of his warm breath hovering over me makes my back bow off the mattress, and then he finally places his mouth there to taste me. His hands go up my arms and down again to catch my fingers in his while his skillful tongue brings me to the brink quickly.

"Tyler," I moan between panting and writhing when I reach my release and close my eyes to relish the feeling.

I'm more than sated while he scoops me up in his arms like a rag doll to lay my head on the pillows again, nibbling on my neck and jaw as my breathing just barely returns to normal. I open my eyes when he lifts his head as another flash of light from the windows plays on the angles of his beautiful face.

There is no mistaking the want in Tyler's low voice while he kisses the spot just below my earlobe again. "I was wrong. Seeing you in my shirt last night wasn't the sexiest thing I've ever seen."

I encircle my arms around his neck, pulling him closer to my lips so that his are poised just above mine. My body flutters and my fingers grip onto his shoulders as he sensually licks my bottom lip.

"Watching and hearing you say my name like that was definitely the sexiest thing I've ever experienced…and when I'm finally inside you and make you say my name like that again, it might kill me," he says before grinding his lower body against my sensitive flesh.

Not wanting to wait anymore, I feel his body tighten above me when I bring my hands down his back to the waistband of boxer briefs. Tyler leans back until he is almost sitting in between my legs and runs his hands up and down my inner thighs while his lust-filled eyes covet every inch of my skin. Following his movement, I sit up and start to kiss and skim my fingers up and down the black swirls on his right arm, shoulder, and upper chest. I stop to look up at him and he cradles my face in his hands.

My voice is laced with need when I say, "I want to see all of you."

"You will."

Gently he pushes us back down onto the bed and reaches across me to his nightstand, never breaking away from my lips. At the sound of the foil wrinkling in his hand, he stops kissing me, props back up, and removes the last article of clothing between us. My eyes take in his gorgeous naked body as he tears the condom wrapper with his teeth and sheaths it over himself.

He licks my bottom lip and I feel his arousal press against me. I wrap my legs around him to try to position myself and I feel his mouth curve into a grin against mine.

"Tyler, please," I almost plead, not caring at all how desperate it sounds.

He positions himself at my entrance and fills me in one stroke, swallowing my moan as his mouth plunders mine at the same time. It's the most perfect feeling I've ever experienced. The sensation is overwhelming, and I can't keep myself from gripping his hair when he begins to move inside me at a deliciously slow pace.

He runs his hand down the side of my breast and further to my hip until he reaches my knee and hitches it higher up his waist. My body starts to respond to his rhythm until he slides into me and stops moving altogether. I almost whimper out loud when I feel his hands burrow underneath my back.

"Lock your ankles together, I've got you," and he lifts me as he goes to sit on his haunches and brings me to sit astride him.

The different position has me feeling even more than I thought possible and I begin to move on top of him, dropping my head back at the contact. His arm angles across my back to grab my shoulder when he brings his mouth to my breast and it's my undoing. As my body starts to tighten around him, he releases my breast and pulls my neck down so that my forehead presses against his. Our eyes lock onto each other's when I finally come apart in his arms.

In my foggy, pleasure-induced state, he lies me back down and kisses me as if I was a glass of water in the middle of the desert. I search for his hands to link mine in his, and he raises them above my head as his pace quickens; I feel him shudder above me and moan into my mouth, finding his own release.

Our bodies stay connected as if we both need to revel in this moment that has taken so long for us to get to. My eyes stay closed while the weight of his body shifts slightly but still blankets mine, bringing warmth to every fiber of my being, inside and out.

He kisses me again, but it definitely feels different. It's soft and soothing like he knows it's exactly what I need from him right now. Dipping his head again, he nuzzles my neck while he unlaces our fingers and frames my face with his hands. He makes a trail with his lips from my ear to my chin; then he lifts his head to place soft kisses on my forehead, my cheeks, the tip of my nose, and eventually my mouth.

Tyler's gravelly low voice vibrates against my lips, and my body hums languidly in response. "Open your eyes."

When I comply, his eyes are soft and fixed onto mine. "That was definitely worth waiting ten years for."

CHAPTER SIXTEEN

My body relaxed, my mind free of thoughts, my limbs entwined with Tyler's is the closest to paradise I've felt in a very long time. The only time we've moved in the last couple of hours was to eat dessert. Well, that's not really true. More like he moved to go get some strawberry ice cream and then proceeded to feed it to me in bed by the spoonful. That task lasted all of maybe ten minutes until I moaned while taking a particular sampling. As a result, he quickly threw aside the pint of ice cream and made love to me again. This is how I ended up being draped over most of his body. My cheek pressed against his bare chest with one of my legs hitched over both of his. He's holding one of my hands over his heart, while the other is drawing figure eights lightly across my bare back.

"Are you asleep?"

Tyler's drowsy voice cuts through the comfortable silence that blankets us. Smiling to myself while I stretch my arm across his torso, I lift my head to rest my chin on his chest and peer up at him through half-closed eyes.

"Not yet," I answer with a contented sigh. "But if you keep making circles on my back, I just might pass out on you."

Amused by my answer, he leans forward a bit and kisses my forehead before settling onto his back again. "We definitely can't have that."

A grin stays on his lips when he stops traipsing his fingers on my back and instead starts to sift them through my hair.

"That might be worse," I say with a laugh.

He chuckles and quickly rolls me onto my back, keeping his head propped up with an elbow. His eyes roam over my exposed chest before he dips his head to place a kiss over my heart. The motion is so simple yet I feel it from the very top of my head down to my toes. A shiver rolls through me, and I weave my arms around his neck to bring him closer to me.

"You liked that," he says and goes on to trace his lips against my collarbone.

"How do you know?"

"Because I can tell by your reaction...here." He pauses to lift his head a fraction so all I see are his beautiful eyes while he glides his index finger across my neck. I know he can feel my pulse jumping out of my skin, and I'm almost embarrassed that he could pick up on it so succinctly.

"And here," his finger now trailing my shoulder and down my arm to point out the goose bumps that have reappeared.

Tyler then brings his finger back up my arm and across my neck until finally reaching my mouth where my breaths are coming now at a quickened pace. While gently swiping his finger over my bottom lip, he whispers, "And here."

I feel exposed and a little scared that he can read me so easily, especially while his eyes are boring straight into mine. Feeling overwhelmed and still embarrassed from my body's reaction to him, I dart my eyes while trying to shift my legs restlessly under the comforter.

"Don't be embarrassed."

"How can I not be embarrassed?" I ask in a quiet voice. "You obviously can read me like a book. It's a little—"

He presses his finger over my mouth to keep me from saying how it's all a little too much. I'm almost mad at him for shutting me up, but what he goes on to tell me is so amazing that I couldn't care less about whatever anxiety I had a moment ago.

"Baby, I don't think you get it. I like that I can make your pulse race. I *really* like it when I make you shiver, too. But what I *really* like is when your breath starts to get all short and uneven, like you're panting just because I'm touching you."

My breath is now completely erratic, and I'm not embarrassed about it in the slightest. That ridiculously sexy grin of his is the last thing I see before he bends his head to bring his mouth to my ear. Now, my legs are even more restless than before, but it has nothing to do with being embarrassed. I latch my fingers onto his hair to bring him closer to me, but he doesn't budge.

"What do you want me to do to you?" he asks in a low voice against my ear.

Without a thought as to how desperate it sounds, I answer back quickly. "Touch me."

"Where do you want me to touch you, baby?"

Tyler's hand is already sliding down my neck toward my breasts and keeps on going until finally stopping at my hip. I'm panting so loudly when he stops just before reaching the exact spot I want him to touch right now.

"There?"

I shake my head while his fingers continue their assault by skimming leisurely down my leg.

"How about there?"

I shake my head again and mewl out loud in protest when his fingers make their way back up my inner thigh before stopping again.

"Tell me."

My fingers tighten their grip on his hair just as his fingers inch up to where I am aching for him. Between moans, I strangle out, "There... please touch me there."

I feel the unmistakable smile in his voice when he breathes against my neck, "All you had to do was ask, baby."

The rest of the night is a blur of pleasure thanks to Tyler's skillful hands, mouth, and body, and not once do I feel the slightest bit of embarrassment in telling him exactly what I want.

The sound of light traffic and a honking horn from the street below wakes me up the next day. My arm slowly creeps across the mattress to seek out Tyler but comes up empty handed. With that, I pop my head up to find that I'm alone in his bed. Before I call out to him, a flash of bright color to my right catches my eye. There, on his nightstand, is a glass vase full of gerbera daisies with a piece of paper balanced atop them, my name scribbled visibly across it. With ninja-like reflexes and a goofy smile plastered on my face, I wrap the comforter around my naked torso and reach out for the note.

I had to run out and get some errands done for the restaurant and didn't want to wake you. I should be back by noon, the latest. Help yourself to anything you need and make yourself at home. I'll see you soon.
Tyler

I clutch the note to my chest and stare at the flowers longingly then literally sigh out loud. Can he be any more perfect? There has to be something wrong with him or a secret life he hasn't shared with me yet. I read the note again and damn it! Even his handwriting is turning me on! I fall back onto the mattress and try to stop the wheels that are spinning in my head. After a moment I glance back at the red, orange, yellow, and white cluster of blossoms and thankfully, my head clears. I'm not going to let my usual over-anxious self drive me crazy. There is no other shoe that will drop as of right now so I'm going to enjoy it because honestly, I think I deserve it. I deserve Tyler.

With that I see the red numbers from his alarm clock staring back at me and jump up to sitting position. I have about forty-five minutes before he's due back so I have to get a move on. In a full-on sprint and keeping the comforter wrapped around me—why, I have no idea, since I'm the only one here—I race into the living room to retrieve my overnight bag. Quickly deciding on an acceptable outfit, I run back toward the bathroom with my toiletries bag tucked under my arm, still clutching the comforter for some reason. I take a lightning-fast shower, get dressed, apply a little makeup, and blowdry my hair.

Not going to lie, I'm completely out of breath when all is said and done. But I smile to myself when I notice the time and see that I have about ten minutes to spare. So, I use that time to make his bed instead of snooping for clues about his secret life as a serial killer. Once I'm done, I head into his living room and plop myself down on the couch. After a few unsuccessful attempts at trying to decipher the remote control, I finally am able to turn on the television. I channel surf absentmindedly for a couple of minutes until settling on an episode of *I Love Lucy*. I'm in a full-on belly laugh at Lucy and Ethel's breadmaking antics when the front door opens and Tyler walks in.

He's dressed casually in distressed jeans and a plain white t-shirt, and he still has his aviator sunglasses on, which make him look even yummier than usual. Smiling as he tosses his keys onto the kitchen island, he lifts the sunglasses to rest on his head and strides toward me. He sits down at far end of the couch and keeps watching me while I turn down the volume on the TV.

"You're a Lucy fan," he says, matter of factly.

"Yeah. I think I've seen every episode a hundred times, but it never gets old."

"My mom was a big Lucy fan, too. One of my favorite memories is how she could make me shake with how hard she would laugh while I was sitting on her lap. It was like being on a ride in an amusement park."

I wipe the tears from laughter and instantly feel guilty. "I'm sorry, I didn't know."

Tyler leans across the cushion that separates us and grips me at the waist. He lifts me until I'm sitting in his lap and cradled in his arms.

"Don't be sorry," he says with a small smile playing on his lips. "It's a good memory."

I lean forward and press a kiss to his cheek before wrapping my arms around his neck to hug him.

"Thank you," I say, my mouth by his ear.

"For what?"

"For the beautiful flowers you left for me this morning."

He nuzzles my neck as he says, "You're welcome, baby."

"How did you get them so early?"

His light laugh against my skin gives me the chills. "I know a guy."

Uh-oh. Here it comes...the secret life that I suspected. Because the only people who say "I know a guy" in the movies never turn out to be an actual good guys. I look at him and ask the dreaded question that could burst my bubble.

"What do you mean, 'you know a guy?'"

"Yeah, I know a *guy*...a guy who owns a flower shop down the street."

"Oh," I say sheepishly.

God, I'm such a moron.

With an entertained look on his face, he shifts me on his lap and gently holds my chin with his fingers. "So, what do you want to do today?"

"Don't you have to go back to the restaurant later?"

"Nope," and kisses the tip of my nose. "I took the rest of the day off."

"I can't let you do that."

He drops his head back onto the couch while he gets a good chuckle out of what I just said. Surprisingly, I find him even more irresistible when he laughs. *Get your mind out of the gutter, Sabrina.*

"What's so funny?"

"Baby, do you really think that on your last night here, I would want to go to work?"

"Well—"

"Well nothing," he says, more seriously now. "You're leaving tomorrow so I'm going to spend as much time as possible with you. So, yeah...looks like you're stuck with me again."

My smile is back in full force. He rewards me by framing my face in his hands and gently pulling it closer to his. Tyler's mouth is so close to mine that I feel his breath against my lips when he says, "You're fucking adorable, do you know that?"

Before I answer with a resounding, "No, I didn't know that," he kisses me, rendering me speechless. When he breaks off the kiss, he asks me the same question as before.

"It's only fair since I got to pick yesterday's date, you get to pick today's. So, what'll it be?"

I know that I would have picked the museum, but he beat me to it yesterday. Instead, when I really think about how I want to spend the rest of my last night with him, the answer is simple.

"Nothing."

Tyler tilts his head and is about to say something, but I steal his move. I put my index finger to his mouth to shut *him* up this time. I feel his lips curl up into a grin against my index finger while he waits for me to explain.

"I mean, can we just do nothing specific? Kind of go with the flow and see where the day takes us, so long as the day ends with a cheesesteak from Geno's. Deal?"

I lift my finger and wait for him to say something. After a couple of seconds, his face turns serious. "It's a deal. But, there is no way in hell that you're getting me to do the *Rocky* steps."

I'm giggling when my lips graze against his to say, "Deal."

With a firm pact in place for no *Rocky* steps, we head out and spend the afternoon sightseeing around the Society Hill neighborhood of Philadelphia that is close to Tyler's apartment. The weather is perfect. The company is perfect. Even the cheesesteak is perfect. And more important, no shoedropping anywhere today… thank God.

CHAPTER SEVENTEEN

The cool air on my back causes me to stir in my sleep as the sheet is dragged down against my skin. I hear Tyler's low chuckle when I stretch my arms above my head while lying on my stomach like a cat just waking up from a peaceful slumber. When I turn my head to face him, I feel his warm lips press softly in between my shoulder blades. He trails kisses down my spine and back up again while his hand fans out on my lower back and rubs small circles just above where the sheet meets my skin.

"Mmmmm," I moan as my body starts to respond to his delicate touch.

I open my eyes and peek through the hair that has fallen over my face to look at him lying on his side propping his head up with his hand. He smiles brightly and brings his hand up to brush the hair off my cheek before bending his head down to place a kiss there.

"Good morning," he says in a husky voice.

Wanting to feel his warmth, I turn onto my side and nestle myself into his arms while he runs a hand through my hair lazily.

"Morning," I mumble into his neck.

"Sleep good?"

Not wanting to lift my head from the crook in his neck where I'm busy taking in his heavenly scent, I nod against his skin instead.

He moves me onto my back and stays propped up on his elbow as his tattooed arm rests atop my stomach. I reach out and trace the outline of the swirls with my finger, wanting to memorize every detail of it while he looks on, amused at my determination.

"I must have thought about this hundreds of times," I say in almost a sigh when I reach his shoulder and make my way back to the black ink on his forearm.

He lifts his tattooed arm off my stomach and gently cups my face in his hand.

"And I've thought about *this* hundreds of times," he says softly before placing a tender kiss on my lips.

I'm falling for him, I think to myself when he pulls himself away from my lips. I'm pretty sure I fell a long time ago, and it scares me to death. He lives here and I live over a thousand miles away. How do I go back to what I knew before him... before all of this? I bite my lower lip in frustration as the thought of leaving him today starts to play out in my head. I've managed to maintain an arm's length from any relationship with a man since Chris. Yet, with Tyler, I've shown all my cards... well, not *all* of them. Yes, the imposed arm's length is mostly by design. But, he's different. He literally walked right back into my life as if he had never disappeared into the night ten years ago. He's turned my world upside down in a matter of days, and I don't think my heart can take him walking away again.

"Is something wrong?" he asks with a concerned look in his eyes.

I'm afraid I'll scare him away, so I decide it's best not to share my deepest secrets yet. "Nothing's wrong, quite the opposite... everything is great."

"Are you sure?"

He turns his hand over to run the back of his fingers softly against my cheek then gives me a feather light kiss on my forehead.

"Absolutely sure," I answer with an easy smile.

"Are you hungry? How about some breakfast?" he asks, which is perfect timing since I think my stomach may start grumbling in a second.

"That would be perfect."

Tyler quickly kisses me again then tosses the sheet off of him and rolls off of the bed. Sweet Jesus. His entire body in all its naked glory is on full display in broad daylight as he stalks over to his dresser to pull out a pair of beat-up black sweatpants and slips them on. They hang low on his waist, accentuating the V of his hip bones, making my mouth water. He comes back over to me as he runs his hands through his mussed hair, and I sit up when he bends to kiss me on my forehead.

"I'll come get you when it's ready. Lie back down, beautiful."

"OK."

I stare in the direction of the door and then fall back onto the bed, flailing my arms and legs against the mattress as if I was a little kid waking up on Christmas morning. Now that I've gotten that completely out of my system, there is no way in hell I'm staying in here. I toss the sheet aside and scan the room for my overnight bag when I hear the Black Keys start playing in the background. My eyes zero in on his white t-shirt lying on the floor from last night, and I quickly throw it on. I stop in the bathroom first for a few minutes to freshen up before making my way down the hall to him.

Tyler's bare back is to me when I go to sit on one of the stools around his kitchen island and watch him prepare our food. From what I can tell, pancakes are in my future. I *sooo* could get use to this.

"That's one of my favorite songs by them."

He turns his head around at the sound of my voice and flashes me a disappointed look.

"You're ruining my surprise," he says.

My brow furrows in confusion before he turns completely around and comes over to where I'm sitting. He swivels my seat and positions himself between my legs and starts to kiss my neck.

"How am I supposed to make you breakfast in bed if you don't stay in bed?"

"Oh, I didn't know," I stammer as his hands run up my bare thighs until he reaches my hips and freezes.

"You're not wearing anything underneath this shirt, are you," he whispers and runs his nose along my jaw.

I shake my head and shift in my seat while he grips my hips tighter.

"We'll eat first, but after that, I cannot be held liable for my actions," he warns and I raise an eyebrow at him.

"Is that a promise or a threat?"

When he lifts his head, he flashes me that sexy grin of his that makes me blush. "Both."

Turning my seat back around, visions of what "both" could be dance around my head like sugar plums, and he goes back to preparing our breakfast. When he's done, he places a stack of fluffy pancakes in front of me and takes the empty seat to my left with a plate of his own. Grabbing the maple syrup that he had left on the counter, I pour an obscene amount over mine and hear him laughing at my side.

"What's so funny?"

He has a forkful of pancakes perched just in front of his mouth still laughing at me. "Nothing at all. It's just I've never seen anyone pour that much syrup over their pancakes."

"Well, what can I say? I like mine sticky sweet."

He takes another bite of food and says, "Didn't peg you for a Def Leppard fan."

Now it's my turn to laugh. "Very funny, and I hate to disappoint you but no, I'm not a fan of Def Leppard. Are you?"

"Not particularly. The hair band scene was kind of before my time."

"Well then, who's your favorite band?"

"The Black Keys. You?"

"The Strokes."

"Who's your favorite singer?"

"The Man in Black, Johnny Cash. You?"

"Alicia Keys."

"Favorite color?"

"Black."

"I'm sensing a theme here, Tyler."

He chuckles and shrugs his shoulders while taking another bite of his pancakes. "What can I say? I'm pretty easy to please."

I take a sip of my orange juice before diving back in with the questions. "Favorite movie?"

"Hmmm, that's a tough one for me."

"Don't you dare say *Black Hawk Dawn* or *Pitch Black.*"

He laughs for a second or two before finally answering. "OK, OK, if I had to pick, I'm going with *The Departed.*"

"Good choice."

"Thanks. How about you?"

"*Godfather Part Two.*"

"Really?"

"Why do you sound so surprised?"

"Figured you pick something more, I don't know... girly."

"I don't know if I should be insulted that I've surprised you with that tidbit of information."

Tyler reaches over to swipe his thumb across the corner of my lips and then brings it to his mouth. "You had some syrup there."

Whatever the hell we were talking about before is completely forgotten while I watch him suck gently on his thumb. The air grows thick around us, and suddenly I'm not that hungry anymore.

"That was so delicious, thank you."

He winks at me, then grabs my plate and goes to rinse it in the sink. With his back to me, he asks if I have to be home by a specific time. I remember that I did promise my parents I would have dinner with them on my last night here so I have to shoot for six o'clock, the latest. He turns off the water and glances over at the clock on the microwave before he turns around and leans against the counter.

"That gives us just over six hours," he says with an impish grin while tossing a dishtowel on the counter. "Anything you have mind?"

He crosses his arms against his chest and tilts his head slightly while I slide off the stool and come around the island to lean opposite him. I'm not comfortable with being this forward with my actions or words, especially with someone of the opposite sex; my lowly track record speaks for itself. But where he's concerned, I can't help it. There is no denying the feelings I have for him both emotionally and physically. I want and need more of him in every way possible and I only have six hours left with him, so I intend to not waste another minute of it.

I hop onto the counter and with my index finger, beckon him to me. His eyes flash with mischief and the side of his mouth curls up as he drops his arms from his chest and takes two steps toward me.

"There is one thing I think I'd like to do," I announce innocently.

Tyler starts to graze his lips against my neck while my hands run up and down his arms. Pausing briefly from his current task, he says, "Name it."

I can do this, I can do this, I can do this. I take a deep breath and then exhale as I let the words tumble out at the same time, "I want to take a shower with you."

Phew, they're out and I didn't spontaneously combust from embarrassment. He exhales sharply against my skin and lifts his head to look at me with such intensity that I feel like I might burst.

Without saying another word, he wraps my legs around his waist and carries me down the hall. He puts me down on the bathroom counter and grabs my face in his hands to kiss me until I'm almost out of breath, then steps back and goes to turn on the shower water. As steam starts to loom around us, he comes back and takes my hands in his to help me down. Trying to keep the upper hand in this, I pull his shirt off of me, and I swear I think I see his nostrils flare when I brush past him to make my way into the shower. All the while his eyes are running up and down my body so intently that it feels as if my skin is ablaze.

Stepping into the shower, I let the hot water rain over me for a few seconds until I feel Tyler's hands grab my waist from behind. He presses into my body and lowers his mouth to my neck to nibble as I close my eyes and drop my head back onto his chest. The feeling of his hands moving up and down my curves while we stand underneath the water is a heady mixture. So much so, that it makes me slightly unsteady on my feet. I bring my hand up and grip his hair as he gently scrapes his teeth against the sensitive spot just below my ear then follows with a light kiss there.

"Stay right there," he whispers.

I open my eyes at the loss of one of his hands to see him reach for the shampoo bottle. For the next few blissful moments, he washes my hair, careful not to get any suds in my eyes in the process. Once he finishes, he turns me around and dips my head under the hot stream of water to rinse. Tyler seems satisfied that all the shampoo has been washed out and takes a step back. I look up at him and then down his body as the water sluices over his muscular frame. He takes a second to run his hands through his soaked hair, and I lick my lips at the sight. I go to reach for the shampoo, thinking that I should return the favor, but he grabs my hand instead.

Tyler's voice is thick when he says, "I'm not done with you yet."

His lust-filled eyes never leave mine when he reaches behind me to grab the soap and begins to bring it to lather in his hands. He takes his time running his soapy hands over every inch of my body until they grip my hips again. I don't think I could ever get tired of feeling him want me so much to the point of possessiveness. The way his hands tighten against my skin, the way his eyes take me in; it turns me on even more than I thought possible.

As the water rushes over me and washes away the soap, I feel his mouth begin to kiss my neck, trailing his way up to my lips. My hands grip onto his shoulders when he nudges me until my back comes in contact with the tiled wall. It feels like I'm leaning against a glacier for a moment but I don't care. I love this side of him. I love that he can't control himself where I'm concerned. I see it in his eyes even before he acts on it and it's a powerful feeling, one that I've become addicted to. His eyes darken when I lean back, silently asking for more. He groans when his mouth follows a trail of running water down my chest and takes a nipple into his mouth while his other hand dips lower and begins to stroke me in an excruciatingly slow motion.

My body is on the verge of splitting in two when he lightly kicks my leg open and wraps one leg around him to position himself at my entrance. Tyler kisses and licks his way up from the hollow of my throat to my mouth where he captures my bottom lip with his. I'm so caught up in the moment that I briefly forget I'm not on any form of birth control and have to stop before this goes too far.

"Tyler," I barely get out between moaning from the sensation of his erection rubbing against me and his lips running across my jaw, "I'm sorry but I'm not on the pill."

When he lifts his eyes to mine he doesn't look as disappointed as I am about this news. It scares me a little that

I am willing to throw away my standards for a second but the idea of feeling him... *all* of him, is exciting. Instead, he reaches over with one hand to shut off the water pouring over us. Before I know it, he lifts me in his arms and I wrap my legs around him. When he opens the shower door, I'm thinking he's going to put me down and grab a towel for each of us, but he keeps right on walking out the door and toward his bedroom.

"What are you doing, we're soaking wet," I screech in surprise.

Even though I'm a bit shocked by what he's doing, I have to admit that it does ratchet up my need for him to a whole other level. He doesn't say a word though when we reach his bed and he tosses me onto it. I land on my back in dead center of it, and he reaches over to his nightstand to grab a condom. My eyes take in his gorgeous body dripping in water while he puts it on, and all thoughts or concerns of ruining his sheets fly out the window like yesterday's news. He kneels in between my legs and enters me immediately before bending over my body to take my breast into his mouth again. The fact that he can't wait any longer and isn't being too gentle about it makes it even better. My hands clamp down onto his forearms and he raises his eyes to mine. His look of raw need is so obvious that my head feels like it might spiral right off my shoulders.

He brings his mouth to mine but doesn't kiss me. "Am I hurting you?"

In my head the answer is no, but my breathing is so out of whack that I simply shake my head.

A wicked smile spreads across his face while he keeps his lips steady over mine. My neck arches when he twists my hair around his hand and pulls back roughly as our wet bodies slide against one another. His thrusts come harder and faster, and it's almost too much yet absolute perfection when my body reaches its peak quickly and he follows shortly thereafter.

I keep my eyes closed and feel his thumb run along my bottom lip. "Are you still worried about the sheets?"

They flutter open while Tyler's mouth glides against my neck and I say completely out of breath, "Fuck the sheets."

CHAPTER EIGHTEEN

I must be in the middle of a really good dream. That's how I feel as I watch Tyler start to get ready for work while I sit on his bed wrapped in a towel after taking another shower, both of us trying to prolong the inevitable. We spent the last few hours lounging on his bed where I think he kissed every single spot on my body like he was trying to commit each piece to memory. We talked, cuddled, ate, and made love until it was painfully obvious that we had to get moving.

Watching him move around his bedroom, I'm not even trying to hide the fact that I'm staring at him. My mind starts to replay the last time we were together in his bed a short while ago...something happened. Not that the times before weren't earth shattering, but this last time was just different. He made sure that I kept my eyes trained on his as he moved slowly above me, his mouth hovering over mine, swallowing my every breath and vice versa. I thought that I saw something in his eyes, an unspoken promise that made me want to stay in his arms and never leave.

"Are you sure you don't mind giving me a ride to the restaurant?" he asks, breaking me out of my thoughts.

During one of our talks this afternoon, he let it slip that he has a motorcycle that he keeps in a garage behind his restaurant. Had it not been for our limbs being totally entangled at that moment, I might have fallen off the bed when the hottest mental picture of him on a motorcycle formed in my head.

"You have a motorcycle too?"

"Yup."

He had been busy with the task of kissing his way from my stomach to my collarbone. "Would you like me to take you for a ride?"

The double meaning wasn't lost on me, especially when he flipped me over and had me straddle him.

"I've never been on a bike before. That sounds like fun."

"It is. There really isn't anything like being on a bike on the open road. The possibilities seem limitless."

"Where is it? I mean, I don't remember seeing a bike parked outside?"

It was becoming increasingly difficult to carry on with the conversation when he had his hands roaming my naked torso, but I was determined to keep talking.

"I keep it in a storage room behind the restaurant. I try to make time on my days off to ride it, but I usually end up working anyway." At this point, he sat up and started kissing and sucking my breasts. The stubble on his face rubbing against me was so heavenly that I barely got the next sentence out clearly.

"I'd love to see it…and ride it," I said and ran my fingers through his hair. "I'd bet any amount of money that it's black."

He laughed and reached over to his nightstand before putting on a condom and then guiding himself inside of me.

"So?" I asked him, somewhat out of breath.

Tyler's hands on my hips had stilled as well as my movement. "So, what?"

"Is it black or not?"

His mouth had curved into a mischievous grin before lifting me and pulling me back down onto him hard. I might have cursed at this point, I can't remember... that's how good he made me feel with just that one stroke.

"Baby, do you really want to talk about the color of my bike right now?"

"Nope."

I gripped his shoulders then and started to move on my own while Tyler buried his face in my neck.

"That's my girl."

That was a couple of hours ago, so, in the guise of wanting to give him a chance to ride it, I volunteered to give him a ride to his restaurant. In reality, I was being a little selfish since I wanted to be able to spend as much time with him as possible.

I get up off the bed reluctantly, clutching the towel around me and walk to his closet, where he's currently standing with a towel wrapped around his waist, eyeing his clothes.

"I don't mind at all. It gives me an excuse to spend more time with you," I say to him while leaning against the frame of the closet door.

He turns his head to look me over. His eyes examine me from head to toe in appreciation, and the corners of his lips curl up just slightly before he abandons the clothing search and comes to stand before me.

Without even touching me his words envelope me in warmth. "You're making this extremely difficult on me, baby."

I tilt my head and smile at his use of his pet name for me. I was never overly fond of pet names, but coming from him, I never want to hear him call me anything else.

"I'm sorry," I say to him. "I'll go get dressed."

When I shove off the doorframe, he captures my hand and pulls me back to him and starts to kiss me. Mourning the loss of his lips, his eyes search mine longingly for a moment before he speaks.

"I would rather spend the rest of the night here in this bed with you. If I could, I would make it so you wouldn't have to leave tonight or tomorrow for that matter. I wish that I could make those things happen right now more than anything."

Smiling at his words, I get up on my tip toes and brush his lips softly against mine. "I wish you could too."

He kisses me one last time, and I let out a contended sigh then set off to get dressed. About a half hour later, I stroll into the living room area to find him thumbing through his cell phone. When I approach him, he lifts his head and looks me over then pockets the phone and asks if I'm ready. I'm too busy ogling him in his black dress pants and charcoal grey button down shirt to say anything so I just nod.

The drive there doesn't take long but the whole time I'm dreading the impending goodbye. My stomach is in knots while I steal a quick glance at him sitting in the passenger seat. Since we hadn't discussed anything further than the ride here, I pull up as closely as I can to the restaurant and brace myself. While staring out at the road before me, I see Tyler's hand take one of mine off the steering wheel. I tilt my head to look at him as he's bringing it to his lips and pressing them softly across the back of my hand. Shifting fully in my seat to face him, he reaches out with his other hand to tuck some hair behind my ear.

"Do you want to come in for a minute?" he asks while stroking my cheek with his thumb.

I hesitate before answering because the tears are right there on the cusp of falling over and would make this goodbye seem like something out of a Lifetime TV movie. The pessimist in me is starting to take over my thoughts on this whole situation. I was fine a few hours ago, but now, the reality of the distance that will be between us is disheartening. I take a quick gulp of air to keep it in check and say yes.

"What's the matter?" he asks.

"Us."

He eyes me warily as his body stiffens slightly. "What about us?"

It takes me a second or two, but I finally admit it. "I don't want to go."

"Then don't."

Is he serious? Didn't he just tell me the other night that he doesn't really do relationships? I stay silent while my heart battles the logical thoughts that keep me from just saying OK to him. God knows I want to, more than anything, but eventually the logical wins out. Even if he was joking about not leaving, which I can't tell if he was or not, I tread carefully in my response.

"These have been the best few days of my life, Tyler. But, it's not that easy...I wish it was, but it isn't. My whole life is there. I can't just pick up and leave after three days. Everyone will think I'm nuts...that we're nuts. I mean, this is nuts...well it's not, sort of, but still. And—"

I stop talking when his finger presses against my lips, cutting me off.

"Baby, this isn't nuts, but I get it." He sighs heavily keeping a watchful eye on me at the same time. "Look, I'm not going to sit here and lie to you that the distance doesn't bother me too. It does. A lot. But who says we have to figure this all out today? I told you that I'm kind of new to all of this so you're going to have to put up with me while we both figure this out together. OK?"

His finger taps playfully against my bottom lip and my mouth opens to say something but he beats me to it.

"Before those perfect, delectable lips of yours say anything else, all you need to be certain of is this: I'm not letting you just up and walk out my life after finding you again." He pauses and takes his finger away to kiss me and keep me from talking. His tactic is working since I can't think clearly when his lips are on mine.

"Now, I'll make you deal," he offers with a sly smile on his face when he pulls back within an inch away from my mine, knowing full well the effect he has on me. "You let me worry about how this is going to work…because it's going to work if it kills me."

"OK," I say, way too breathily and embarrassingly so.

"Why don't you come in for a minute?"

"OK."

Tyler chuckles then steps out of the car and waits for me on the sidewalk. When I reach him, he takes my hand in his and laces our fingers together before leading me to the entrance. There are only a few people here since the restaurant isn't open yet for the night. A couple of them give quick glances our way and go back to whatever it is they were doing before we walked in.

"My office is back that way," he says motioning with his other hand to the far end of the restaurant.

I have no idea what he needs me to see in his office, so I just let him lead me through the bar area. I'm taking in all the decor that I really wasn't able to appreciate last night when a man's hurried voice calls out, "Tyler, thank God you're here. We've got a problem with the delivery from earlier today."

Tyler curses under his breath, stops walking and turns us around to see where the voice is coming from. A handsome, older man with a frustrated look in his eyes is stalking toward us. I'm guessing this must be Jimmy. He's dressed nicely with a pair of dark slacks and sky-blue button-down dress shirt, carrying a stack of papers in his hand. He's about to start talking and then notices me standing next to Tyler and stops suddenly.

"Oh, I'm sorry, I didn't realize you were busy."

"Don't worry about it, Jimmy," Tyler says and starts to introduce us. "Sabrina, this is Jimmy, my right- hand man. Jimmy, this is Sabrina…my friend I was telling you about."

I catch him with a stunning smile as the description escapes his lips and it makes me momentarily forget my manners. Flustered, I put my hand out to shake Jimmy's. "Nice to meet you. I've heard a lot about you."

"All lies, I'm sure," Jimmy chuckles and takes my hand in his. "Hello, Sabrina, I'm so sorry, but can I borrow him for a minute or two."

"Oh, sure," and I sneak a peek at Tyler when he asks Jimmy to give us a second.

"I'll be at the bar," he says then turns to me with a friendly smile. "It was very nice to meet you, Sabrina."

Tyler turns around and I follow him when he walks toward one of two doors in the very back of the restaurant. He takes his keys out to unlock the door and turns on the lights. His office space has basic furniture with just a few stark personal touches here and there, nothing fancy.

"I'll be right back, OK," he says just before he kisses me on my cheek and leaves.

As soon as he disappears from my sight, my mind goes into hyperdrive. What the hell does "friend I was telling you about" even mean? This should make me a little happy because he's talking to someone about me, but just a couple of days ago he was telling me that he's not use to relationships... or a girl-friend. The word alone is almost exotic to me and makes me even more anxious than before. I haven't been a "girlfriend" to anyone in so long that I'm not even sure what that entails anymore. I realize that it seems silly that a twenty-eight-year-old woman doesn't know the first thing of how to be in a rela-tionship with someone. A long-distance relationship one, at that, but it's the sad truth. I already know I'm falling for him, which is half the battle, I think. Who am I kidding? The way I'm feeling, I've already fallen flat on my ass for him.

I go to take a seat in one of the chairs facing the dark oak desk and dig through my purse for my cell phone. I'm in the middle of sending a text to my mom to let her know my arrival time when a woman's voice from behind me makes me stop.

"Look who's here."

The hairs on the back of my neck stand at the sound of Ava's voice. Before I turn around, I already hate the fact that I'm not dressed for this standoff. My selection of comfort over beauty due to a long drive ahead of me won out earlier. So, the low rise jeans, distressed Blondie t-shirt and my favorite pair of black Converse sneakers are not exactly prime battle armor right now.

When she comes into view, her ruby-red lips curl up in an almost snarl while she leans in the doorway and puts one hand on her hip. For a woman I know I don't like, I hate to admit she's gorgeous. Her black dress pants ride low on her hips, while her black fitted dress shirt is tucked to reveal that hour-glass figure that rivals Marilyn Monroe's. Her brown hair is swept up in a ponytail with a slight poof, accentuating her striking blue eyes and high cheek bones. I study her closely while conjuring up images of her being doused with water and melting to the ground, leaving only her steaming clothes behind before she starts talking again.

"I don't think I've ever seen Tyler bring one of his girls here. You must be *special*," she says with a lilt in her tone.

"What do you want from me, Ava?" I ask quickly and put my phone on Tyler's desk to give her my full attention.

She smiles as she drops her arm from her hip and pushes off the door to sit in the chair opposite me. Crossing her legs so that one can dangle precariously within inches of my shin, she leans back as if she hadn't a care in the world. I can't fool myself, this is bad. Not like I had enough to worry about with the logistics of a long-distance relationship, but to know that she is here and I'm not...it's really bad.

"He's got you fooled, doesn't he? Tyler's never been in a serious relationship. He's more of a love 'em and leave 'em kind of guy. You are no different."

As she uncrosses her legs and leans forward, she scrutinizes my face carefully to make sure her words have left their mark. And they most definitely have. My heart drops and my palms start to sweat as I think of some of the things he's told me, almost in a panic: He doesn't want to see me walk out of his life; he's going to kill himself trying to make this work between us. Why would he lie to me? He has nothing to gain by stringing me along, especially since I don't even live in the same freaking state.

"Did I hit a nerve?" she asks in a concerned voice that is laced heavily with amusement. She smiles and waits for me to say something, anything. I would like to say a lot of things to her at this moment, but all of them would give her the satisfaction she is trying to achieve. Instead, I opt for the cool approach, even though it takes all of me to not smack the stupid smile off her face.

"It looks more like I'm the one who strikes a nerve," I say as I mimic her slightly by leaning back in my chair and crossing my legs. "If not, you wouldn't be in here looking as desperate as you do right now."

"Keep telling yourself that, if it helps," she shoots back evenly.

My cell phone vibrates on Tyler's desk, and Ava eyes dart over at the same time mine do and see that it's a text from Alex. I curse my iPhone for previewing texts on a locked screen since it reads as clear as day for the world to see.

Dinner date when you get back?

Why did he have to pick this exact moment to text me? All he had to do was wait a few more minutes. But no. I could never be that lucky. That would be asking for too much.

"Does Tyler know about this Alex person?" she asks way too interested for my liking. "Looks like someone isn't so saintly after all if you're stringing men along like this."

Her smile deepens and she tilts her head to the side, glancing momentarily at the phone then back to me. Keeping her eyes trained on mine, she takes her hand and smoothly runs it over the surface of the desk, stopping just short of caging me in on one side.

"You can pretend all you want that you're special to him, but trust me, as soon as you leave, he'll go right back to doing what he does best."

"And what's that?"

She lets out a hasty laugh and then says, "Honey, if you have to ask, then I really feel sorry for you."

Most definitely jealousy has reared its ugly head and I'm reeling.

Score one for Ava.

"Please, just leave," I faintly say focusing my attention on the desk instead of her.

Her sardonic, low laugh brings my attention back to her when she pulls herself up to stand and strides casually toward the door.

"Have a safe flight home, Sabrina. I'll make sure to watch over Tyler while you're gone," and then winks at me before leaving the room for good.

I turn to face the desk again in a daze. How many times has he been with her? It would seem as though to her it's recent enough to stake some sort of claim on him. And when I look at her, even I couldn't blame him. I can't compete with that! The girl is beyond sexy and alluring and...ugh!

I take my palms and press them against my eyes to try and erase the vision of Tyler and Ava together. Who am I kidding? Not enough bleach in the world could wash it away now. It's permanently etched into my brain like a tattoo.

"Sorry I took so long," Tyler says when he comes into his office to meet back up with me. He takes one look at me and hones in like a beacon on the worried look on my face. "Are you OK?"

What can I say to him? *Um, yeah, the girl you told me you occasionally used to sleep with just came in here and threw down the gauntlet. Nice, right? I thought so, too.* That might not be the wisest thing to say since I don't want to sound too jealous or insecure, even though the feeling is running through my veins like a runaway train. So, what do I do? I lie. I lie like a rug. I take my hands away from my face, put on a fake smile, and chalk up my mood to being tired. I know it's a cop out, but really, what good does it do for me to get into this with him now, right before I'm set to hit the road?

He asks if I'm sure that's all it is and sits across from me in the chair that had been tainted by Cruella de Vil. The entire room is laced with tension, and I stand up, unable to stay a second longer.

"I've got to start heading out to beat some of the traffic," I announce, knowing damn well how lame that sounds.

He remains seated and takes both my hands in his, pulling me to stand in between his legs. When he looks up at me, I wish that for once I wasn't such a sucker for those brown eyes of his because they have a way of making me feel like he's ransacking my heart.

"Whatever you're thinking in that head of yours...whatever doubts you have about this...*whatever* it is, I can see it in your eyes and you need to know that I'm going to do everything I can to prove you wrong."

He stands and cups my face with his hands, caressing my cheeks with his thumbs and softly says, "I knew the real you was going to be so much better than whatever I could dream up in my head, and there is no way in hell I'm letting you get away this time."

"Tyler, when you say things like that it makes it even worse," I respond, sounding defeated.

"How is it worse?"

"It just is. I mean, I'm flying home and...I don't know how this could possibly work."

"What the fuck happened from the moment I left this room a few minutes ago to now?"

Even though this is my perfect chance to tell him about Ava, I chicken out, again.

"Nothing happened. I'm just...I don't know...scared?"

That's not really a lie so I don't feel too guilty not spilling my guts about Ava's visit. I am scared. I'm utterly terrified at how he's already set up shop in my heart, and my thoughts are saturated with him to the point that I'm second-guessing every little thing he says or doesn't say.

Tyler rests his forehead against mine, takes a quick breath and exhales. "I'm going to let you in on a little secret. I'm scared too."

"You are?"

"Sabrina, the things I've said to you, I've never said to anyone else. The way I feel when I'm around you, I've never felt anything like it before. I want to be a part of you...your life, because everything...every little piece of me was always meant to be yours." And he slides his hand to stop just above my heart before pressing a light kiss on my lips. "So, yeah, all of that scares the living shit out of me."

It's a huge leap for me but one that I want to take so badly that I can taste it. Life sometimes is about taking risks, and this is one that I'm willing to throw the dice on. I want to trust him and forget about Ava, the distance, and the other myriad of reasons or doubts I have.

"I believe you and I want the same things, but—"

"But nothing. We'll figure it out. You just have to have a little faith. Can you do that for me?"

The pushover in me sighs because she knows when she's beat. "Do you always get what you want?"

A boyish grin comes across his face as the words fall out of my mouth and I giggle at the sight.

"What's so funny?" he asks.

"Nothing. You're just... how do I put this?" I'm stalling, while he wraps both his arms around me bringing me closer to him.

"I'm just what?" he asks, raising his eyebrow in curious amusement.

"It's just funny that back in high school all of us girls thought of you as a 'bad boy,' but here you are, saying some pretty romantic things to me. It's sweet."

He brings his lips to my jaw and kisses a trail to my ear. "I can still be a little bad for you, if you want? Maybe I was just waiting for the right girl."

My hands come up to grab hold of his hair, pulling his lips to within inches of mine. "Promise?"

"Most definitely, promise," he says with a devilish twinkle in his eyes before his mouth covers mine in a searing kiss that makes my toes curl.

Reluctantly, I'm the one that breaks off the kiss. "I don't want to be the one to say this, but I really have to get going," He runs his index finger from my temple to underneath my chin, his eyes following the motion in deep concentration. His brow furrows slightly when he nods in agreement and then bends his head down to press a quick kiss to my lips.

I grab my purse and pull my keys out as he takes my other hand in his, walking me back through the restaurant and eventually to my car, thankfully with no other Ava sightings.

"Drive safe, baby," he says and pulls me in for one last hug. I nuzzle into his neck and take a deep whiff of his delicious skin before I let go for good.

Driving away, he stays standing on the sidewalk watching me. Jesus, this is like something from the movies. I swear if I sneak a peek in my rear view mirror I'm going to start crying like an idiot. So what do I do? I look. And there he is. The tears come with every inch of distance I put between us, until I take a turn at the end of the block and he's gone. I angrily wipe them away before putting on my sunglasses and settle in for the long drive ahead. When I reach the highway a few minutes later, my phone buzzes with a text from him.

Have some faith xo

It's exactly what I needed to hear. The smile on my face is so wide that I probably look like the Joker right now to anyone driving by, but I don't care one bit because Tyler "Willy Wonka" Anderson is mine... *finally.* I think.

CHAPTER NINETEEN

Laundry sucks. No person in his or her right mind will tell you that laundry is the most fun thing to do, ever. And if there are people out there like that, they need to get their heads examined.

I'm back at my parents' house, having arrived about an hour ago and decided to wash my clothes so that I wouldn't have to when I get home tomorrow. In retrospect, I probably should have just put it off because I absolutely detest doing laundry. Too late now, I think to myself and gather up my whites to toss into the washing machine. One article of clothing sticking out of the pile catches my eye. I snatch it back out of the machine and bring it to my face to inhale the sweet smell of Tyler.

Yeah, I stole his t-shirt.

I couldn't help myself. It was just begging for me to swipe it. I'm sure he won't miss it either. It's just a plain old white t-shirt. Plus, guys in general must have dozens of these so with one less lying around, I probably did him a favor. Now, not only do I get to have him with me, albeit in a weird way when I get home, but I got new pajamas out of it. Because I'm definitely going to be sleeping in it until the smell wears off.

God, I really need to get a grip, but I can't stop, it smells…glorious.

"What are you doing?"

My mom's voice scares the living crap out of me since my eyes are closed and I am sniffing away at Tyler's t-shirt like a hunting dog. So much so that I jump a little and drop the t-shirt to the ground. I quickly gather it back up and turn around to find my mom staring at me with a very curious look.

"Mom, you scared the shit out of me!"

I shove the t-shirt behind my back and onto the top of the dryer that has a pile of clothes from my previous load waiting for me to fold.

She cocks her head to the side to try to get a glimpse of the t-shirt. "Were you sniffing that shirt?"

Going straight into defensive mode, I respond, "Yes. Yes, I was. Is there something wrong with that?"

My mom covers her mouth with her hand to keep from laughing. She doesn't do a good enough job since she's currently doubled over and laughing so hard she can barely get a word out.

"Oh, sweetie, I wish you could have seen your face," she says, wiping the tears from her eyes. "It must smell really good, huh?"

I purse my lips to keep from smiling and choke out my answer. "Yes, it does."

"Well, don't let me interrupt," she adds and turns around to head back upstairs, still laughing. "I was just coming down here to tell you that dinner will be ready in about an hour."

"OK, thanks," I say to her legs that are disappearing up the basement stairs.

Great. Now my mom thinks I've officially flipped my lid.

I turn back around to start folding my pile of clean clothes, being careful to extract Tyler's t-shirt first. Once that's taken care of, I place it to the side and tackle the rest. In between the shirt-sniffing and laundry-folding, I forgot that my cell phone was tucked away in my back pocket until it vibrates. I dig it out to see that I have a text from Tyler.

I know you just left, but I already want you back in my bed . . .

My Joker-like grin is back with a vengeance while I quickly type out a return text.

Miami isn't that far away ;)

He answers me back just as fast.

Anywhere but here is too far xo

The sigh that escapes me borders on ridiculous as I text back a simple "*xo*" to him and get back to folding my clothes. By the time I finish, the second load is done with its rinse cycle. I transfer it into the dryer and haul myself and my folded clothes up the stairs to start packing. When I turn the corner into my old bedroom, there's a knock at the front door. I toss the pile of clothes onto my bed and yell out to Mom.

"I'll get it."

She must be busy cooking since she doesn't even answer me back. As I approach the door I can hear her and my dad arguing about what temperature a grill should be for steaks. So, I guess we're having steaks on the grill tonight. With that I open the door and see Chris in mid-freeze with his hand in the air ready to knock again.

"What are you doing here?"

At least he looks a little better than he did a few nights ago at the reunion. I don't know why that makes any difference to me since I can't stand him, but even I have to admit the man is still pretty darn good looking. He pulls his sunglasses off his face and there they are…the baby blues that I use to get lost in. Before I get too upset at him for showing up here, not to mention if my parents see him they may kill him, I ask him one more time.

"Chris, what the hell are you doing here?"

"I came to apologize," he says and shoves his hands in his jeans pockets.

I dart out onto the porch and close the front door behind me, careful not to make too much noise so that my parents don't notice.

"I appreciate that, but you already tried doing that the other night and it didn't go over too well. So what I'd like for you to do is just turn around and leave and never come back here again."

He runs his hand through his hair, visibly stressed over this. Do I care? No, not really. He made his bed and now he has to lie in it. It's not my problem that he shares that bed with the most awful person in the free world. As Julia would say, "sounds like a personal problem to me."

"Sabrina, look, I know I shouldn't have said anything to you at the restaurant and I sure as hell know that I shouldn't have said anything to you at the reunion," he says as his voice gets quieter at the mention of the reunion. "It's taken me ten years to realize that I've made some pretty shitty decisions in my life, but in the end, I know that I'm the one who made them."

It's then that I see it in his eyes as he flashes them my way. The authenticity he's trying to express through his apology. It's funny how words can perfectly relay how you feel. They can be the exact thing you need to hear or know at any particular moment. But sometimes, it's the person delivering those words that makes all the difference in the world. Their eyes shine with whatever emotion they are trying to convey. It can be love, hate, happiness, or anger. In Chris's eyes, I see nothing but regret.

I still don't trust him *or* like him, but even I can't be this cold. I guess when it comes down to it I have to let it go, and I mean let it *all* go, even if it means forgiving the one person who broke me.

His head bows down, but he keeps his eyes on me when he breaks the heavy silence without any agenda. "I'm so sorry I hurt you, more than you'll ever know."

And I feel it. I feel his apology really run through me. I know the last couple of days with Tyler have played some part in allowing me to let go of my anger toward Chris. So his apology is more than I had hoped it could be and it's what I needed from him to completely move on. I'm not sure if he needs to hear the words from me more than I need to say them to him because I truly mean it.

"I forgive you."

"Thank you. I don't think I deserve that," he says, "but I'm glad to hear it."

A wisp of a smile appears on his face at the same time I hear my dad's voice clamoring behind the front door and getting closer. There goes the thought of being able to relish this poignant moment. As much as my mom thought it was somewhat amusing when my dad said he would kill Chris if he ever saw him again, I know he wasn't joking. Now it's of critical importance to keep him breathing and my dad out of jail, so I need to get him out of here.

"No offense, Chris," I mumble, "but you should probably leave now."

I step forward to force him to walk with me down the front porch steps. He looks confused when we reach the final step, that is, until we hear my dad's booming voice as clear as a bell and that's when it registers why I'm rushing him off. Thankfully, Chris's car is parked on the street and he's in it in no time. He lowers the driver's side window while starting the engine and looks over my shoulder to make sure there is no threat.

"Thanks, Sabrina."

"For what?"

He exhales before saying, "For letting me get that off my chest, finally."

Surprisingly, it's not difficult for me to respond because I mean it wholeheartedly. "You're welcome."

With that he pulls onto the street and drives away, and not a moment too soon. The front door swings open behind me and I turn around to find my dad in his barbeque cooking apron waving a pair of tongs in his hand.

"What are doing out here? The food is in the backyard not the front yard."

I shake my head and smile up at him while walking across the front lawn and back up the steps. When I try to go around him, he grabs hold of my hand with the one that isn't making clacking noises with the tongs.

Even with his usual quiet demeanor, my dad is pretty damn good at telling it like it is and I love that about him. I guess you can say that growing up, I was kind of a daddy's girl. He's always been so patient with me, and we were thick as thieves until the day I moved away. Although I've been away from home for years and I see my parents when they come to visit me—which is often enough—I know the distance has put a strain in our relationship. And as much as I can point a finger to Lisa and Chris for what they did as an excuse for staying away for so long, I really only have myself to blame. I should have never let them come between me and my only family. So, right then and there I make a promise to myself to come home more often instead of making my parents make the trek to Miami.

"Is everything OK?"

My dad's brow creases with worry as he studies my face. Instead of answering him, I hurl myself into his arms and hug him so hard that he's the one who's choking for a change.

"Everything's great, Daddy," I say between a laugh and tears. "Never been better."

He pats my back with his free hand, and I let go of him only to have him wipe a tear that got away down my cheek.

"Why are you crying then?" he asks.

"I'm just so happy to be home again."

Never one to be able to handle my tears, he smiles and kisses my forehead before saying, "I'm glad you're home too, baby girl."

Just as I'm about to find my voice, he speaks up again.

"Even if it's just for a little while, I'm happy having you back here."

How I don't completely lose it after my dad says that to me, I don't know. All I can manage to say back is evidently enough for him, proof positive by the big smile on his face.

"Me too, Daddy."

I wipe the corners of my eyes when he starts clacking together the tongs and we both chuckle. "Come on. Let's

get back inside before your mother burns down the backyard just so she can get her steak medium well."

He swings the front door open for me, and we make our
way to the patio where my mom is turning the knobs on the
grill just as he suspected. I grab a bottle of beer from the
outdoor cooler and then take a seat while my dad winks at
me before sneaking up on Mom.

"Woman," my dad shouts playfully, "if I've told you once,
I've told you a thousand times: the grill is my domain. Please
step away and let me work my magic."

I watch them from my seat as she smacks him on his arm
before he grabs her by the waist and plants a big wet one on
her cheek that makes her giggle in delight. I look on and
smile because I'm so deliriously happy with not only how
everything has gone so far on this trip: from Tyler to what
just happened with Chris, but for this—right here, right
now. Being home with my family, I've missed *this*. More than
I thought. And one thing's for certain, I'm never going to
miss out on this again.

CHAPTER TWENTY

Home sweet home. I took a cab from the airport instead of calling Julia so I could beat her here. I texted her earlier in the day before my flight left to see if she wanted to have dinner tonight. She agreed, too eagerly, I might add—chomping at the bit to get more details on the whole Tyler situation.

God, I miss him terribly already. I knew when I left him standing there on the sidewalk, that it would kill me. And now that we have so much more distance between us, it makes that pain of missing him more palpable. Because I know he's not a quick drive away and vice versa. But, like he asked of me before I left, I'm keeping the faith or at least I'm doing my best damn impression of it.

I only have an hour before Julia gets here so I take a quick shower to wash away the travel scum and plunk down onto the couch to veg in front of the TV.

"Lucy, I'm home," Julia says in the absolute worst Ricky Ricardo voice of all time, but it still cracks me up.

I mute the TV while she drops her purse, laptop bag, and keys in the foyer and hustles over to the couch. Kicking off her heels, she props her feet up on the coffee table and studies my face for a second or two before I see a smile creep up at the corners of her mouth.

"You had sex," she says coolly.

How the hell can she tell I had sex? Is there a giant sign on my forehead or something? I open my mouth to answer her but she stops me.

"Wait, don't tell me the details just yet." She stands up, almost tripping over herself in the process to go get her purse and rummage through it until I hear her say, "Ah-ha!"

With a pen and her checkbook in hand, she comes back over to the couch and starts to write.

"I'm just going to round up to the nearest hundred," she says to herself then tears off a check and hands it to me.

I look down at the check and burst out laughing when I see that it's made payable to me in the amount of four hundred dollars. But the best part is the memo, which says: *For finally getting laid.* And with a smiley face, no less.

"I appreciate it, but I can't take the money." And I hand her back the check, but she puts up her hand to intercept it.

"Seriously, you're cashing that check," she says and pushes my hand away. "A bet's a bet."

I tilt my head to give her the fake evil eye and resign myself for now that she's not willing to budge on this. But, I'm so not going to cash this check. I'll tear it up later when she's not looking or never deposit it. Either way, it's not happening.

"So, dinner?" I ask, trying to change the subject.

"Hell yes! Give me twenty minutes to get ready."

We arrive at LuLu's in The Grove and grab a seat on the sidewalk since the tropical weather is cooperating tonight.

The waiter arrives at our table and takes our drink order while we look over the menu. Julia and I decide on some appetizers instead of a full-on meal when he brings us our drinks and finally leaves us alone for a stretch. Taking a taste of my drink, I notice the flowers on the table between us. The vivid yellow and orange hues bring to mind the flowers that Tyler gave me while I was staying with him. I'm beaming at the memory and lost in thought until Julia clears her throat to get my attention.

"I have to say, girlie, I've never seen you this happy. You're almost glowing," she says before taking a quick sip of her mojito. "Now, before you tell me what happened, please say you have at least one picture of him for me to properly fantasize about. Because that high school one isn't quite cutting it anymore."

"It's your lucky day," I taunt and then fish through my purse to find my cell phone. I pull up one of the two pictures I have of Tyler. The first one is of him lounging in his kitchen. He has on his old pair of black sweatpants and that's it. His dark brown hair is a perfect mess and it looks incredibly sexy and his smile is. . . .

"Wow! He could make an old lady's panties melt with that smile," Julia says, loud enough for the people behind us to start chuckling.

"Shhh! Jesus, everyone can hear you."

I go to reach for my phone but she already has scrolled over to the next photo, which I didn't want her to see. Tyler had taken my phone after he took a photo on his and snapped a picture of us together in bed. The sheet covers me, just barely, but it's obvious that neither of us is wearing any clothes.

"Well, well, well," she announces and pops her head up to look at me, "seems like someone went from having no sex at all to taking porn shots."

The guys in the seat behind Julia whip their heads around to look at us as I'm dying of embarrassment. Seriously, she has no filter. "Oh my God, Julia, would you please keep your voice down," I mumble and bury my head in my hands to deflect the looks we're getting from the guys behind her.

She leans forward so that only I can hear her. "Sabrina, I've known you for seven years and you're like a sister to me. I only want the absolute best for you. So don't mistake me busting your chops for anything other than that I'm over the fucking moon for you right now. OK?"

Shit. She had to go and throw out the sister card. I lift my head from my hands and say OK as her attention goes back to my phone in her hands when it vibrates.

"Someone's got a text from the sex god," and she's back to her normal self, just like that.

I snatch the phone away from her before she has a chance to read it out loud.

Hope you got home safe. I'll call you later tonight . . . xo

I text him back when the waiter comes over with our food.

Safe and sound. Looking forward to it ;)

"Wink face? Come on, just put 'Love, Sabrina' and call it a day," she says as she starts to nosh on some truffle French fries. "It's written all over your face. You are head over heels in love with him."

I wrinkle my nose at her and she laughs because she's got my number on this one.

"What about you?" I ask, casually trying to move the topic of conversation in another direction. "What happened to this last guy you met on Match?"

Julia, for as gorgeous and smart and funny as she is, has always had difficulties finding a good guy. He's either too this or too that. She started experimenting with Match. com recently and in the last few months her dates have not gone off so well. Honestly, I don't know how she does it anymore; every guy seems to be worse than the last one. My self-esteem would be on the floor if I was her, and that's saying something, since mine can get pretty damn low.

"Ha! You mean the scientist?"

I nod and brace myself for some dating horror story. "Well, the first couple of times we went out, he was cool. Very nice, actually. Had impeccable manners, the whole bit. Then he told me about the science project he's working on, and I immediately cut my losses."

How her dating life can possibly be more pathetic than how I feel in my current situation, and I technically have a "boyfriend," is beyond me. I lean forward in rapt attention and say, "It couldn't have been that bad."

She raises an eyebrow in defiance, ensuring that this story is going to be a good one.

"His 'project' was to save his farts in sealed containers to see if he could 'capture the wind' or some crazy shit like that," she says, as serious as a heart attack. "I should have taken a picture of his laboratory for you. It had Tupperware galore."

"You're joking," I sputter, laughing. "That cannot be a true story."

"Do I look like I'm joking?"

I'm laughing so hard now that I have to wipe the tears from my eyes. I look over at her to see her not evening cracking a smile, so I quickly compose myself and apologize. "Sorry, Julia. That really sucks."

"Yeah, whatever," she says dismissing the light chuckles still coming from me. "Enough about me. Spill!"

So, I spill. I don't tell her everything, but she's got the gist. When I tell her about the battle royal I had with Ava in Tyler's office though, she sits straight up like a rocket in her seat.

"What a bitch!"

"I know," I say uncomfortably. The incident is still plaguing my thoughts. I'm trying to let Tyler's words and actions win out, but it's just not that easy for me.

Carefully, she asks, "Are you really in love with him, Sabrina?"

"Julia, I think I've been in love with him for ten years. I gave him my heart—"

"Please don't say, 'and he gave me a pen,'" she smiles sincerely before going into her little pep talk, breaking it all down.

"Listen here, girlie. It honestly sounds like he feels the same way about you. I really don't think he'd go through all that trouble for just some random girl. You have to be able to put aside all that crap about Ava too. It's like a poison. I know it's a lot easier said than done, but jealousy will eat you up from the inside out like a cancer. And before you know it, she wins, even if she doesn't have him. You're going to hate me for saying this, too, but you're actually going to have to do the one thing you've never been able to do."

"What's that?"

She tilts her head to the side while eyeing me carefully. "Trust him."

Trust. That's a big one for me. It's been a deal breaker over the years while casually dating. And if I'm being honest with myself, I don't know if I completely trust him. I want to, I really do, but then I think of the wildcard in all of this...Ava. I know I sure as hell don't trust her. The way she touched him that day I first met her to the way she spoke to me that day in his office. Just something about her does not sit well with me. I mean, who goes around saying, "I'll watch over him for you while you're gone," or whatever the hell she said. Either way, her meaning was crystal clear to me; she still wants him.

The rest of dinner goes by without any more embarrassing moments, compliments of Julia, thank God. We get home a little after eleven o'clock. I'm pretty tired after such a long day, and I still have to unpack. Leaving Julia on the couch to watch her nightly dose of *Seinfeld* reruns, I say good night and head to my bedroom.

An hour or so later, after I've unpacked and have been able to decide on an appropriate outfit for work tomorrow, my cell phone rings. Before I grab it off my nightstand, I already know who it is and the butterflies in my stomach start swirling around. I let it ring a couple of times since I don't want to appear too eager, so on the fourth ring, I finally answer.

"Hello," I say trying to sound as unaffected as possible while my heart is racing wildly.

Tyler's deep come-hither voice washes over me instantly, soothing the ache somewhat I feel from being away from him. "I didn't wake you, did I?"

"No, I was just getting into bed."

"Sorry, I just got home from the restaurant, and it was really busy tonight so I didn't get a chance to call sooner."

I look at the clock on my nightstand and see the time is just after midnight as I pull back my comforter and settle in with my phone carefully cradled on my ear.

"It's OK."

"Do you want to go to sleep? I can call you back tomorrow if you're too tired."

"Nope, I want to talk to you. I…"

"You what?" he asks softly.

"I kind of miss you."

"*Kind of* miss me?" he asks teasingly.

"OK, OK," I say, knowing I'm busted and might as well let it all hang out. "I miss you."

"Good to know. Because I miss you too, baby."

His admission brings warmth to every fiber of my being and helps to alleviate some of my apprehension. I relax further into my bed and almost giggle out loud like I'm eighteen and not a twenty-eight-year-old woman who has to wake up in less than six hours for work.

Our conversation for the next hour is seamless. There is no lull, and it would seem that we both have a lot more in common than I previously thought. Case in point, movies. Tyler is a pretty big fan of them, good ones too. We now have a "date" to watch all three *Godfather* movies the next time we get together. And he got even more brownie points by agreeing with me that the third installment in the franchise is kind of a throwaway but a necessary evil, so to speak.

I stretch and yawn into the phone, the sleepiness starting to creep in. "I'm sorry, that yawn came out of nowhere."

"I've kept you up past your bedtime again," he says suggestively. "Go to sleep, I'll call you tomorrow, OK?"

"OK, good night, Tyler."

"Good night, baby."

I smile in the dark as I place my phone on the nightstand. So satisfied I am in fact, that I'm pretty sure my smile stays put until I wake up.

The next morning, I roll out of bed at the sound of the shower being turned on and make my way to the kitchen to turn on the coffee maker. I grab my "The Truth is Out There" mug and hop onto the counter to wait it out. A few minutes later, Julia strolls in her robe and her hair wrapped in a towel looking way too bright and sunshiny for my liking.

"Don't give me that look," she says with a huge grin and pointing her finger at me, "I didn't tell you to stay up all hours of the night on the phone like a teenybopper."

"Yeah, yeah, yeah," I say to her as she reaches over to grab her own mug.

"So, Mulder, did you partake in some phone sex at least?" She wags her eyebrows and leans against the counter, trying to keep her cackling down to a minimum but not doing a very good job of it.

Instead of answering her, I slide off the counter and fill my cup, ignoring her assumption and laughing fit completely. If this is any indication of how my day is going to go, I'd much rather crawl back under the covers. I'm pretty beat still, but it was worth it. I'd do it again if it meant spending some sort of time with Tyler, even if it's not in the physical sense.

"Nothing to say for yourself?" Julia asks, full of humor, while I take a sip of my coffee.

"Nope," I say, "but thanks for your concern, Scully."

She's still chuckling when I leave the kitchen and go back down to my room to get ready for work.

I pull into the gallery parking lot at eight o'clock, and thank God for once the stars have aligned in my favor because no one seems to be here yet. I have been prepping myself for seeing Alex again, since when I left last week I kind of left things up in the air. Up in the air is probably the very nice way of saying that I led him on and then left town for almost a week with no contact. Whoever would have thought my personal life could be like an episode of *90210*? And the good *90210*, not that new crap that the powers that be try to pawn off as *90210*. I'm talking Brenda/Dylan/Kelly kind of angst. I shake my head and smirk, accepting my fate that I've officially lost my mind, realizing I'm sitting in an empty parking lot comparing my life to that of Brenda Walsh.

Alright, enough! Time to put on my big girl panties, get out of the car, and get this over with.

Over one hundred emails later and a couple more cups of coffee from the community pot, I'm as caught up as I'll be for now and no sign of Alex yet. I lean back in my chair and swivel it an inch or two to my left as the framed print on the wall of Picasso's *Blue Nude* catches my eye. Instead of letting it bring me down, it makes me smile. Julia is right; I have to trust Tyler, I have to let go of my fear of the unknown and welcome the warm fuzzies. If it was New Year's Day, that would be my resolution: trust Tyler. I repeat it in my head, *trust Tyler, trust Tyler, trust Tyler,* 'til I hear someone clearing his throat to get my attention, snapping me back to reality.

Alex appears before me with a charming grin. Really? Why, for the love of God, does he have to be so good looking? There he is, in all his glory, wearing a black three-piece, pinstriped suit and perfectly matched tie. I swear, he looks as if he just stepped out of the pages of *GQ* magazine, which is not making this the least bit easy for me.

"Welcome back," he says smoothly and takes a seat opposite me.

I turn my seat back around to face him and see his eyes full of mirth until they take one good long look at my face. It's almost as if I can feel him shut down on me. Jesus, is it that obvious? Does it make me a bad person that I almost feel relieved? I hope not. Because I do, just a tiny bit.

"Good morning, Alex," I say nervously. "I'm sorry I didn't get a chance to text you back or anything while I was gone. I was really busy."

I'm an awful person and a terrible liar. Although, I really *was* busy so it's not a complete lie; it's more like a half-truth. He leans forward and puts his elbows on his knees, the corner of his mouth curling up to reveal a dimple. How have I not paid enough attention to know he has dimples in his arsenal? Wait, what the hell am I saying? I try to focus by grabbing my almighty pen and twirling it in my fingers to keep me distracted from staring at that dimple.

"You don't need to explain anything to me, Sabrina."

He's letting me off the hook? He's even nicer than I originally gave him credit for.

"I'm sorry," he says. "I didn't mean to put you on the spot."

He pauses, carefully considering his next words. This just makes me more anxious, and my pen-twirling has gone on to a whole new level.

"How about we discuss this over dinner tonight?"

"Alex, under normal circumstances, I would say yes. But, I have to say—"

"No," he says, finishing my sentence for me while his gaze drops to the floor momentarily then back up. He puts on a faint smile when he goes to stand up, and I open my mouth to say something. I have no idea what exactly, but something profound, no doubt, given my stellar performance in this conversation so far.

"Sabrina, I really don't want this to come between our working relationship and our friendship. And as much as I would like the opportunity to change your mind, I can tell that it's of no use."

"I'm so sorry," I say. "I never meant for this to get so messy."

"In matters of the heart, it's always messy," he says as a good-natured chuckle escapes him.

With those parting words, he turns on his heel and leaves my office. I hear him down the hall, calling out to Sarah our receptionist, then I drop the pen and exhale. I sink further into my chair with an immediate sense of relief washing over me. God, how I hate confrontations. And truthfully, I don't think I could have ever been comfortable enough to look past the whole employee/boss dynamic. I must be crazy because Alex has everything a woman could possibly want in a man: gorgeous, successful, nice, and sexy. The list goes on and on. But for all those things, he's missing one key ingredient… he's not Tyler.

CHAPTER TWENTY-ONE

I don't know how people do this long-distance thing on a regular basis, but it's starting to work on my already-frayed nerves. Even though the last three weeks have been wonderful getting to know Tyler, albeit over the phone, it's been agonizing not having him close enough to touch me, kiss me, or hold me.

At first, our conversations were spent learning simple things about each other, like a progression of twenty questions. In a way, our relationship is somewhat backward. We were lucky enough to spend three and a half perfect nights together almost in a cocoon. No outside interruptions. No slowly easing your way into it. We went straight past go and collected our two hundred dollars. And I'm not complaining because I loved every minute of it. But, there's something to be said for finding out all there is to know about the person with whom you want to spend every waking moment.

For instance, he has the most perfect middle name ever. It came to me a couple of days after I was home that I didn't know this information and that I needed to know it. So in the middle of a late-night phone call, I asked him.

"I'll tell you mine if you tell me yours," he answered.

"Is yours that bad?"

Tyler laughed at my very real assumption that his was pretty rough. "No, it's not bad at all. I actually really like it. I just don't tell anybody."

This had me even more curious. "Why don't you tell anyone?"

"No reason, I don't know…maybe because nobody's ever really asked me."

"OK, now that is ridiculous," I said as seriously as I could without laughing.

"It's James."

"Tyler James," I said in a daze because I thought it sounded so lovely. "That's kind of perfect and I love it. I may have to call you that from now on."

A chuckle escaped him before he said, "I'm glad you like it, but don't expect me to answer to that."

"We'll see about that."

So ever since that conversation, whenever we talk on the phone late at night I always end the call with, "Sweet dreams, Tyler James."

And for the record, he hasn't complained once, so it's stuck.

As for the phone calls, we've worked out a schedule of sorts that seems to work for us. During my commute in the morning, I call him and we talk until I get to work. At night, he calls me when he gets in from the restaurant. That doesn't take into account all the texts during the day and night and everything in between. At first, I kind of felt terrible about waking him up so early, seeing as he puts in long hours at night. I discounted those concerns fairly quickly when he told me his reasons.

"Baby, if you haven't been able to tell yet, yours is the first voice I want to hear when I wake up and the very last thing I want to hear before I go to sleep."

My answer was pretty awesome. "OK."

I was lucky to have gotten that one word out because I had literally swooned from hearing him say that to me. Most assuredly, the sisterhood would have revoked my privileges if they knew how I reacted after he told me that. But, do I really give a damn what the sisterhood thinks at this point? Nope, not really. They're not around to help navigate me through all of this, so screw them.

In the last couple of days the volume of texts has been increasing because of Tyler's visit in four days. This visit is such a nice surprise because I had already resigned myself into thinking that I would probably not see him again until Thanksgiving. So when he brought it up late one night on the phone, about a week ago, I jumped at the chance.

We had been discussing nothing of extreme importance when all of a sudden we both had gone quiet. Not an uncomfortable silence but enough that I thought perhaps that he was getting sleepy. I was about to tell him to go to bed when he spoke up and caught me by surprise.

"I want to see you," he said in such a way that my body almost fused to the mattress that I was laying on.

I couldn't hide my reaction when I answered him. "I want to see you too."

I knew that his trademark sexy grin was in place without even seeing him in the flesh.

"What can we do about that?"

"Um...." I couldn't say much of anything. One, because I had just taken a week's vacation and two, his voice was driving me crazy, in a really good way.

"Baby, I want to see you so bad that it's all I think about. I need to see your beautiful smile with my own eyes, and I want to feel you in my arms."

"I want that too," I said in a hushed voice, "more than anything."

"Well, your wish is my command."

My body responded before my mouth did by knifing up in the bed. "What does that mean?"

"I'm coming to see you."

"When?"

"I'm thinking the weekend after this one coming up. How does that sound?"

It took all of me to not squeal into the phone at this news. In fact, I was trying so hard not to that I remained quiet.

"Baby, are you still there?"

"I'm here," I finally answered.

"So, what do you think?"

My heart beating wildly in excitement, I quickly responded this time. "I think it's the best news ever. I can't wait to see you."

"That's my girl."

So, he bought his ticket, and we made plans to see each other in just over seven days. I'm so excited about it that I've been totally counting them down as if it was "Dick Clark's New Year's Rockin' Eve." Today is no different. While I sit at my desk looking over plans for a new exhibit in the fall, my phone vibrates, and the lovesick grin that always accompanies that magical sound is starting to make my face hurt. I abandon my work, yet again, and read his latest text about ten times.

I'm sure Miami is great, but we may not leave your room.

Oh my.

The sex fog that's clouding my brain is pretty thick. I should respond but don't have an inkling as to what I should text back. I could go for the gusto and say something naughty but don't want to come off as cheesy. I give up and pick up my work phone to dial 911—or at least the closest thing to it.

Julia answers, "What's up?"

"So, just got a text from Tyler and not sure how I should answer him," I say excitedly.

"Hit me," she says, all business-like.

I read her the text and she asks me to repeat it, and then repeat it again. When she asks a fourth time, I kind of lose it.

I grate my teeth in frustration. "I think you've got it by now."

"Relax," she says. "This is an easy one. The question is, do you want to be a bad girl or a good girl?"

The devil on my shoulder perks its head and looks around as if awoken from a deep sleep. I want to be bad. Hell yes, I want to be all kinds of Jessica Rabbit bad with him.

"Bad."

"Did you just say you want to be a bad girl?" Julia is almost as shocked as I am by my admission. "Can't say that I blame you, really. After seeing his picture I'd want to be a bad girl, too. That man is one hot piece of ass."

"Julia, focus. And please do not refer to my boyfriend as a 'hot piece of ass'…at least not around me."

"Alright, alright. Well, you can't just jump headfirst into the deep end, you know. Let's dip your foot in the shallow water and check the temperature."

I groan into the phone, "Listen, Jacques Cousteau, just tell me what I should say."

Her wicked cackle makes me roll my eyes.

"Text him back something like…hmmm…I got it! Say this: *But what will we do if we get hungry?*"

"Huh? That's all you've got? That's not even close to being bad, that's just…sad." I start to giggle at my own rhyming capabilities when Julia says "ahem" loudly into the phone to get my attention.

"Oh ye, of little faith," she says, all holier than thou. "Trust me."

So I grab my cell phone and text him exactly that, verbatim. Julia stays on the line, gabbing about her day so far, when my phone vibrates a minute later. I gingerly pick it up and stare at it as if it was an alien device.

I finally find my voice, interrupting Julia's current ramblings about somebody on her staff. "He texted back."

"What did he say?" she asks in stealth mode.

I open the screen and read it. My jaw drops open while my panties start to feel too tight in the process.

"I can't read it out loud to you," I say quickly.

"Oh, no you don't. I don't have anything going on in my sex life at the moment, so read that text to me this very instant, young lady!"

"Julia…um," I mumble, "it's embarrassing."

She chuckles, "Good, I hope so."

"OK then, this is what he said back." I clear my throat and drop my voice so low that I can barely hear myself. *"Baby, after I get you in that bed, the last thing on my mind will be actual food."*

"She shoots, she scores!" Julia is as proud as a peacock, and I can picture her bowing to a make-believe audience in the middle of her office.

"Should I text him back or leave it be?" I ask while she's still patting herself on the back.

"You damn well better. If you don't, I will." She's sounds almost appalled that I even would entertain the idea of not responding.

"Chill out. I'll text him in a minute when my brain is functioning properly."

She sighs before she says, "My work here is done. Enjoy your sexting. See you at home, girlie."

I hang up and for some reason I think back to when we were younger and specifically that one horrible night, when the only bright spot was him. You really couldn't take your eyes off him back then. His rough exterior would make you take pause, but in a good way. A very good way. And now that I have the real thing in my life, it's even better than any dream I could have ever imagined.

I reread his text and think of how to answer as my body responds and my mind wanders further on its own. My pulse quickens at the memory of my body welcoming his, being underneath him as his hands explore every inch of my skin. The taste of his lips and tongue flicking against mine and...this is crazy! If I keep this up, I'm going to go up in flames in my office just on a memory.

Drawing on my steamy daydream, I give in, handing over the reins to my inner bad girl and typing a text back to him.

Can I at least be dessert?

God bless modern technology. It takes him all of twenty-three seconds to respond. I know, because yeah, I counted.

Baby, you have no idea…

Now, I'm the one patting myself on the back and kick back in my chair as a goofy grin covers my face. I relish in the moment for a minute or two before finally getting back to work.

The rest of the day goes by at a snail's pace, aided only slightly by the flirty text banter with Tyler. I did have to abandon it at one point and really concentrate. It was getting close to his time to go into work anyway. But, I'm thinking maybe a little foray into phone sex territory later might be in order. Yes, most definitely need to think about that later tonight when he calls. We've never done "it" over the phone. We've gotten pretty close to all gooey for each other occasionally, but this would definitely be a first and not just for us, but for me in general.

I'm so tired by the time I get home from work that I head straight for a long hot shower. I collapse onto the couch alongside Julia to watch a movie, each of us with our favorite kind of Hot Pocket on opposite ends of the couch. The movie drags on, and I should have known better than to agree to watch it with her since she got to pick tonight. All I know is that Gwyneth Paltrow better get her head out of her ass and just run on over to Ben Affleck's house pronto. Or at least in the next ten minutes since I'm starting to get a bit sleepy.

In the middle of a yawn, Julia smacks her lips in annoyance. "It's not that bad, quit the theatrics."

"I can't help it if I'm tired, although I will say this movie isn't doing it for me at all," I say then stretch my limbs and reposition myself on the couch.

"Well, it's almost over so *shhh.* Don't you know silence is golden," she says sarcastically.

I stick out my tongue at her then curl up more comfortably on the couch and go back to watching the movie. My eyelids grow heavy and before Gwyneth can figure out the mess that is her life, I fall asleep. A soft poke wakes me, and I instantly regret falling asleep on the couch. My neck is achy and I rub it while I ask Julia what time it is.

"Almost one," she answers quietly.

"Why are you whispering?" I ask in a same hushed tone.

She giggles. "I have no idea. I'm going to bed, girlie, have a good night."

"Good night."

While I'm still rubbing my neck with one hand, I grab my cell phone off the coffee table and scroll through it for missed calls or texts from Tyler. His nightly call usually comes around eleven thirty, midnight at the latest; and if he's running late, he'll shoot me a text letting me know. Nothing. Not one message or phone call since his last text, which was hours ago.

Funny how the mind works; mine automatically starts thinking the worst and worrying that something might have happened to him. Maybe he took his motorcycle and got into a horrific accident. *Calm down, Sabrina... maybe he's just running late and had a really busy night.* That's what I try to tell myself when I nervously pick up the phone and call him, hoping he's OK and not laying in a pool of blood somewhere in the middle of the street.

Anxious doesn't even begin to cover how I'm feeling as his phone rings. When the call actually connects and I hear his fumbling to pick it up, relief washes through me. But that relief is short lived and quickly replaced by heartbreak.

"Hello," Ava says groggily.

My heart hurts in response to her voice answering his phone at this time of night. I'm finding it difficult to say even one word to her. In the few seconds of hearing her, the walls around my heart, which I so diligently had constructed over the years and demolished for him, build back up to rival that of Fort Knox.

"Is anybody there?" she asks, forcing me to acknowledge her.

Somehow, I find my voice. Its sounds weak and barely audible even to me. "Is...is Tyler there?"

"Yes." She pauses and I hear Tyler's low, sleep-filled voice in the background. When she tells him to go back to bed, I know I've heard more than I ever wished to hear in a lifetime. I'm still frozen with shock, when I hear a rustling on the line.

"Sabrina."

I wish that I didn't love the sound of my name rolling off his tongue so easily. The same tongue that's been doing God knows what with Cruella tonight. My stomach turns at the thought, and I think I'm really going to be sick when he starts talking again. Tyler's voice is slightly slurred, but there is absolutely no doubt that it's him.

"How is Alex?"

I'm so caught off guard by his question since I'm still trying to wrap my head around Ava answering the phone to begin with. What could Alex have anything to do with this? I'm still in shock and lost in the confusion when he speaks again in a more biting tone.

"Your date with Alex...how was it, baby? Did he treat you good?"

"I don't know what you mean, Tyler."

"Did things not work out with him and you want to go *slumming* for old time's sake again?"

"What are you talking about?"

"Was that what this was between us, Sabrina? Because if it was nothing, I wish you would have told me a hell of a lot sooner."

Ava says something in the background to him but I can't make it out clearly. Then I hear another quick noise that sounds as if the phone has been dropped.

I feel Ava's evil smile across the line crawling over my skin when a lone tear escapes my eye and she asks, "Is there something you needed, Sabrina?"

I hang up, further humiliation unnecessary, and my heart goes on official lock down. Quietly, sobs start to leave my throat and I cover my mouth to silence them in an effort to not wake Julia. I curl up into a ball on the couch, overwhelmed by the pain that is all-consuming, my mind flying in all kinds of directions.

I'm not sure what just happened. Does he really believe that I've been seeing Alex all this time? How he can think that, after what we've shared together, hurts me even more. Perhaps I should have brought up Alex to him, but since it stopped almost as quickly as it had started, it didn't seem important. Especially since I've made it perfectly clear that he is all I've ever wanted. Willing myself to somehow magically transport back to a few hours earlier when everything was perfect, I stay that way, crying silently in the dark until sleep starts to claim me again, asking myself the same question over and over... Why?

CHAPTER TWENTY-TWO

"Wake up, girlie."
My eyes slowly open and adjust to the sunlight streaming into the living room. I feel slightly disoriented with my surroundings until I hear Julia's voice again coming from the kitchen.

"Did you fall asleep out here?" she asks.

I throw my legs over the couch and rub the heels of my hands against my eyes in an effort to wipe the memory of what happened last night out of my mind. When I peel my hands away, I hope upon hope that it worked, but like hitting a rewind button on a DVR, it's all still there. It wasn't a nightmare. It all happened. Tyler was with Ava last night and effectively smashed my heart into smithereens.

"You better start getting ready," Julia says while slamming a cupboard closed, "it's getting late."

If I open my mouth to answer her, I'm sure that the crying jag to follow will never stop. Right now, my silence is keeping everything contained under the surface. The pain of losing any chance I may have had with Tyler leaves me utterly speechless for fear of having to actually come to terms with it. I'm just not ready to do something like that.

The vibration of my cell phone on the coffee table jerks my head to stare at it. I can tell from where I'm perched on the edge of my seat that Tyler is calling and the restraint I had lets loose. I'm not prepared to hear his voice let alone hear what he has to say after the accusations and assumptions that he so casually tossed around last night. I wrap my arms around my stomach while tears cloud my vision until the ringing stops. Only a temporary reprieve, since as quickly as the ringing had ceased, its starts back up again.

"Aren't you going to answer him? I'm sure loverboy wants to say good morning to you." Julia is now standing directly behind the back of the couch, and the ringing stops again.

When it starts back up immediately, Julia walks from behind the couch to sit beside me. I keep my eyes instead trained on the phone as it vibrates, not able to look at her yet. From the corner of my eye I see Julia put her coffee cup on the table and go to make a grab for the phone.

I sound panicked when I say to her, "Don't touch it."

"Sweetie," she says, "you're acting really strange. What's going on?"

When the ringing stops this time and he doesn't call back, I officially lose it. My body convulses with heavy sobbing as the pain infiltrates every single part of me. I feel Julia wrap her arms around me, pulling me toward her and start to rock me like a child. I don't know how long I stay that way, but she doesn't say a single word until the phone rings again.

"Sabrina, what happened?"

I raise my head when the ringing stops and go to clean my face, which I'm sure is futile at this point. Julia's small smile at my poor attempt makes me almost laugh out loud.

She tugs on the sleeve of her robe and wipes my tears. Afterwards, she takes the other sleeve and shimmies it over her hand then goes to cover my nose with it.

"Blow," she commands.

"That's gross," I say between a hiccup and a sob, "I don't want to ruin it."

She raises an eyebrow in warning and I'm in no mood to fight over this so I blow my nose on the sleeve of her robe.

"Do you think you can talk now?" she asks carefully and I nod in preparation.

Like tearing off a Band-Aid, I let the words fly out of my mouth. "I think Tyler might have slept with Ava last night."

Her eyes grow wide as she covers her mouth with her hands in utter disbelief when my cell phone vibrates again. This must be what having an out of body experience is like as curiosity gets the better of me and I answer it. I don't say hello. I don't say a single word to him. My breath hitches, and I know he can tell I'm crying.

"Sabrina."

Somehow I had hoped that all of it was just my imagination, but hearing him say my name laced with remorse confirms it all. The little composure I had gathered long enough a few minutes ago disintegrates.

"Baby, I'm sorry."

"I...I...ca...can't." I barely finish that incoherent sentence when Julia rips the phone out of my hand.

"You fucking, no-good, piece-of-shit cocksucker," she pauses to take a breath, and I can tell Tyler is trying to get a word in edgewise.

"Who am I?" she shouts." I'm your worst fucking nightmare! I'm the best friend who's going to tell your 'baby' to never talk to you again." Julia glances over at me when I scramble to the far end of the couch while I hear him again trying to say something to her. "Ha! Nice try, asshole. Go fuck your whore now with a clear conscious and don't bother Sabrina again. If you do, I swear I will get on a plane so fast and personally plant my foot so far up your ass that you'll taste leather in your fucking throat for a week."

She ends the call and chucks the phone with enough force that it skips across the coffee table like a skipping stone across the water. It lands with a thud, face down on the far side of the living room. She turns on her side and scoots over to me then reaches out to wipe my face again.

"I'm so sorry, sweetie," she says full of concern. "What can I do for you?"

I shake my head, bringing my feet underneath me. "Nothing. I think I'm just going to stay home today."

Julia sighs thoughtfully. "Do you want me to work from home today and keep you company?"

I think about it for a second and realize that as much as I love Julia and everything she's done for me, I really want to be alone today.

"I'll be OK by myself," I say. "I just need to call work and let them know I won't be in."

She says OK and smiles weakly one last time then disappears into the hallway. She returns a moment later with a box of tissues, placing it on the coffee table then quickly changes her mind and puts it on my lap for easier access.

When she leaves the room again, I quietly tiptoe over to my phone, grab it and hurry back onto the couch. I scroll through the contacts and call the gallery, keeping my fingers crossed that no one will answer this early.

"Good morning, may I help you?" Sarah's chipper voice makes me curse in my head that the girl is so goddamn punctual sometimes.

"Sarah," my voice cracking and I quickly clear my throat before I continue. "It's Sabrina. I'm not coming in today. Can you please let Alex know that I'll be monitoring my email from home instead?"

"Are you OK? You sound awful." She's clearly fishing but there is no way I'm sharing anything with her unless I want all my business to be on a billboard any time soon.

"I'm fine, thanks for asking," I say quickly back to her. "If you need me for anything, just shoot me an email, OK?"

"OK, feel better." I hang up not wanting to expel further energy on moving any part of me, even my lips.

Julia comes out a few minutes later dressed for work with a blanket tucked under her arm. She pulls it out as she approaches me on the couch and unfurls it. I recognize this ratty thing from our college days. I didn't even know she still had it.

"This is my lucky blankie," she says seriously, and I look at her funny before she explains. "Don't laugh. This blankie has helped me through many a break-up, and I'm entrusting you today with its magical powers."

I let her throw the blanket over me while I stretch out on the couch and sink in as deeply as possible into the pillows, wishing they could swallow me up whole.

"Get some rest, sweetie. If you need anything—I mean it, *anything*—call me, OK?"

I snuggle with the blanket and say yes as she gives me a sympathetic once over before turning around and gathering her things to leave for work.

I don't even bother with the television and have no concept of how much time has gone by when exhaustion finally overtakes me. A vibration from underneath me coaxes me to open my eyes. On any other day, I would go digging through the cushions to see his text or pick up his call. Hell, this time yesterday I was busy having a mini text war with him. How stupid am I? For all I know, he could have been sleeping with her this entire time.

When the phone vibrates again, I can't take it anymore and sit up to find it. I yank it out from the far cushion that my feet are propped up on to see that I have four texts from Tyler. Why I am such a glutton for punishment? I have no idea, but I do the dumbest thing possible and read them all in order.

9:06 AM—I never meant to hurt you. Please call me.

9:28 AM—Baby, please talk to me. I know I fucked up bad and need to explain.

10:02 AM—I'm going crazy over here, please call me back.

10:08 AM—I would give anything to hear your voice, please call me.

What kind of explanation could there be? He didn't even try to hide it, and he wants me to believe that he never meant to hurt me? I feel my anger growing like The Hulk as it roars through me, and I want to punch him in the face so bad that my hands start to shake. Who the hell does he think he is? And as this question turns over in my mind, my fingers, seemingly of their own free will, start dialing his number.

"Baby," he says, relieved after picking up on the first ring.

"Don't ever call me that again. You lost that right last night when you were with *her*," choosing not to say her name out loud. "I'm only calling to set you straight on something and to say that after that, I never want to hear from you again." Yeah, right. The thought of him never calling me again stings, and the emptiness I feel looming over my head begins to settle. But I need to get this out as difficult as it is and as angry as I am. I owe myself that much.

He sounds mournful when he says, "OK."

"For ten years—*ten years*, Tyler—I waited for you. I trusted you. And when I say I trusted you, I don't think you understand what that means to me. Because during every single one of those years, ever since that one night, I've never really been able to trust anyone after what happened to me. So, of all the people in the world, you are the *very* last person I ever expected to do this to me. One of the hardest things I've ever had to do was let my guard down and open myself up to you. I entrusted you with my heart, but you threw it away." I have to take a quick breath before I go on since the tears are starting back up again. "God, I'm so stupid! I fell in love with a memory...a fucking ghost!"

Now the crying is getting the better of me and I really should just hang up, but his raspy voice cuts through any logical reasoning I have and keeps me on the line.

"I fell in love with you too, Sabrina. Please don't do this. Let me explain."

That just pushes me over the edge of what little control of the situation I have left. The anger intermingled with the heartache is killing me, and my body feels like it's on auto-pilot when I stop him from doing just that.

"You love me? You know what, don't even answer that. You don't know what the hell love is, Tyler. If you did, you wouldn't have done what you are claiming to be so sorry for. It wouldn't even have been a fleeting thought. If you did actually love me, you would know how much this would kill me. You would know that I would never forgive you. So please don't say that you love me, because it's obvious you don't have a clear grasp of what that word means."

With an edge to his voice, he asks, "Who's Alex?"

"He's my boss," I say defensively, "not that it's any of your business."

"Do you have something going on with him?"

"I guess you're just now remembering what you said to me last night. Do you have any idea how humiliated and hurt I felt after hearing you talk to me like that? Look, I'm only going to explain this to you once so listen carefully. Alex is my boss. He was...*was, as in past tense*...interested in me and before I left for the reunion, he let me know that he wanted to pursue something. But, being the goddamn fool that I am, the moment I got back home I told him no because of *you*. Because of the way I feel about *you*."

"Ava said...," he trails off because just the sound of her name from his lips makes my stomach lurch in response and I cut him off.

"I don't care what she told you, Tyler! If you have a problem with something that concerns me, about us, then you man up and ask me about it."

"Did you or did you not go on a date with him since you've been back home?"

"No, I didn't! Didn't you hear a single word I've just said to you? Do you honestly not believe me right now? Because that would be perfect, considering what you said to me last night."

"I was drunk, I didn't mean it."

"Is that supposed to make me feel better?"

"I told you when you were here…I warned you that I'm not use to this shit. I fuck up, that's what I always do."

"So you get to go 'slumming' then you apologize and blame it on being drunk? I'm supposed to just accept your apology and forget about all of this because you love me so much, is that right, Tyler? Did I leave anything out?"

"Cut the sarcastic bullshit, Sabrina," he says in a huff. "Look, I never said that I was perfect. I told you from day one that I was a selfish bastard."

"Are you fucking kidding me? Are you really going to sit there and tell me that because you're not use to *this*, that I should have known better? That I should have seen this coming?"

I don't know how I manage to stave off the sobbing; perhaps the rage I'm feeling is that strong. Whatever it is, I'm done. I'm so done with this conversation that the silence doesn't even register until he says my name.

"Are you still there?" he asks.

"What do you want from me, Tyler?"

"You."

"Please…just leave me alone," I say expelling what little energy I have left.

He sighs and I can picture him on the other line running his hands through his hair in frustration. "I can't do that, baby. If you won't let me explain, then at least let me say one thing."

I don't say yes or no. All my words have been used up. I've reached my quota for the day and he notices since I don't hang up. Instead, I stay on the line and listen in morbid curiosity to what he has to say.

"I'm not giving up, Sabrina. If it takes every day for the rest of my fucking life, I'm going to fix this."

"Did you fuck her?"

He stays quiet for too long then exhales loudly before answering. "Yes."

A small part of me had been hanging on to the tiniest of hope that maybe he hadn't actually done the deed. But with his one little-word answer, everything crumbles around me all at once. I'm exhausted, completely defeated, and between tears when I choke out, "Then it's too late. Goodbye."

I hang up the phone and turn it off this time, not wanting to be bothered any longer today with texts or calls from him or anyone else for that matter. The anger and hurt over him openly admitting his betrayal is rushing through me so fast that I feel lightheaded. I wish I could make it all stop. I wish that I had never given him my heart with a goddamn bow on it only to have him squander it at the first obstacle thrown his way. With that, I throw Julia's magic blanket over me again and get into a fetal position on the couch. My crying has died down a little when I eventually close my eyes and hope that this blanket can really make all the pain go away forever.

CHAPTER TWENTY-THREE

My vision is blurred after staring at my work monitor for an hour. The words are all jumbled and nothing is sinking in. I'm not able to accomplish much of any work that will help me catch up from my unscheduled day off yesterday. My day off that consisted of crying, followed by more crying, and followed up with some more crying.

I'm all cried out. At least I hope I am while I'm at work. Nothing more embarrassing than my fellow co-workers witnessing an emotional breakdown. The only reason I think I've been able to hold off the tears this long is by keeping my phone off so that I'm not tempted to call him.

There's one side of me that wants to hear his voice again and tell me it was all some crazy mix-up. That side is obviously delusional. The other, logical side of me knows I can't do that because it's not some crazy mix-up. A mix-up to me is more akin to ordering a Diet Coke and they bring you a Coke instead. Or when you get your neighbor's mail by mistake. This doesn't qualify in that category at all. This is full-on, hot-mess soap opera, the I-wish-I-was-in-a-padded-room kind of crazy mix-up. The kind that doesn't go away when you close your eyes to try to erase everything by squeezing them so tightly that they hurt. This kind of mix-up is the kind that stays with you forever. Always in the back of your mind, no matter how much you wish you could forget about it, even if for only a few minutes of temporary blissful ignorance.

I look away from my monitor only for a moment to rummage through my desk to find something to snack on. I haven't eaten anything since... God, I don't even remember. I'm pretty sure a copious amount of White Chocolate Macadamia Nut ice cream doesn't count. Between Julia and me, we polished off the entire half-gallon while sitting in my bed after she got home from work yesterday. Only problem with that is that I'm pretty close to starving now but not in the mood to get up and go anywhere to get myself a bite to eat.

My hand digs to the back of my file cabinet that I use for useless junk and finds a granola bar. It's just going to have to do for now. As I take my first bite, I open up my personal email account to send off a quick note to my parents, who I'm certain have been trying to reach me but since my phone is off, they've probably started to panic.

I efficiently type out a few lines explaining how busy I am with work and then throw in a quick blurb about having an issue with Tyler without providing any details. That should appease them for a day, maybe two, if I'm lucky. Common sense tells me that this will come back to bite me in the ass later. Knowing my mom, as soon as she reads that something is wrong with Tyler, she'll not only call me immediately but she'll send me a care package loaded with God knows what. Oh well, too late now. Probably should have thought out my email better, but under the circumstances it was the best I could do.

At two minutes to five, it's a race against time and I start to gather my belongings so I can drive home and crawl back into my bed. My computer starts to shut down, and I snatch my keys from inside my purse when I look up to see Alex standing in the door of my office.

"It's not like you to leave any earlier than six; you must not be feeling well." He hesitates a second before stepping inside.

I'm not feeling well. I'm feeling like total and utter shit right now, thank you very much. I just want to be left alone and contemplate life and what a complete idiot I am. I nervously tuck the loose strands of hair that have fallen out of my chignon behind my ear and put on the best smile that I can muster before I answer him.

"No, I don't."

I drop my head and go to walk around my desk, which brings me to within inches of where he's standing now. I'm hoping he doesn't notice my overt attempt to hide my misery but seeing as I'm wearing my crushed heart on my sleeve, I doubt it.

"You look pale and you're shaking."

"I'm fine. Just need to get home and get some rest."

I tilt my head up so that my eyes meet his. Big mistake.

"Sabrina, are you crying?"

"No."

I'm totally crying now after seeing the sympathetic look on his face a second ago.

"What's wrong?" he asks and goes to put his hands on my upper arms.

He stops just shy of doing so when the ugly cry finally makes an appearance. I cover my face with my hands to sob and sink into one of the guest chairs I have in my office. The sound of my office door closing registers, and I'm relieved that he's left me and my breakdown alone.

"Here, take this." Alex's voice is soft and surprisingly close. I peek through my fingers to see him crouched right in front of me holding out a handkerchief.

When I don't take it, he inches closer and pulls my hands down slowly one at a time from my face. The tears have stopped while he starts to wipe my cheeks with the handkerchief.

Keeping his eyes on the movement of his own hand, he asks, "Is it because of him?"

"Yes."

Satisfied with the job he's done, he tucks the handkerchief back into the breast pocket of his suit. His jaw flexes when his clear blue eyes lock onto mine. His hand reaches out to cup my jaw and he rubs his thumb gently over the apple of my cheek.

"Did he hurt you?"

"Yes."

"Do you want to talk about it?"

"No."

The corner of his lips twitch to keep in a smile. "Because of…"

"Yes, because of…," and my eyebrows rise to emphasize the "us" that's so blatantly missing from that sentence.

"Try me." I don't know if it's the way he said it or the look of melancholy in his eyes that pushes me to want to tell him everything. Whichever it is, I know I feel safe enough here with him in this tiny office to unload all of my drama on him.

"Tyler was the one. The moment we met up again, it was like finding that missing piece to a puzzle that I never could find with anyone else. It was like magic. Or at least I thought it was."

I drop my eyes to my hands, which are in balled fists in my lap, and take a quick breath before continuing.

"He slept with someone else and broke my heart. He smashed it into a million tiny little pieces, and every single part of me hurts so badly that even taking a breath is painful."

Before the first tear can escape down my cheek, Alex tugs at my upper arms and pulls me closer to him until he can wrap his arms around me. My hands grab onto the lapels of his suit for dear life as if it was my own personal life preserver in the middle of this never-ending pit of pain that I'm feeling. He holds me for as long as I need him to, long after the tears dry up and definitely longer than is necessary to comfort me. His strong arms never once breaking their tight hold of me, I let go of his suit and bring my arms to encircle his neck. Even I know this is dangerous territory and not at all what I should be doing, but the thought seeps into my head anyway. I want him to take all my pain away. I want him to make me forget. No, I *need* him to make me forget.

Rational thought process completely thrown to the wayside, I lift my head and before he can make any kind of decision, I make it for him. My lips graze his, and he flinches for a second before he cups the back of my head with his hand and kisses me. My mouth opens to taste him when the kiss turns deeper. It remains at a slow pace, which isn't nearly as fast as I need it to be. I run my hands through his hair and grab onto it roughly while I lean back in the chair and take him with me. I have to have Alex now so that my head will hopefully clear itself from thoughts of Tyler. My skirt rides up when he better positions himself in between my legs so I can wrap them around him tightly. For a brief second, I think I can't believe I'm actually going through with this. Then the moment his hand goes to stroke the skin of my exposed thigh and he drags his lips down my chin, I'm not thinking anymore. My body is on autopilot to tune out any doubts I have of whether or not this is a good idea. I let go of his hair to start undoing the first few buttons on my blouse when all of a sudden his lips stop moving along my skin, and he covers my hands with one of his. We remain frozen and entwined in each other for a few seconds in complete silence.

"Why did you stop?"

Keeping his face tucked against the skin on my neck where I can feel his breathing trying to return to normal, he says, "We shouldn't be doing this."

"But, I want to."

"No, you don't, Sabrina. If we do this, you'll regret it, and the last thing I want to be is somebody you regret."

He lifts his head and I'm so embarrassed by how terrible I am, thinking that I could use Alex to help me forget about Tyler, that I avert his eyes until I feel him move again. Removing his hand from covering mine, he pulls away from me slowly, taking care not to disturb my clothing too much more than it already is. He tugs at my skirt until it is back to normal and then goes to take the seat next to me.

"You love him."

Even I think I sound like a petulant child when I answer him. "No, I don't."

"It's OK to admit it. I can see it written all over your face, clear as day."

"I do, I love him…but I don't want to."

"It's not that easy, Sabrina. Love isn't something you can switch on or off. Trust me, I've been where you are right now."

The look on my face must reveal the question in my head and he smiles. "No, I didn't mean that I love you or that you even love me. Do I care about you? Yes. Am I attracted to you? Obviously…but I don't love you, Sabrina. What I meant was, I was in love once. I won't bore you with all the details since it's been years, but I can tell you the one thing I regret most about her…I gave up. I should have fought harder for her, for us…but I didn't. I just gave up."

He just hit the nail on the head. In frustration, I rub my face with my hands. "I don't think I want to fight, Alex. I don't know anymore if he's even worth fighting for."

"That's what you need to figure out on your own," he says quietly. "The answer may not come to you today or even tomorrow, but it will. If he's 'the one,' like you said, then it definitely deserves some time for you to think about."

"I already feel like a real jerk for before and now I just want to go out and buy you a puppy or something." His laugh is so infectious that I can't help but laugh along with him.

"Seriously, how is it that you're still single?" I ask him.

"I haven't met 'the one' yet," he says through a dimpled smile and winks at me. "Will you be OK driving yourself home or can I give you a ride?"

"I'll be fine, Alex. Somehow you've managed to make me laugh on an otherwise shitty day, so driving should be a piece of cake."

Standing up, he chuckles one last time as he says good night and opens the door to leave my office. I stay planted in my seat trying to make heads or tails of what just happened and thank God that he had the sense to stop it all when he did. There is no scenario where sleeping with Alex could have erased Tyler from my mind or heart. He's moved in and taken up permanent residence around the fortress that I've built back up.

My head drops back and I slouch in my seat when the painting of *Blue Nude* on the wall catches my eyes. I feel like the woman in the painting, sheltering herself from pain by wanting to curl herself up in a protective ball. I imagine that maybe she must have been heartbroken or wronged. Or perhaps she's simply trying to forget something that's happened to her. As if seeing it for the very first time, I understand the grief, captured by Picasso's brush strokes, that must have caused the woman so much misery. Unfortunately, I have my own misery to thank for being able to see it with such clarity.

Sighing, I sit back up, gather my purse from the floor, and fish my keys from inside of it. I leave the office using the back entrance reserved for employees and deliveries only so as to not run into anyone. I consciously choose to listen to upbeat music on my drive home, not wanting to torture myself again with listening to Joss Stone's "Spoiled" for the hundredth time today. The music change works because my mind is absent of Tyler-related thoughts. I'm home before I even realize that a whole thirty minutes have gone by without having driven myself further into insanity, so I guess you could say that's good.

I feel a small sense of victory at my progress and walk inside my front door. Dropping my laptop bag, purse, and keys, I let the scent of fresh basil lead me toward the kitchen. Thank God Julia is cooking tonight! My stomach grumbles in response to the amazing smells in our house, and I find her stirring a huge pot of her delicious homemade spaghetti sauce.

Without looking up she asks, "Wine?"

"God, yes."

She puts the spoon on the counter and reaches over to the cupboard to take out two wine glasses and places them on the island. She turns on her heel and goes to the far end of the counter to grab an open bottle of cabernet sauvignon. Pouring both our glasses, she raises hers in the air then clinks them together when she says her toast.

"To men. Can't live with them. Can't kill them either."

I smile weakly and bring the glass to my lips to taste and almost choke on the little amount in my mouth when she asks, "So, are you going to tell me why I can see your boobies or do I have to guess."

"Oh my God!" I quickly put down the glass and start to redo the buttons on my blouse that I had undone while trying to seduce Alex.

"I gotta say, for years you've been quiet with your dating life. But for the last couple of months, I don't know what's going to come out of your mouth when you come home. I hate to say it, but I'm kind of looking forward to it."

"Very funny," I say dryly. "I'd really rather not get into it right now, if you don't mind. I just want to eat, shower, and go to bed."

Bringing the glass back from her mouth, she grins and raises her one eyebrow in curiosity. "That good, huh?"

"I really don't want to talk about it, Julia."

"OK, OK," she says retreating back to the stove, "but you promise that you'll provide full details tomorrow?"

"Fine, it's a deal."

The rest of dinner goes by without either one of us speaking about my personal life. I don't know how we manage it, but I'm so relieved that she doesn't bring it up. I'm sure the wine helps to take the edge off and not think too much about what's happened over the last couple of days, but I'm not complaining in the slightest for the temporary amnesia. After we've cleared the plates and Julia retreats to the couch, I take a quick shower before calling it a night and heading to bed.

I toss and turn for a while, trying to find a comfortable position when the whole "inquiring minds want to know" thing makes me reach over to my nightstand and turn my phone back on. The main screen tells me I have twenty-eight unread texts, missed calls, and voicemails. Between my mom and Tyler, my phone has been blowing up. I open the last text from him which was sent about an hour ago, and my eyes blur with the tears that I have been able to keep hidden for a few hours.

I love you. Please talk to me.

Indulging myself in the idea that the last two days never happened, I start to type out a response back to him.

I love you too.

Quickly backspacing the entry before I ever press send, I turn the phone back off and put it on my nightstand. I roll over and make a decision right then and there. When I wake up in the morning, I'm going to look at this with fresh eyes and think about what my next move will be. Alex is right; if I thought already that Tyler was "the one," I at least owe myself that much.

That settled, I wipe my eyes with the edges of my comforter and smile weakly to myself in the darkness when one of my favorite movie quotes comes to mind. "*After all, tomorrow is another day.*"

You're goddamn right it is, Scarlett.

CHAPTER TWENTY-FOUR

Willing myself to keep my promise from the night before, I try to bring some semblance of normalcy back to my life by stopping at Sergio's for my *café con leche* before heading into work. I plug my iPhone in the audio jack when I get back into my car and press shuffle but skip any song that will no doubt lead me into a downward spiral. I simply click the button and tell Siri to skip, and if I have to say skip the whole ride in and end up listening to dead air, so be it... I refuse to listen to anything that will make me depressed today.

I arrive at work feeling somewhat rejuvenated and dive in, hoping that it will keep me occupied. Now, I'm perfectly aware that I should be thinking about the whole Tyler mess, but I need to allow myself one day of peace and quiet before I can go back there. Thankfully, the constant buzzing of my phone has stopped, and I'm hoping he's giving me some breathing room to do just that. This new exhibit I'm working on for a fresh local artist is just what I need to keep me busy long enough that I don't even notice when it's time to go home.

When I arrive home, Julia is getting ready to head out for an event her company is planning, and she is dressed to kill. I remember I was with her when she bought this

Bottega Veneta dress months ago; I loved it then, but now I'll definitely have to ask to borrow it.

"You look amazing, Julia."

"Thanks, girlie. What are you doing tonight?" she asks as she runs from room to room gathering her belongings.

"Um, nothing. Staying in and watching a movie, maybe do some more work on this new exhibit."

From the other room she yells out, "Oh yeah. I forgot to tell you, Alex called my office today and wanted to book me for it."

"That's great."

She finally comes back into the living room and looks around it one last time before she settles her eyes on me already sitting on the couch.

"Are you going to be OK here by yourself tonight? I feel bad leaving you in your time of need."

"Don't be silly. I'm a big girl and like I said, I do have some work to do anyway."

"Tomorrow is the weekend, and he who shall not be named was supposed to come," she says cryptically and goes to sit next to me. "I was thinking we can go to the beach if the weather's nice and then maybe some retail therapy. What do you think?"

She really is the *bestest* friend ever. "Sounds like a plan."

"Awesome!" She stands up with a huge smile on her face and tells me to have a good night as she picks up her keys and leaves.

Keeping with my earlier theme, I stay away from any TV show that could possibly get me to think of him. This doesn't leave me with many options, so I settle instead on *Househunters* on HGTV. It's mindless and good background noise while I open up my laptop and get some work done.

An hour later, I take a break from working and open my personal email account to see if my mom has responded. I knew it! Her response to my telling her I was having an issue with Tyler is that she will be sending a care package. I email her back letting her know that we have stores here too, but knowing her, she was probably at the post office first thing this morning.

Instead of closing my email, my eyes go to scan over my inbox, which is loaded to the hilt with spam, and then zeroes in on one email in particular. It was sent just after three o'clock this morning. Good to know the rat bastard was not able to sleep either. It gives me a small amount of satisfaction to know this but isn't nearly enough to appease the hollow I feel in the pit of my stomach.

My hand, as if detached from my body, points the cursor at his email and before my brain and heart can catch up to its movements, opens it. My mouth goes dry, and my tear ducts constrict when I read the first sentence. And even though I'm fully aware that I should stop this self-torture, I can't. I'll be the first to admit it; I'm weak and I'm my own worst enemy.

Sabrina,

The words I'm sorry will never be enough. I've been able to talk my way out of every kind of mess I've ever made in my life, up until now. This time I can't say it wasn't me or I didn't do it. I could explain how and why this happened, but it wouldn't matter. Just the memory of it is a constant reminder of how I lost you and how fucking stupid I am. I will never forgive myself for the pain I've caused you. For the rest of my miserable life, I will do whatever it takes to earn back your trust and your love. I know it's not going to be easy but I can't walk away from you. I did it once and I'll never do it again.

Love always,
Tyler

Each word hurts more than the last. Like a glutton for punishment, I read it over and over again to the point that I can probably recite it back to myself from memory. What catches my eye most of all is the "Love always" at the end. I want to believe the phrase means something, but his actions spoke louder to me than any typewritten words could ever say. Now I want to kick myself for even opening the damn thing because the ugly cry is right around the corner. As much as my mind is being controlled by my heart, I attempt to veer it toward work instead of reading his email again by repeating in my head: *I'm not going to cry, I'm not going to cry, I'm not going to cry.*

I might be a little crazy. Because one part of me wishes I hadn't read his email and that he would just go away, while the other part of me wants to read it again and then pick up the phone to call him. That's the other thing that's kind of bugging me now…why hasn't he called? I know this for a fact since my phone has been on all day today and hasn't beeped or vibrated once. His silence made me think that maybe I didn't have to make any kind of decision at all. It appeared that he was giving up and cementing his status as a liar in my eyes. But then I see this email, and I'm so pissed and hurt all over again. I shut down the laptop and focus my attention to the mindless drivel on TV for the next couple of hours until sleepiness takes hold, forcing me to climb into bed a little after midnight, before Julia ever makes it home.

The next day at the gallery is filled with meetings and goes by even quicker than the day before. Throwing myself into work was a brilliant idea. The second I have downtime he infiltrates my thoughts and it forces me to find something productive to do instead. So, needless to say, my office has never been tidier and my work has never been more caught up.

A few people from the office are heading out for happy hour and invite me to tag along. At first I say no because as much as I want to believe that I'm doing better, I know that lying in wait under the surface of my "everything is OK" exterior lies a pile of heartbreak that I'm just putting off until I can properly deal with it. It isn't until Sarah pleadingly convinces me to stop by for a couple of drinks that I agree to go. Plus, it is a Friday night, and I don't have to wake up early tomorrow anyway, so why not. Before I head out to meet up with them, I send Julia a text to see if she's interested in joining us.

So tired from last night, thanks anyway. Still on for beach tomorrow?

I grin and type out a "hell yes" response to the beach question then grab my keys to head on over to Cooper Ave in South Beach.

A "few people" ends up being more like twenty. Between all of us from the gallery and some significant others, we stake a claim at the far corner of the bar. We're packed like sardines in here and as I try to finagle myself to the actual bar to order another drink, I feel a man's hand grab onto my upper arm. Turning around to see the rest of what's attached to Mr. Arm Grabber, I come face to face with a semi-decent looking guy. However, as soon as he opens his mouth to speak, I smell the alcohol as if he had bathed in it.

"Who are you and where have you been all my life," he slurs.

Really? Men and their sorry-ass one liners…it's really insulting to women everywhere.

I free my arm carefully and smiling, I point to the bar, hoping that he understands bar speak from someone that has no desire to talk to him. Turning around again to attempt my original task, he grabs onto my arm with a little more force.

"Come on, don't be such a bitch," he says with a sick smile on his face, clearly enjoying himself.

Before I can say anything back, Alex appears next to me. Smoothly, he puts his arm around my waist while keeping his eyes on Mr. Arm Grabber.

"Take your fucking hands off her." Alex's dead calm voice is scary even to me, and I'm the one who's being rescued. If I was this guy, I would run for the hills. Drunken guy immediately lets go of me and puts his hands up as if to say, "no harm, no foul."

Retreating back to the hole he crawled out of, he says, "Sorry, man, I didn't know she was with anyone."

"Are you OK?" Alex asks, dropping his arm from my waist and coming to stand in front of me.

"I'm fine," I say, relieved. "Thank you for that."

Shrugging his shoulders as if to say it was nothing, he puts his hands in his pockets and grins. He looks over toward the bar to the group we belong to and then back to me before he says, "Come on, let's get you to a safer spot."

There's a rule somewhere that whenever someone puts a shot glass in front of you, you must drink it. When I go to grab what I think is my third shot of a very yummy concoction that tastes like a Jolly Rancher, Alex gives me a stern look.

"Slow down," he says in a fatherly tone.

"I'm totally fine," and I go to get up from my bar stool to show him that I still have my wits about me.

I teeter a bit and giggle at my attempt to try to stand straight when I know I'm officially a little tipsy.

"OK, that's enough," he says through his crooked grin. "Let me drive you home."

"Pish posh, I can drive myself home."

His eyebrow rises when he laughs and says, "Did you just say 'pish posh?'"

"Yup, I did."

"Now I know it's definitely time to get you home. Let's go."

I keep on giggling as he maneuvers us through the crowded bar until we are outside. He tells me to stand by the door and wait while he goes to bring his car around. The first few droplets of rain start to fall on my head when Alex's car roars up to the curb, and I get in before the deluge begins.

I stay silent and stare out the window at the fading lights of South Beach through the heavy rain and darkness when we get on the A1A. Maybe it's the alcohol or the general gloominess from the weather, but the thought of what I was supposed to be doing tonight and this weekend starts to play with my head. On the verge of losing it again in front of Alex, I start wishing that the car could move faster so I could just hide under my covers and cry in solitude. Doesn't help that the drive that usually takes about a half hour is longer tonight because of the heavy downpour, but we finally arrive and luckily it's without one tear shed.

Alex pulls up behind a car I don't recognize already parked in the driveway next to Julia's. I'm about to put a kibosh on her alone time with whoever it is she's got in there. Doesn't really matter since I plan to go right to bed anyway.

I look over at Alex, who, God bless him, has put up with my silence, and say thank you, when just over his shoulder I make out two people at my front door. It's hard to discern who's who since the window is covered with rain, but I know one of them has to be Julia. It's not until the other person takes a step back and looks over at Alex's car that it registers who it is. My head that was clogged with alcohol is clearing up fairly fast when I see this figure striding toward us, still sitting in the car.

"Shit. Shit. Shit."

"What's wrong?" Alex asks, and he turns around to look at what's caught my attention.

Before he turns his head back I'm already out of the car and walking to where Tyler is standing in the middle of my front yard in the pouring rain. He runs his hand through his hair and goes to take a step toward me, but I put my hands up in defense.

"Don't come any closer," I say through the tears that are intermingled with the rain that's pelting my face. "Why are you here?"

He looks tired and miserable, evident by the five o'clock shadow on his face. Good, I hope he's as miserable as I've been. I want him to feel just an ounce of the suffering I've had to deal with since he betrayed me. He goes to open his mouth and say something, when from behind me I hear a car door slam, and I know that the shit has officially hit the fan.

"Who the hell is this?" Tyler asks as he eyes Alex up and down menacingly.

Alex ignores him completely and tugs at my hand to pull me to the front door where Julia is still standing with her hands on her hips.

I go to walk by her when under her breath, so only I can hear, she says, "See what I mean when I said I have no idea what to expect when you come home anymore."

"Julia, please," I say a little too defensively. She tries unsuccessfully to hide the smirk on her face, so it's obvious she finds humor in this mess.

Tyler is right behind us and only gets one foot in the house when Julia is on him like a rabid dog standing in his way. "I told you, get the hell out of here! She doesn't want to see you!"

"Let her tell me that herself," Tyler yells over Julia's voice.

I sink down onto the couch and cover my face with my hands to shield myself from the scene playing out before me when I hear Alex's calm voice over both Julia and Tyler's.

"Take it easy."

Tyler's voice is beyond agitated when I hear him say, "Get your fucking hands off me."

A scuffling noise makes me pop my eyes up to see Tyler right in Alex's face looking like he's about to tear his head off. Julia tries to get in the middle of them by patting Alex's shoulder and saying, "Alex, calm down."

"Alex? This is Alex?" Tyler asks out loud to no one in particular but looking over at me, still frozen in place on the couch. "I thought you said there was nothing going on."

Julia answers for me at the top of her lungs when she finally gets enough space in between them, "There isn't anything going on, you jackass! He's just her boss and a friend! And who the fuck are you to even ask who he is, anyway? The last time I heard, your dick was in some random skank!"

Oh my God! That's it! I can't take another second of this craziness! The alcohol has completely worn off, and my head feels like it's going to crack open when I wipe my face and stand up. All three of them shut up and turn to look in my direction as I walk toward them, still dripping wet from the soaking I got a few minutes ago.

I look into Tyler's eyes, which is a huge mistake, because I see the pain I feel in my heart looking right back at me. I knew even ten years ago those eyes of his would be the death of me and here they are, boring holes into the depths of my soul that is aching to be comforted by the same person who destroyed it.

"Give us a minute," I say quietly, keeping my focus on Tyler.

Julia quickly gets in front of me. "Listen, girlie, if you think for one minute I'm going to leave you alone with this piece of shit, think again."

"Julia, I appreciate it, but I'll be fine...I need to talk to him." I hear myself but it's like I can't believe it's me I hear.

"I don't like this," she says as she steps aside and looks over at Alex. "Alex, I need you to stay here just in case I need someone to kick his ass."

Alex's mouth curls up when he goes to move by Julia and says, "Doesn't look like you need any help, but I'll stay just in case."

"Well? Go ahead and talk to him," Julia says. "We're not leaving."

I roll my eyes at her, and she gives me the "I don't think so" look while putting her hand on her hip. I motion for

Tyler to follow me instead to my bedroom for the privacy that we require to have any kind of conversation. He follows me in and walks past me as I close and lock the door behind me.

I lean my back against the door when I ask softly, "Why did you come?"

"I needed to see you."

"Why? Hurting me from over a thousand miles away wasn't good enough? You had to do it to me in person too?"

He takes a couple of steps toward me, and I push off from the door and past him to sit at the foot of my bed.

"I didn't come here to hurt you. Sabrina, I'm—"

"You're what? You're sorry?"

He inches closer to me, his large frame making me feel so small in my own room that I want to fall back into my bed and disappear. Once he is standing right in front of me, he crouches down to his knees so that our faces are almost eye level.

"Yes, I'm sorry, but that's not why I came." His hands carefully reach out to touch me, and I flinch so he lowers them to the bed on either side of me.

"Every time I hear or see you cry, it kills me just a little bit more because I know it's me who's to blame for it. I know I'll never be good enough for you...I knew it back then, and I fucking know it for sure now. I know I don't have any right to ask, but if you give me another chance, I swear I will spend the rest of my life trying to put that beautiful smile back on your face. Because what I came here to tell you is that I need you...I need you like I need the fucking air to breathe."

Tyler drops his head to rest on my lap, and his arms encircle me. I can't say anything back to him. My vocal chords are temporarily robbed by the emotions I'm feeling. The pain in the pit of my stomach is appeased only slightly by his words that I want to believe so badly. I pull my arms out of his embrace and put them just over his dampened hair. They hover there while I struggle with wanting to soothe him and wanting to hurt him. In the end, they fall to my sides, careful not to touch the bare skin of his arms.

"Please just go."

He lifts his head slowly and brings his lips to my forehead to press a soft kiss there. I close my eyes at the contact, not wanting to look into his when he backs away and goes to stand up. Hearing his feet walk the few steps to my door, I keep my head down and my eyes tightly shut so I won't even be tempted to stop him.

I can tell he's opened the door and is about to walk out when he faintly says, "Whether you want to believe it or not, I do love you, Sabrina."

The heartache of wanting to hear those words for so long from him brings a new wave of tears, and I go to bury my face in my hands, but not before I manage to say one last thing to him before he leaves.

"I love you too... but right now, it's just not enough."

CHAPTER TWENTY-FIVE

I wake up to the sound of rain outside my bedroom window. So much for a day at the beach. It's just as well. I couldn't lift a limb if I tried. All my energy is drained, and I'm so uncomfortable from falling asleep in my clothes. I roll onto my back and stare blankly at the ceiling, hoping to find some answers there to the questions in my mind.

I never made it out of my room, even after Tyler left last night. I heard some murmuring, which I assumed to be Julia and Alex for a few minutes, but I didn't want to face either of them after what happened. I locked my door and just buried myself in a cocoon in my bed and cried myself to sleep.

The sound of footsteps approaching and stopping outside my bedroom door makes me abandon the staring contest I'm having with my ceiling. I look over to the clock on my nightstand to see that it's past ten in the morning. I know that Julia must be busting at the seams to talk.

I sigh and push my hair out of my face before I find my voice and say, "You can come in."

She immediately goes to open the door but it's still locked, which forces me to throw the covers aside and unlock it for her. I crawl back into bed as she opens it and stays in the doorframe with her arms wrapped around herself, assessing the damage.

"I'm sorry, sweetie," she says sympathetically. "Can I get you anything?"

I shake my head no when she starts to take a few steps closer until she's sitting on the side of the bed and smiles weakly at me.

"Did he say anything to you when he left?"

She tilts her head thinking of something, then says, "No, not really."

"So he said something to you. Tell me."

"I don't know if that's a good idea, Sabrina."

I sit up in the bed intrigued by whatever information she's choosing not to share and wish that I didn't want to know so badly, but at the same time needing to hear it.

"Fine," she says giving in to my request. "He apologized to me and said that I was an amazing best friend for looking out for you and that if you changed your mind that he'd be staying at the—"

"Stop! Don't tell me. I don't want to know."

"I hate to admit this, but I kind of felt sorry for the guy when he came skulking out of here looking like his dog died. He deserves it and all, but seriously he looked pitiful. What did you tell him?"

Thinking back to the moment he wrapped me in his arms and I was so close to giving in but couldn't, my eyes water. Ugh! Jesus Christ! This constant crying at the drop of a hat is even annoying me. I groan out loud, utterly frustrated with the knowledge that my heart is in complete control of me right now and has been since the second he stepped onto that gazebo a month ago.

Julia sounds confused when she asks, "What? What does that groan mean?"

"I'm so tired of all of this, Julia. I'm tired of feeling like a wet mop all the goddamn time. I'm tired of crying all day and night. I'm tired of trying to pretend that I'm OK when I'm not. I'm tired of not wanting to admit to myself that I should have seen this coming. But most of all, I'm so fucking tired of loving him with everything that I have when I know I shouldn't after what he did."

"This is the last time we'll talk about this, so whatever you choose to do, I'll support you regardless, OK?"

"Last time ever, or just today?" I ask sarcastically.

She grins and I know she's dying to say something equally biting, if not worse, in return but she keeps it in check.

"You have every right to feel everything you are feeling right now. Because what he did...no bullshit...I'd want to go Lorena Bobbitt on him too. But...."

"But what?" I ask, propping myself up on my elbows.

"But, it took a lot of balls to come here. I've never felt like that for someone that deeply where you fly across the country and—"

"It's isn't across the country," I say quickly, correcting her.

"Fine," and she rolls her eyes at me before she continues, "fly down the eastern seaboard to apologize to someone in person."

"He already had the airline ticket."

"True, he did, but he could have easily kept his unwanted ass at home too. But he chose to come here and fight for you. That says a lot."

"This coming from the person who wanted to kill him last night when he showed up here," I say, reminding her of the scene.

She lets out a dry laugh, then says, "Well, as the best friend, that *is* part of my job description. Don't get me wrong, he's still on my shit list. But maybe, just maybe, he fell to the number two slot."

I fall back onto the bed with such force that the pillows give a big "poof" sound and I put my arm across my eyes. As soon as I do, I see Ava and Tyler wrapped in each other's arms. His mouth kissing and nipping at her neck as her head falls back in ecstasy while her hands grip onto his hair roughly.

"Every time I close my eyes, Julia, I see them together. It's like it's on constant rewind, and I can't make it stop long enough to listen to what he has to say."

"I'm sorry, sweetie. I don't know how to fix that."

And that's it in a nutshell. Nobody can fix it.

I slide my arm off my face and let out a big breath. "I don't want to talk about it anymore, if you don't mind."

She turns the imaginary lock closed over her lips, trying to get me to smile, and it works for a half a second before I notice my crumpled clothes.

"I need to get out of these and shower."

Julia goes to stand and starts to walk out of my room. "I'll have some coffee ready for you when you get out."

"Julia?"

Her hand on the doorframe stops her progress, and she turns her head around to look over at me.

"Yeah?"

"Thank you, for everything."

She winks and says, "What kind of best friend would I be if I didn't take care of you?"

Her long blonde hair goes flying behind her when she leaves my room and heads to the kitchen to make that cup of joe. I kick the blanket off of me and make my way to the shower, staying under the hot stream of water until I realize my fingers look like prunes. Throwing on a pair of yoga pants and a tank top, I pull my wet hair into a messy bun on the top of my head and stalk to the kitchen to join Julia. Waiting for me is my filled *X-Files* coffee mug with steam flowing from the top as promised.

I hop up to sit on the kitchen island and Julia goes to grab a refill when something occurs to me. "Oh my God! Alex!"

With her back to me, Julia snickers then says, "Yeah, I was wondering when you'd ask about that."

"I can't believe he saw all that drama." I put my hand to my head in disbelief and embarrassment. "What did he say when he left?"

"Nothing much," she says with a little grin. "He hung around for a few minutes after Tyler left then went home to his bat cave or wherever the hell he lives. I think I freaked him out a bit, to be honest."

"You kind of freaked me out too. I thought you were going to slice and dice Tyler right in our living room, and I was going to have to start collecting bail money for you."

As she breezes past me and starts walking down the hall, she says, "Well, bros before hos and all that jazz."

I yell out to her, "I think you mean sistahs before mistahs."

"Semantics," she yells back.

I finish my coffee while thinking of things to do to occupy myself today. When my bare feet hit the hard-wood floor after sliding off the counter, I decide to take on a huge project that I've been putting off forever. With renewed vigor, I set off down the hall to tackle the task of cleaning out my closet. This ought to keep me busy for a while. It's packed so tightly that it's screaming for a good reorganizing.

Several hours later I'm staring at an empty closet and piles of clothes, shoes, and handbags scattered all over my room. I've somehow managed to move the mess from a contained mess to a nuclear bomb mess. What the hell was I thinking? I'm never going to get this crap straightened up and in semi-decent order then back into a tiny closet to boot. I see myself sleeping on a pile of clothes later tonight because this has got to be the stupidest idea I've ever had.

The sun already set, I've made a minor dent in just the shoes when Julia pops her head in and lets out a long whistle.

"Holy crap, girlie," she says, chuckling. "Bored much?"

"At least I've got some of the shoes organized," I say, a little happy at my progress. "You should have seen it when I started hours ago."

"I'll take your word for it. I was going to heat up some leftover pasta, do you want some?"

"No thanks, I'm really making some headway here and it's helping to keep me mind off of—"

She cuts me off, keeping me from breaking my own rule while turning on her heel and walking down the hall. "La la la la la. Sabrina is talking but I'm not listening to Sabrina."

I laugh and walk over to sit down on the one bare spot on the floor but before my ass touches the ground, I curse myself for not thinking of something sooner. I grab my iPhone off the nightstand, which has no messages, thankfully, and dock it into the alarm clock to listen to some music.

Those seven dwarfs were onto something with that whole "whistle while you work" thing, because the music motivates me to get even more floor space cleared in a matter of hours.

Now all that's left is a small pile of handbags that I've transferred from the floor to my bed. I grab a couple of them and go to put them on the top shelf in my closet when that goddamn box of "old stuff" from high school gets in the way. I look up to the ceiling, hoping for some divine intervention to keep me from having to touch it, but no such thing happens. I pull the corner of the box to the edge and take it down without glancing inside of it, bringing it to the furthest corner of my bedroom instead. Out of sight, out of mind.

At just after midnight, I look over my now spotless and reorganized closet with pride. I walk backwards out of it until I fall onto my bed exhausted. I sit back up just as quickly though, not wanting to fall victim again to sleeping with my clothes on. In doing so, I notice that box in the corner. And just like that, all the work of keeping myself busy was for nothing because Tyler is all I can think about now.

I sit and stare at it too long for it to be normal. All it does is bring more questions. Why? Why, if you love me so much that you need me like the air to breathe, would you sleep with someone else? It doesn't make any sense whatsoever. He's an enigma that I cannot seem to figure out; he does one thing but says something else. I want to kick myself for sitting here and trying to decipher it all—the pieces that make up Tyler. There's too many to count and nothing seems to fit. I grow increasingly agitated with every thought while I stare at that goddamn box that feels like it's taunting me. Pulling my eyes away from it, I look down at my hands that are clenched in fists. I know there are no answers in the box just like I know that none will magically appear in my head. Only one person can give me the answers I'm looking for.

I snatch my phone from the dock and slip on my Converse sneakers before bolting out of my room. I reach the front door after bending down to pick up my purse and keys before it dawns on me that I have no clue where I'm supposed to be going and that my car is still parked by the bar from last night. Running back down the hallway, I stop outside Julia's bedroom door and tap my knuckles softly against it. I'm surprised when I hear her voice, clear and alert, that says to come in.

She tears her eyes away from her laptop, takes one look at me and says, "The Delano, room 1408, and my keys are in my purse."

"Thanks."

She shouts a "you're welcome" that I can barely hear because I'm already in full sprint toward the front door.

CHAPTER TWENTY-SIX

The drive to The Delano Hotel takes me less than twenty minutes, but to find a parking spot in South Beach on a hopping Saturday night takes another fifteen. It's not until I'm in the elevator and the door closes that I see my reflection. Shit, I should have thought this out a little better. I don't even have time to fix the messy bun on the top of my head before the doors open again on the fourteenth floor.

Of course his has to be the very last door, and the walk down the hallway feels like a death march. I stand there as if I was wearing a pair of boots made out of cinder blocks until I lift my hand up to knock. Adrenaline is racing through me, making a dull pounding sound in my ears that barely drowns out the clink of the lock being undone on the other side.

Tyler opens the door wearing a black tank top and black pajama bottoms. His thick brown hair is a perfect mess. But what catches my attention more than anything are the old-school Ray-Ban eyeglasses on his face. Lord, help me. No one should look this good in the middle of night, especially with a pair of glasses on.

"I didn't know you needed glasses," I say, sounding like a complete idiot.

"I wear them for reading," he answers with a small shrug and goes to take them off. "Do you want to come in?"

He swings the door wider for me to walk by him, closing the door before he goes to stand at a small desk to my left. Putting his glasses on a pile of papers there, he leans against the desk and watches me closely while I put Julia's keys in my purse and drop it to the floor. I walk to the windows to stare at the ocean view, choosing to keep my back to him when I blurt out the reason I came here.

"I need to know exactly what happened with Ava."

"I'm sorry, but I can't tell you that."

"Why not?"

"Because I know anything I say is going to hurt you more, and that's the last thing I want."

I drop my head against the cool glass, still locked in a trance with the ocean waves hitting the sand down below.

"Tyler, I know it's crazy, but please ... I need to know how and why it happened."

He stays silent for so long that I'm forced to turn around and look at him still leaning against the desk with his arms wrapped around himself. I walk over to stand in front of him and try not to take in his pained expression as he struggles to find the right words to explain himself.

"A few of us were hanging out at the bar in the restaurant after we closed for the night. Little by little, it was only the two of us left. That's when she told me about Alex and how she saw some text you got from him that last day when you dropped me off. I didn't believe it at first, since you never mentioned to me that you had spoken to Ava at all. Why didn't you ever tell me about that?"

I quickly say to him, through clenched teeth, "So this is my fault because I never told you about Alex?"

"No, that's not what I meant."

"Why then? It wouldn't have made any difference," I say, matter of factly.

His jaw flexes when he answers me back. "For starters, I would have fired her back then instead of having to wait three weeks to do it."

I feel a small sense of happiness and relief at that piece of information, but it doesn't take away from the path of destruction she left in her wake. He pulls himself off the desk slowly to come closer to me but with every small step he takes forward, I take one backwards. I swing around him and put my palms on the desk, keeping my back to him when I take a deep breath and exhale, remembering the reason I came here.

"Go on. Tell me the rest."

He lets out a string of curses under his breath before he finally goes on with the blanks I need filled.

"One drink led to another. I was pretty drunk, and she offered to give me a ride. The part of me that still thinks I don't deserve you and lets me fuck everything up in my life without a second thought…yeah, that part let her convince me that you were still with Alex. So when she drove to her place instead, I didn't say no." He pauses then continues. "I kind of passed out…after. When I woke up in the morning, she filled in the blanks for me. She told me about the phone call and what I had said to you."

I feel him coming to stand right behind me. So close that I can feel his warm breath on the back of my neck when he starts to talk again.

"Baby, I knew in that very moment that I had seriously messed everything up. I'm so fucking stupid for ever doubting you even a single second. I should have gone home, called you, and asked you myself. But I didn't and I can't take that back. I want to more than anything, but I can't."

The hurt in his voice cuts through to me somehow. I want to hate myself for it, but I can't control the feelings I have for him. My emotions have been in the driver's seat since I came knocking on his door a little while ago, and I know if I turn around to look in his eyes, I'll be a goner. Keeping my attention trained on the papers on the desk, I barely notice his movement behind me. It's not until I feel his right hand lightly rest on my hip that I snap out of the trance into which I've talked myself.

He dips his head and brings his mouth to my ear and, in a voice that cuts me to the core, says, "Tell me what I can do to make this right, baby. Whatever it is…please tell me and I'll do it."

"I don't know," I whisper.

His other hand gently pushes me to turn around, but I keep my head down. My heart is racing with our bodies being pressed so closely together, and the pounding in my ears has reached an all new high. He cups my face with both his hands and gradually lifts my head so that I have no choice but to stare back at him. I see something that I would assume is regret and sadness across his face, but I don't know if he fully realizes that the gravity of what he's done deserves more than an "I'm sorry." He broke my trust in him and once it was violated, I knew it would be the most difficult thing to repair. Like a flower that needs the right amount of sunlight, water, and care to bloom, trust requires the right amount of nurturing to flourish. How, after all of this, can I ever trust him again to accomplish that? Will I always question every little thing he does or doesn't do, or will I be able to look past this one day?

"You once told me that you saw the real me." My voice cracks at the memory from that night. "Well, what if *that* was the real you? What if everything you showed me about yourself was just smoke and mirrors?"

He smiles faintly and rubs my cheeks with his thumbs. "There are only two people in my life who have ever seen the real me. One of them died when I was six years old, the other one is standing right in front of me."

I close my eyes the moment he presses a kiss against my cheek, and I bring my hands up to grip onto his wrists. When he goes to pull away, I surprise myself by running my hands up his arms and encircling his neck, pulling his head back down so that his lips are just an inch from mine. Both of us hesitate for just a second before our mouths finally meet.

At first our tongues move slowly but it quickly escalates, each of us wanting more from the other to help dull the pain. I arch my neck when his mouth moves down toward the exposed skin on my chest, my hands in a death grip around his neck to keep him as close to me as possible. He takes a step forward, pushing me against the edge of the desk so I hop up to sit, and he stands in between my legs.

Tyler's eyes look conflicted, but my body, with a mind of its own, craves more. I put my hands underneath his tank top to touch the bare skin of his rippled stomach. Slowly,

I move them higher, taking the fabric with my movement, until something catches my eye.

There, on his right upper chest, is calligraphy-style lettering in black ink that says "Sabrina." With my heart in my throat, my fingers graze the edges of the raised skin around it that looks like it's still healing. I never thought I'd be the kind of girl that would be touched by something like this, but I can't lie—I think it's amazing. If I can get my thoughts to stop whirling around long enough, I might be able to say something to him about how much it means to me that he did this to himself. So much so, that I'm utterly speechless.

"Do you like it?" he asks softly, running the back of his fingers across my cheek.

"When did you do this?"

"The day after you left."

I stare at the expressive curves of the letters that are permanently branded onto his skin, completely captivated by the beauty of it.

"It's beautiful...I love it." And for the first time in what feels like an eternity, I look up at him and smile.

"No. That right there," he says acknowledging my smile, "is beautiful. I didn't think I'd ever see that smile again, and God knows I don't deserve it."

The corners of his lips curl up just as he dips his head to kiss me again, but I stop him by putting the tips of my fingers there.

"I can't, I'm sorry. I want to...obviously...but I need some more time to think about everything and if we do what we were about to do, it will just confuse me more than I already am."

He grabs hold of my fingers that are still touching his lips and kisses them tenderly before placing it above his heart.

"Baby, you don't ever need to apologize. I should be the one on my fucking knees begging for forgiveness."

I smile weakly as my eyes well up, and I search his face for the answer I need more than any other. He had said those magic words to me yesterday but at the end of the day, they're just words. I need to feel those words blanket me just like the warmth of his body does. And right now, I need that more than anything.

"Do you really love me, Tyler?"

Without a second of hesitation, he whispers, "With all that I am."

He dips his head to rest his forehead against mine, and I close my eyes to relish the closeness for a few moments. The confirmation of his feelings for me is like a salve on a wound that won't heal no matter how much I want them to. I try to clear my head of all the thoughts I have swirling inside of it like a tornado but it's of no use. I need to give myself some time to carefully think things over, since there is no way that I can decide to forget what happened just like that.

"I should go," I say, sounding as exhausted as I feel.

"Can I see you again?"

"I'm not sure that's a promise I want to keep right now."

He lifts his head, causing some of his hair to fall onto his brow. On instinct, I go to brush it out of the way but let my hand fall onto my lap instead. I try not to let the bleak look in his eyes affect me when I slide off the desk, taking some of the papers with me. I bend down to gather them at the same time Tyler does, almost bumping our heads together in the process. I start to hand him the ones I picked up as we both go to stand and then yank them back to me when I make out what they say.

"Why...what are these for?" I stammer.

I shuffle each piece of paper in my hand. Back and forth and back and forth, again and again, but he doesn't answer. I settle on one that shows a commercial property for sale about two blocks from where we are right now. Feeling completely thrown for a loop, I look up at him to find him run both his hands through his hair and lace his fingers behind his neck. He looks like a child who's been caught with his hand in the cookie jar when a meek smile appears across his lips.

"I told you that I would do anything to fix this, and I meant it."

Confusion, frustration, joy...take your pick. All of those emotions and then some are running through my mind like I switched on a blender. I don't even know where to start.

"So, you're going to move here? Just like that...without even telling me," my voice almost sounding as panicked as I feel.

"No. I was going to tell you about it when the time was right. Plus, I haven't decided anything yet."

I try to find some calm in this shit storm that just keeps getting more complicated by the minute. "You can't just up and move here. I can't let you do that. I need time to think. And who's to say that when I do think about all of this that I decide not to—"

"Don't say that." He closes the space between us quickly, taking the papers from my hands and throwing them onto the desk. Turning my chin up with his thumb and forefinger so I can't escape his penetrating gaze, he looks me dead in the eyes when he speaks again.

"If you move tomorrow to Timbuktu, then guess what, I'd be looking at restaurant spaces there too. Do you know why?"

I shake my head while he still has a hold on my chin.

"Because wherever you are is where I want to be. You can take all the time you need to think, but I'm not giving up. You and I...we belong together, and I'll wait for however long it takes because I love you."

I need to stand my ground here, which is more difficult than before when he says things like that to me. I love him, but like I told him last night, it's not enough...at least right now with my head and heart flying in all kinds of different directions, it's not.

"Tyler, I've never been in a real relationship before, but I'm pretty sure moving across the country after a month isn't normal. Especially when one of us has already cheated."

His mouth opens to say something but I continue, not wanting to be swayed further by him. "Trust isn't something that I can just turn back on overnight. I need time and I need for you to give that to me, no matter how long."

He thinks over what I'm asking of him for a second or two while he takes my face in both of his hands, finally nodding yes with a slight sadness in his eyes. The uncertainty is so thick all around us that even I don't know if this will be the last time I ever see him. I get up on my tiptoes and bring my lips to his, wanting to taste him once more before I walk out of this room. He wraps his arms around me possessively, and I cup his stubbled jaw with my hands, kissing him as if there was no tomorrow.

When we break the kiss, the first few tears start to stream down my cheeks. His thumbs wipe them with care. "Don't cry.... this isn't the end. I promise."

He lets go as my arms drop down to my sides, and I grab my purse from the floor where I'd dropped it. Tyler follows me to the door, holding it open for me, and I cross the threshold back into the hallway then turn around to face him one final time.

My voice wavers only slightly when I say, "Goodbye."

"Goodbye, Sabrina."

The walk to the elevator is even more difficult knowing that he's watching me. When the elevator doors open, I hit the button for the lobby and turn to look out at him. Both of us soak in every second we can before the doors shut completely. I'm left staring back at my own reflection again, wondering how strange it is that after ten years, I'm the one who's deciding to walk away this time.

CHAPTER TWENTY-SEVEN

"OK, Mom," I huff into the phone, pretty much giving up on getting a word in edgewise in this conversation.

"Sabrina, now you know you need to take better care of yourself. You're running yourself ragged with that job of yours. I think the best medicine is a nice long vacation."

My mom, God bless her. If she could only understand that my job is the one thing keeping me sane right now. Ever since I walked away from Tyler in that hotel hallway a couple of weeks ago, my heart has been on a seesaw. One day it's up and I'm more than willing to jump off, feet first, into the unknown. The next day it's so down that I want to throw in the towel, forget about him, and move on with my life. Today, for all intents and purposes, it's down.

Rubbing my eyes while the phone teeters on my shoulder, I grab it just in time before it drops on my desk. "Mom, I just took a vacation about a month and a half ago. I can't take another one again that quick."

"That may be so, but you sound like you need to do something, sweetheart. Is everything alright? How are things with Tyler?"

Surprisingly, my mom has been "Team Tyler" ever since I told her we were on a break. Actually, what she said when she found out was, "You mean like Ross and Rachel on *Friends*?" I had to clarify for her that Ross and Rachel were technically on a break when said cheating occurred and that I would prefer she not compare my personal life to that of two fictional characters. I further clarified for her that Tyler's cheating happened when we were not on any kind of break at all and is *the* reason behind what has put us in the holding pattern that we're currently in.

Taking in a deep breath through my mouth and then loudly exhaling through my nose, I try to explain to her again why things are not looking up at the moment.

"I haven't spoken to him since he left a couple of weeks ago, so I would say that things between us are about the same as when I talked to you last...which was, what...yesterday, right?"

"I didn't talk to you yesterday."

"I know you didn't, Mom. I was trying to be funny."

"Sabrina, there is nothing funny about this," she says seriously. "Obviously the man loves you enough to want to move down there. What else does he have to do?"

I answer her question with a silence so thick that it borders on screaming because I don't know that he has to do anything at all. The whole "it's not you, it's me" thing is exactly what this has come down to. I have trust issues, plain and simple. I've had them my entire adult life, and it's not something that I can just snap my fingers and make all better from one day to the next. What kills me is I've actually tried to do just that. But every time I think I want to break down the fortress of solitude around me long enough to believe in Tyler, I second-guess myself. Then, like a dog chasing its tail, I'm right back where I started. It's exhausting.

"Mom, I don't want to talk about it anymore, if you don't mind."

She sighs loudly on the phone then says, "You know, there is a saying about forgiveness, Sabrina. 'To err is divine, to forgive is human.'"

I try to contain my laugh at her mistake. "You got it backwards. It goes, 'To err is human, to forgive is divine.'"

"Even better," she says triumphantly.

"Alright, Mom," I say still grinning, "I have to get back to work. I'll call you later this week, OK?"

"OK." There she goes sighing again like I'm dismissing her. "Take care of yourself, sweetheart. Love you."

"Love you too, Mom. Bye."

Putting the phone back in its cradle, I'm still amazed that my mom is rooting so strongly for Tyler. Little does he know that not only is my mother supporting his cause, but his biggest cheerleader is the least likely of suspects.

Julia.

After choosing to leave my heart on the fourteenth floor of the Delano Hotel, Julia is convinced that I'm making a mistake of epic proportions. No one is more shocked than I am at this strange turn of events. I mean, the girl almost tackled him in our living room and wanted to tear him to bits, limb from limb. Only to make a complete about-face a couple days later so suddenly that it almost made me dizzy.

I swear, if Julia wasn't as successful as she is in her event planning business, she'd make a fantastic lawyer, because every chance she gets she's pleading Tyler's case. Her biggest argument for being "Team Tyler" is the same as my mom's: he's willing to move. To her, that shows a tremendous amount of commitment on his part and I can see that, really, I can. But it doesn't erase all the stuff before it that led him to think about doing something so drastic. When

I tell her this, she goes into a long-ass-winded explanation that drives me absolutely crazy.

First, she starts off with the whole thing about Tyler thinking he's not good enough for me. After everything I've told her about his childhood, she thinks that it directly affects some poor decisions he's made in his life, including this last one. The problem I have with her argument is how long someone can blame their current mistakes on the past. I'm not trying to be unfeeling or uncaring in the slightest, quite the opposite, and my heart breaks every time I think of him struggling as a child. What worries me is if every time he gets the slightest hint of doubt about how I feel toward him—and I can't even begin to fathom how he could— who's to say he doesn't jump into someone else's bed just as quickly as he did with Ava?

Ava. Just thinking of her name makes me vomit a little bit in my mouth. Which brings Julia to her second point in the case of *Sabrina Chandler v. Tyler Anderson*: he fired her. Awesome! Way to go, Tyler! My rebuttal is easy on this one: he slept with her *before* he fired her. He did say that he would have fired her on the spot, had I told him about the impromptu meeting she decided to call that day in his office. I'm not sure if I totally buy this answer from him, though. He did see my reaction to her just a couple of days before, when she showed up unannounced at his apartment. Tyler knew how upset I was, having to stand there and watch while she put her hands on his stomach as if she was a cat marking her territory. Even with all of that evidence, I couldn't have asked him to get rid of her because of the jealousy she spiked in me. God knows I wanted to, and I'm glad he eventually did, but I'm aware that would have been a completely unreasonable request on my part at the time.

This brings Julia to the closing arguments of her case: the tattoo.

The most crucial piece of information to her is the date that he got the tattoo. The fact that he did this the day after I left him in Philadelphia is a pretty big deal. If anything, it helps him in my eyes. It may seem juvenile or even stupid to some, but to brand your own flesh willingly and permanently, so close to your heart…well, to me, it's downright romantic and that's not lost on me either.

So, as I've explained to Julia on almost a daily basis for the last couple of weeks, the jury is still out on Tyler. I know it's not fair to leave him hanging so I need to make a decision sooner than later. The problem with making a choice is that I could have my heart broken either way. I love him so much that it's what keeps me from wanting to decide. I'm so afraid that he'll hurt me again that it's got me in this state of limbo where I know my heart is safe and under constant guard.

Tired and hopefully done with today's latest pity party, I push my seat back and grab my purse, already running a bit behind for an appointment I have with a local artist at his studio. I'm thankful to be kept occupied by work but not nearly as much as I'd like to be. As the saying goes, an idle mind is the devil's playground, or in my case, Tyler's playground.

When I walk back into the gallery at just past four o'clock, Sarah, our receptionist, is staring back at me with a huge smile on her face. Her bouncy, usual self is extra bouncy when I approach her while putting my sunglasses on top of my head.

"Oh my God! Oh my God! Guess what?" She's so excited that she's practically falling out of her seat.

I smile back at her, not having any clue what could be the cause of so much exuberance. "I have no idea, what?"

She shuffles some things on her desk and picks up a message pad, quickly tearing off the top page, and handing it to me. I grab it and look over her handwriting on the tiny scrap of paper, not understanding the big deal right away until I read it again.

My eyes still on the message, I ask her, "When did he call?"

"About an hour ago."

I look up at her and mirror her huge smile and say thank you then head back to my office, closing the door for privacy. Sitting at my desk, I breathe in and out a few times to calm myself down, long enough to pick up the phone and return the call.

A woman answers on the second ring and her greeting makes my smile even wider.

"Good afternoon, may I speak to Dennis Forrester, please?"

She puts me on hold for a few seconds until a man's voice comes on the line. "This is Dennis Forrester. How may I help you?"

"Mr. Forrester, this is Sabrina Chandler, returning your call."

"Thank you for calling me back so quickly Ms. Chandler," he says warmly.

"It's not every day that the head curator of the Philadelphia Museum of Art calls you personally, so I assumed it must be important."

He laughs, putting me more at ease. "I suppose you're right."

"What exactly can I do for you, Mr. Forrester?" I ask, my curiosity more than piqued.

"Actually, I'm hoping *you* can do something for me. I was wondering if you'd be interested in interviewing for a position here at our lovely museum."

I look around my office for any signs of a hidden camera so I can ask it if I'm being punked when he says my name again to get my attention.

"I'm so sorry, Mr. Forrester, you just caught me by surprise." Digging down to find my most professional voice under the circumstances, I say, "May I ask what position?"

"Assistant to the head curator."

Holy shit. Before my brain can catch up to my mouth, I answer.

"Yes, of course I'd be interested in interviewing for the job. Thank you so much."

"Great. Just looking over your résumé, and I must say, I'm very impressed."

Wait a second, how did he get my résumé? Hell, I haven't even seen or updated it in years. While he's looking over his schedule for the next few days for a good time for a phone interview, steam is already coming out of my ears.

"Is that good for you, Ms. Chandler?"

"I'm so sorry, can you say that again?" I recover quickly.

"How about tomorrow, Wednesday, at three o'clock. Does that work for you?"

I don't even look at my calendar, I say yes because as pissed as I am right now, I'm not a complete moron.

"Sounds great. I'm looking forward to it, Mr. Forrester."

We end the call with the usual pleasantries and when I hang up the phone, I immediately pick it back up to make another one to the one person who I know must be behind this.

"Hey, girlie, what's up?"

Gripping the phone so tightly that it might shatter in my hand, I speak through my gritted teeth. "Julia, did you send my résumé to someone at the Philadelphia Museum of Art?"

"Um, why?"

"They just called me to schedule a phone interview for Wednesday, that's why. The best part about it is that he mentioned my résumé was impressive. Which I thought was funny because I haven't updated it since before I started working here."

"Huh, interesting."

"That's it. That's all you're going to say about it? Are you serious?"

She's quiet, too quiet, which translates into being caught red-handed.

"Please say something, Julia."

"Congratulations?"

"I'm so mad at you right now, I can't see straight. So, before I hang up on you I'm warning you that I'm hanging up on you, OK?"

She knows better than to say anything else other than a sorry sounding, "OK," before I slam the phone down.

I love her to death, but she's nuts! Does she really think that this is going to solve all my problems? And I'm crazy for sitting here even contemplating it. Could I truly be qualified enough to warrant a phone interview for my dream job without any help from her? Maybe I'm the one who's nuts. This gets me to thinking that I must get my hands on a copy of that résumé she sent out. Who the hell knows what she put on that thing!

I angrily snatch up my purse and leave work on a mission to see this résumé for myself... and kill Julia.

CHAPTER TWENTY-EIGHT

I've paced from the kitchen to the living room so many times in the last half-hour that I've burned off over a thousand calories while waiting for Julia to get home. Fuming doesn't come close to covering it. How dare she pull a stunt like this? For her to go behind my back and try to force me to make a decision in favor of Tyler by dangling a huge carrot in my face is so unfair. Best friend, sister, and partner in crime—no more. This crosses the line a tad more than I'm comfortable with and goes beyond her usual level of meddling.

Come to think of it, her meddling is what got me into this mess to begin with. If it wasn't for Julia's little pep talk almost four months ago, I wouldn't be here plotting her demise. As soon as I got that stupid invitation I should have torn it into a million pieces and then burned it until it was nothing but a small pile of ashes. But no, what did I do instead? I let her little Tony Robbins act get to me. I was convinced after her speech that it was my destiny to go see Tyler again and confront Lisa and Chris. Like I was supposed to go and kill two birds with one stone. What a joke! Now, the only killing will be of Julia as soon as she walks through that door.

The sound of her keys jangling stops my pacing. She opens the door slowly, only popping her head in first to check to see if the coast is clear. When she sees me standing with my hands in balled up fists at my sides, her head disappears like she's going to turn around and leave. As if!

I'm so mad that my voice goes eerily soft when I speak. "Get in here. Now."

Julia comes in and goes to sit on the couch after leaving her purse and laptop bag in the foyer. I come from around the back of it to stand facing her, trying my best not to jump over the coffee table and strangle her to death.

"Sabrina—"

I put my hand up, stopping her.

"I...I don't even know where to begin. I'm so mad that I just want to choke the living shit out of you right now. Can't you understand that this is *my* life you're playing with? This isn't some TV show, Julia. This is real life!"

I run my hands through my hair, and I start to pace again in the small space between the coffee table and the television.

"Let me explain—"

"Uh-uh, you don't get a chance to explain right now. I mean, seriously, what did you think I would say when I found out? Did you think I would pack up my shit tomorrow, start my new job, and go live happily ever after with Tyler? Because if that's what you were thinking, I hate to disappoint you, but it's not going to happen!"

"Why not?" she asks defiantly.

I laugh, because surely she can't be serious. "Are you kidding me right now? Do I really need to spell it out for you?"

She nods her head yes.

"Fine. First off, I'm not qualified for this job. The only reason I'm being considered is because you called in a favor.

I don't want to get my dream job by someone pulling strings for me. I want to earn it, fair and square. Not to mention this job is in another goddamn state! It's not like I can just take it and start in two weeks. I would have to move my entire life and start all over again from scratch."

"You're from Pennsylvania," she deadpans.

I raise my eyebrow to warn her to keep her mouth shut before she gets herself into any more trouble with me.

"Second, this whole crusade you've got going on for Tyler and me has got to stop! I've told you over and over again that I can't just switch off how I feel. As my best friend," I pause to turn and look at her for emphasis, "*you* should respect that and leave it alone already."

We both stay quiet until she leans forward, putting her elbows on her knees and clasping her hands together.

"Can I talk now?" she asks.

"Knock your socks off, but it won't make one difference."

"Ever since we met in college, Sabrina, you've been in hiding because of what those assholes did to you. I've sat here and watched you beat yourself up for years... right here, on this very couch. So, the moment I saw that light switch on in your eyes when you came back from seeing Tyler, I was beyond happy for you."

I go to sit on the edge of the couch since my legs start to feel wobbly.

"If you think for one second that I'm going to let you give up on that after everything you've been through, you're sadly mistaken. Because *that's* what best friends do. They look out for each other."

Tears start to well in my eyes when she turns in her seat to face me and takes my hands in hers.

"Sabrina, you've been waiting for a job like this for as long as I've known you. This is an opportunity of a lifetime. With all due respect, you would be an idiot for saying no," she says with a crooked smile. "Who cares if Alex sent in the résumé I gave him for you? It got your foot in the door."

I tear my hands away from hers while I wipe my eyes angrily and stand up from the couch. "What did you just say?"

Julia looks confused and asks, "Which part?"

"The part about Alex sending in the résumé. I thought you did all of that."

She curses under her breath and drops her head in her hands. She brushes back her bangs when she says, "I thought you knew it was him."

"No, I had no idea he was involved! What the fuck is going on around here? How did Alex get mixed up into this mess? "

She puts her hands up. "Sabrina, calm down."

Calm down? Is she really telling me to calm down? Not only did she doctor my résumé, which I still haven't seen, but now she's got my boss involved in her plans and schemes.

"Julia, start talking or, I swear on everything that is holy, I will kill you!"

She exhales and stands, coming toward me with her hands still up as if she was approaching a skittish animal.

"It's not as sneaky as it sounds. He came to my office last week for a meeting, and you came up in the conversation. I didn't tell him anything other than I was trying to get one of you to move your asses and get back together already."

"How does that turn into...this?" I say motioning with my hands into the open air all around me.

"Kind of as an afterthought he mentioned that he knew, or someone in his family knew, I can't remember which one, the head curator at the Philadelphia Museum of Art. So...."

"So what?" I say trying to get her to finish.

"So," she says, "I told him as a joke that if he could get your résumé to the right person that my company would work any event of his choosing for free."

I don't even know what to say to her. I open my mouth to say something but nothing comes out. I'm speechless or shell-shocked, take your pick. I cannot believe she did all of this and dragged Alex into it for good measure. It's official, my quiet, uneventful life has gone down the rabbit hole never to be heard from again.

"Yeah," Julia says sheepishly, "I kind of owe him now. Big time."

A nervous laugh escapes me, and I think it's because I've lost my mind. Turning on my heel, I make a beeline to my room with Julia right behind me.

"Sabrina, you're going to do that interview," she says when I reach my door.

"No, I'm not." I slam the door on her face, putting an end to the conversation.

I fall onto my bed and stare at the ceiling. This poor ceiling has gotten an eyeful in the last few months. I'm sure it's sick of me looking up at it either crying or silently willing it to answer me. Tonight is no different, with all its slight imperfections that I've committed to memory; it just looks blankly back at me, forcing me to make a decision all on my own.

The next morning I do my best to ignore all of Julia's attempts to get me to talk; I'm still upset and I can hold a grudge for a pretty long time. I make it through our usual morning mug of coffee without even a peep to her and leave for work on a mission to talk to Alex. If anything, this was one of the best things that Julia could have done for Tyler's cause, because now she and Alex sit atop his ranking on the good ol' shit list.

I get to the gallery relatively early and dump my purse and keys on my desk before heading down the hallway to Alex's office. The door is closed so I tap lightly and open it, not waiting on his answer of whether or not I can come in.

As soon as I see him sitting at his desk, he stops moving the mouse with his hand and grins when I close the door behind me.

"Good morning, Sabrina. I would ask you to come in, but you already did that."

I grin, equally smug right back at him and say, "I'm sure you know why I'm here anyway, so excuse me for not being in the best of moods this morning, Alex."

He leans back casually in his chair and adjusts his tie, watching me while I put my hand on my hip, the universal sign for "I'm pissed off."

"Aren't you going to say anything?" I ask.

"What do you want to hear? The part where I tell you that I was the one that called Dennis and asked him to look at your résumé? Or, the part where I tell you that you should do the interview."

"So, you admit it?"

He chuckles. "Of course, I admit it and I'd do it again."

"I'm so glad that you find humor in this, because I'm not finding any of this remotely funny."

Alex goes to stand but I'm already walking to the door to leave. "Don't bother getting up, I'm going."

"Sabrina, wait."

I don't turn around when I hear him come up behind me at first. Between him and Julia, I'm so close to murdering someone that my fingers are twitching. What I want is to get out of here and back to my office so I can punch something to take the edge off. I swing back around to see Alex, his dimpled smile on full display, clearly enjoying himself and making me see red.

"What you don't know is that I didn't ask him to give you an interview for the job. He only agreed to look over the résumé and if it was up to par, he'd think about it. It was you, Sabrina, and no one else who got that interview."

That does change things, but only by the smallest of margins. It doesn't take away from the real reason that Julia used to get this ball rolling. That just makes me wonder why Alex would want to help her with her crazy hairbrained scheme in the first place. Granted, we agreed to just be friends, but we do kind of have a past together, albeit a minor one. Maybe not as sordid as how that just sounded in my head, but a past is a past, right?

"Why would you agree to do this, Alex?" I ask him out of curiosity.

His expression is amused as he tilts his head. "You mean besides getting to use Julia for free whenever I choose?"

Nodding yes with a half-smile, because the thought of Julia being at Alex's beck and call is pretty funny, and I secretly hope he puts her through the ringer for all of this.

He puts his hands in his pockets and says, "Maybe I'm just a sucker for a happy ending."

Alex reaches out to open the door for me while I stand there somewhat slack-jawed by his answer. My feet finally start to move, and I take a few steps out of his office when he calls my name again.

"Good luck on the interview later today," he announces, looking pleased with himself, and closes the door again.

Walking back to my office in a bit of a daze, I drop into my seat and wonder what in God's name just happened back there. My head is throbbing, and I rub my temples in an attempt to ward off the impending headache that has been brewing since yesterday. I can't fall back on the good advice of Scarlett because tomorrow isn't another day anymore. Today is *the* day to decide my own fate. I can't pussyfoot anymore or make another ridiculous excuse. Without a moment's hesitation, I pick up the phone and make the call that I've been putting off for the last couple of weeks.

Tyler picks up on the fourth ring, sounding groggy. I look at the clock to realize that it's only just after nine in the morning and I've probably woken him up.

"Did I wake you?" I ask apprehensively.

"If it's your voice that's waking me up this early, I don't mind in the slightest."

My stomach does a little flip flop and a smile creeps across my lips at the sound of his voice. Closing my eyes, I envision myself in his bed, wrapped safely in his strong arms. The thought is so real that I can briefly imagine his scent flooding my senses.

"Sabrina?"

"Yeah," coming out of my fantasy, "I'm still here."

I can tell he's smiling when he says, "Good, I thought I lost you for a second there."

"No, you didn't lose me."

"Are you sure about that?" he asks quickly.

Not positive if his question is supposed to have a double meaning, I answer just as vaguely. "Yes, I'm sure."

Before this conversation goes somewhere I never intended it to go, I blurt out, "I'm sorry, I shouldn't have called so early. I'll let you go."

"Wait. Can I call you sometime?"

"I don't know."

My heart aches when he says after a short pause, "I miss you, Sabrina."

"I miss you too," I admit in a quiet voice before I say bye.

I hear his goodbye while my hand goes to put the phone back on its cradle. Dropping back limply into my chair, I stare at the phone like it's going to jump off the desk on its own. Not sure if hearing his voice has helped me make any kind of decision in regards to the interview, I check the time again and count how much time I have left to decide what my next move will be.

Approximately five hours and forty-three minutes.

That's how much time I have to decide what mine and Tyler's future will hold. In the grand scheme of things, it's not a lot. In the same amount of time I could be doing something fun, like driving to Disney World or catching the next flight out to Vegas, I have to figure out if I love him enough to look past everything and if whatever this is between us could ever work after what he did. I, Sabrina Chandler, the same girl who gave her heart away ten years ago to a dream, has to decide whether the reality is worth the heartache and forgive him.

Damn. I wish I had more time.

CHAPTER TWENTY-NINE

Seems for every box I've unpacked in the last week, I've taken a two-hour break. At this rate, I'll be completely unpacked and settled in by Halloween. I absolutely adore my new one-bedroom apartment in the Old City neighborhood of Philadelphia. Filled with historic landmarks, art galleries, boutiques, fine restaurants, Old City has just the right amount of eclecticism for my tastes. To give credit where credit is due, had it not been for my mom's stealth apartment-hunting skills with the few requirements I gave her, I would probably be living with them temporarily and not in this awesome apartment. I love them with all my heart, but I think I'd much rather stick needles in my eyes than live with them again for any extended period of time.

The top requirement for my mom in the short amount of time I gave her to look for an apartment was the most crucial to me: proximity to my new job. I still can't believe I work at the Philadelphia Museum of Art. On my first day, I had to actually stop and pinch myself because I thought I was in a dream. Now, here I am on Friday night, a full week under my belt, and I still can't quite wrap my head around it all.

The last month has been nothing short of a whirlwind. After I called Mr. Forrester that day in my office for the

interview, which took almost an hour, he called me back the
very next day and asked if I'd fly up for a face-to-face interview. At first, it sounded too good to be true. Even though
I was still ticked off at Julia for all her interfering, I'm not
that dense. I thought about it for all of ten seconds then
said yes. My flight to Philadelphia was booked within the
hour for that very weekend. To say it was a whirlwind would
have been an understatement. I literally flew in, took a cab
straight to the museum, met with Mr. Forrester for a couple
of hours, was formally offered the job, accepted it, then took
a cab right back to the airport where my flight was scheduled to depart later that evening.

As much as it pains me to say it, Julia was right; it is the
opportunity of a lifetime. I couldn't very well let her stay in
the doghouse too long after that. Especially after she found
out and started to cry and tell me how much she was going
to miss me. I kind of had no choice but to stop being mad
at her at that point. Then she went right into party planning
mode, promising that she was going to throw me the biggest
going-away party ever. I made her swear up and down that if
she did that, that she'd be right back in the doghouse again.
Much to her dismay, she agreed, but only if she could help
me with the actual move.

When my parents found out, well, I think the hearing
in my left ear is still experiencing some light ringing noises
from all the screaming my mom did on the phone that
day. My dad, as even-keel as ever, got to say a quick, "I'm
so proud of you, baby girl," until my mom tore the phone
away from him again so she could scream some more in my
ear. Mom began apartment hunting immediately and luckily stumbled upon this gem on about her third try a few days

later. She had all the papers drawn up for me, and all I had to do was receive a fax and sign on the dotted line.

That gave Julia and I just shy of three weeks to get all my stuff packed up and shipped out, including the furniture. Thankfully, the apartment was already empty and the landlord was accommodating enough to let the furniture and boxes be unloaded before I arrived. All under the very watchful supervision of my mom, of course. That only left Julia and me to drive my car from Miami to Philadelphia. We left a sweltering, hot-as-hell Miami a week ago, late Thursday night, and between taking restroom and sleeping breaks every few hours, made it in early Saturday morning. She left the next day, and it was quite a scene at the airport between us. You would have thought we were Siamese twins being wrenched apart the way we were both carrying on like bumbling idiots. Needless to say, we've been texting and calling each other all week, and since she left, she's been constantly hounding me to get my computer hooked up so we can Skype. But at the rate I've been unpacking, that probably won't happen anytime soon.

One of the first things Julia wanted to do when we got here was do a drive-by of Tyler's apartment and restaurant. I can't believe I actually entertained for a millisecond the idea of us doing that, like we were gonna case the joint, but sanity prevailed and we stayed away. That didn't stop her from continually bringing him up before she hopped on her flight. And, persistent as only Julia can be, she's been texting me once a day since she left to ask if today will be the day I go and see him.

Honestly, I don't even know what's taking me so long. I want to see Tyler more than anything, but something always stops me. Like an invisible force field comes out of nowhere and knocks me on my ass when I've thought about seriously going to see him after work a few times. We have spoken twice since that day of the interview, but I never told him that I was moving, and we didn't touch on anything about us either. I was very careful to make sure the conversation didn't veer into that direction this time. With the stress of moving and the new job, I couldn't bear the thought of one more thing added onto my already full plate. I know that sounds selfish, but it's the truth. As a result, a part of me is afraid that so much time has gone by, that maybe he's already moving on. The fact that he doesn't even know I'm here, just a few miles away from where he probably is right this very second, is killing me inside with guilt.

Guilt is a fickle bitch, too. I feel guilty for making him wait when he's the one that broke my heart. Then as that goes through my mind, I don't feel guilty at all. I feel like he *should* be waiting for however long it takes me to decide I'm ready to take a chance again. Then I feel even guiltier for thinking he's waiting. See what I mean? The guilt alone is going to kill me. I rack my brain over and over again, driving myself into a panic until the dust settles, long enough only for it to start up from the beginning.

What I wouldn't give to just wake up tomorrow and realize that this is the day. Instead, here I sit, alone in my apartment on a Friday night a few miles away from Tyler, surrounded by boxes and not having the faintest idea of when or if I'll make the first move.

This vicious-circle shit is getting really old, even by my standards.

Angry at myself, I shove the box I was making very little progress with away from me and watch it as it slides across the hardwood floor. It comes to a stop in front of another set of boxes marked "living room" that I haven't touched yet either; I decide to call it a night, hoping that when I open my eyes in the morning, I'll be able to overcome whatever it is that's keeping me away from him.

When I wake up the next day, I decide to take a walk around my new neighborhood, wanting to partake in the early fall-like weather that I've been missing out on for the last ten years while living in Miami. I stroll for about an hour, trying to clear my head with no specific destination in mind until I realize that I should probably get back to unpacking. I decide to stop at a local flower shop for a fresh bouquet of gorgeous sunflowers that would look lovely in my new dining room and then pop over to the coffee shop next door before heading home. With my flowers bundled in one hand, I reach for the door to the coffee shop just as it's being opened. I don't look up when I say thank you to the person holding it open for me.

"Sabrina, is that you?" Shit, I've been made.

I look up to find myself face to face with Jimmy, Tyler's partner at the restaurant. Momentarily flustered, he smiles kindly at me, making me just a tiny bit more comfortable at the situation.

"Hi, Jimmy."

"What are doing here? I thought you lived in Miami."

Another customer is trying to enter the coffee shop so we both step aside to give them room. Then, and I have no idea why, but I suddenly let the cat out of the bag. "I just recently moved here."

He looks surprised before he asks, "Tyler doesn't know, does he?"

I shake my head and answer him at the same time. "I would appreciate it if you didn't tell him."

"Of course, if that's what you want."

What do I want? Oh God, I'm going to lose it right here on the street if my mind starts to go down this path again this early in the morning. So, instead I mumble a quick thank you.

"It was really nice to see you again," I say, and I'm already turning toward the door of the coffee shop. The door knob feels cold against my now sweaty palm when Jimmy speaks up again.

"Sabrina," he says, "may I let you in on something?"

I'm still gripping onto the door knob for dear life when I turn my head and shrug my shoulders.

"I've known him for a very long time. And in all that time, I've never seen him head over heels for anyone like he is for you." He smiles faintly before he adds, "I mean, the boy is a goner."

My defensive side perks up, and I let go of the door knob to face him.

Jimmy puts his hands up and says, "I can tell that I've upset you, and that wasn't my intention at all."

"He made a choice, and it wasn't me. Is that all you wanted to tell me, Jimmy, because I can't handle this right now?" I strangle out and instantly feel terrible.

"Look, I know what happened," he sighs and I almost burst into tears. "When he told me, I almost killed him. I warned him from the start that Ava was bad news." Pausing to take a breath, he nervously goes on to add, "But, I also

300

told him that he shouldn't quit. That if he loved you as much as he says he does, he should fight for you."

Now I'm officially crying. Tears are streaming down my face, and I can only imagine what anyone walking by is thinking, seeing this scene play out.

"I'm sorry," he says, "I shouldn't have said anything."

He reaches into his pocket to pull out a tissue and hands it to me. His eyes search my face with concern before he turns on his heel to head down the sidewalk. I let him get a couple of steps away from me before I call out to him.

"Yeah," he answers, turning back around to face me.

I close the distance between us while I'm using the tissue to wipe my eyes. When I reach him, I can see that he really does care for Tyler and only meant well.

"Thank you, Jimmy."

I mean it, too. Even if things don't work out between Tyler and me, at least I know that he has someone who's looking out for him.

"You're welcome, Sabrina."

Jimmy's barely-there smile is the last thing I see before I quickly turn around to head back toward my apartment. If I had stayed a second longer, I would have asked him to take me right to him, and I can't do that yet.

When I reach the safe confines of my box-filled apartment, I don't even put the flowers in a vase. I'm still in a daze from my brief conversation with Jimmy. I sink to the exact same spot on the floor that I was sitting in last night, just staring at nothing and feeling more defeated than ever.

It all feels empty.

The rooms, my life, my heart—all of it, empty.

CHAPTER THIRTY

The following Monday at work is fantastic and worth all the misery I've been heaping onto myself at night when I'm alone. I'm working closely with Dennis—I'm still not comfortable calling him that, even though he insists I do—on a new exhibit of Van Gogh's latter years that will begin its run in February. Everything is falling into place, or at least the career portion of my life is. If only the rest of it would follow suit as easily.

Just like my apartment, my new office still has a couple of boxes left to unpack. The space itself is about the same size as my office at the gallery in Miami, so I really have no excuse other than I've just hit the ground running with my new job and been too busy to devote any time to it. Since my first day, I've spent most of my lunch hour roaming the museum. I've been here as a visitor so many times in the past, but somehow it's different now that I work here. It's like I'm seeing everything with a new set of eyes. But today, I've promised myself that I will not randomly wander the building, but will dedicate the time to get at least this done.

With a few minutes to spare in my lunch hour, I take a step back and admire my handiwork. A bookcase that came with the office now has all my little knick knacks and framed photos of my parents, Julia and I, and a few from when I lived in Italy after college. I've interspersed the photos with other little personal items that I've collected over the years. My favorite one is an official NHL hockey puck from the first Flyers game my Dad ever took me to. I've never been a huge sports fan, but the memory of my Dad taking me at eight years old to see a live game was one of the best days of my life and always brings a smile to my face.

"All settled, I see," my boss, Mr. Forrester, says from behind me as I place the hockey puck in its rightful place on the bookcase. *Dennis, Dennis, Dennis...* I repeat instantly in my head to correct myself.

"Yes, finally," I say relieved that I'm done.

He cheerfully takes a couple of strides in my office and comes to stop at the one item I haven't touched yet. Still wrapped in brown parcel paper and twine is the framed print of *Blue Nude* by Picasso, which I was planning on tucking away into a corner somewhere.

He pulls it off the wall it's leaning against and picks it up. "Looks like you forgot something."

Quickly wanting to get it out of his grip, I reach out with my hands and say, "Maybe when I have more time I'll hang it up."

He puts it back down before I can grab it and says he'll be right back.

Shit.

Dennis comes back a minute later with a small hammer and a wall hook, looking as determined as ever to get the damn thing hung on the wall.

"You don't have to do that, Dennis," I say as my voice wavers on me. "I'll get to it eventually."

"Don't be silly. We'll do this right now so you can be completely settled into your new office."

I can't very well say no, can I? I'm stuck and can't talk my way out of it now. The picture is going up whether I like it or not.

"Here, hold this," he says handing me the hammer.

He backs up a few steps to look at the blank wall, picks a spot, and then gets to work. In a matter of minutes, the hook is in place. Dennis asks me to tear off the paper that is carefully guarding my memories that are now associated with this painting. Ever so slowly, I make a small tear in the corner and, like Charlie getting that first glimpse of the Golden Ticket, I smile faintly at the blue strokes of color.

"One of my favorites," Dennis says while I remove the rest of the wrapping. "May I?"

He gingerly takes it from my hands before I can answer and lifts it up to hang on the wall. Stepping back a couple of times to ensure that it's centered until being completely satisfied with his job, Dennis now stands beside me studying it carefully.

"Such an exquisite piece," he says. "Picasso really had an ability to express his complex emotions with one simple shade of blue, don't you think?"

I say yes, but my mind is not thinking at all about the complexity of Picasso's emotions. My head and heart are vaulted back to Tyler's apartment where it hangs above his bed, simply because it reminded him of me.

"A shame that the original belongs to a private collector in Paris. What I wouldn't give to have it here for the world to see and admire," Dennis says regretfully.

I'm still holding the brown paper it was wrapped in; he takes it out of my hands and tosses it in the garbage for me.

"Oh well, enough daydreaming," he laughs. "Now, you're completely moved in."

I emit a small hooray and try to divert my eyes from the picture while he tells me that we will be cataloging some of the older paintings in one of the museum's archive rooms for the rest of the afternoon. Relieved that I won't be stuck in my office to torture myself, I reach over to my desk and grab my supplies before following him down the hall.

The rest of the afternoon goes by rather quickly, but there is no question that I feel distracted. My thoughts are elsewhere, and I can't blame it all on the painting either. Sure, it brought it back to the surface a little while ago, but who am I kidding? They've been there ever since I last saw him. I'm right back at the proverbial crossroads where I can never seem to decide which direction to take. Tired of feeling so lost, I rub my eyes with the heels of my hands hoping that it will help me see more clearly. Opening them up again, all seems exactly the same, so I pack it in for the day shortly after six o'clock.

I nervously grip the steering wheel while I weave in and out of rush hour traffic as if my car had a mind of its own. It drives through some of the smaller, cobblestone streets of Philadelphia until I reach a familiar area. Looking for a parking spot relatively close, I finally find one about a half a block up and across the street. I kill the engine and stay in my car for a minute or two, silently willing myself to get out. When my body doesn't respond, I think that I've made a mistake and go to start my car again. I freeze though when I happen to look up and catch a glimpse of the lit sign of Tyler's restaurant up the block.

I reach from my purse, fish out my cell phone, and call the one person who won't think I'm crazy.

Julia answers on the second ring. "Hey, sweetie," she says cheerfully. "And just so you know, this doesn't get you out of our Skype session later."

I ignore her comment and just cut to the chase.

"Julia, do you believe in signs?"

"What do you mean signs? Like actual signs on a street or big-picture, life-altering signs?"

"I mean big-picture, life-altering signs."

"Hmmm," she counters, "will my answer directly affect whatever the hell it is you are or are not about to do?"

"Well, since I'm sitting in my car staring at Tyler's restaurant, then yes, it very well could."

She squeals in my ear so loudly that I pull the phone away.

"OK, OK, I've got it out of my system," she says excitedly. "Go ahead and tell me about these signs."

"I ran into Jimmy, Tyler's partner over the weekend—"

"You didn't tell me that," she interjects.

"I know I didn't; just let me finish please," I plead.

"Sorry, go ahead."

"OK," I say getting more anxious by the second. "So, I ran into him, and he told me how Tyler's head-over-heels in love with me."

"Well, I could have told you that, Sabrina."

Sighing into the phone, she shuts up quickly and lets me continue. "Then today I was unpacking my office and had no intention of hanging up that print that I told you about."

"The Picasso?"

"Yes," I confirm, "that's the one. Anyway, I wasn't going to hang it up and then my boss zooms in and makes me open it and proceeds to hang it up on my wall for me."

She's quiet for a second or two before I cut in again.

"So, what do you think?"

"What do I think about what?" she asks.

"About all these signs? I mean, Philadelphia is a big city, what are the odds that I would run into Jimmy in such a big city?"

She laughs lightly before she answers me. "That is true."

"And the painting," I explain further, "I really was planning on keeping it sealed and putting it away instead of hanging it up."

Julia laughs again, but this time more heartily, and it kind of bugs me.

"What's so funny?"

"Sweetie, you said you're parked outside his restaurant, right?"

"Yeah, and?"

Sounding slightly amused at how I haven't connected the dots on my own, she says, "Sabrina, the heart wants what the heart wants. Fuck the signs."

And just like that, I know I'm right where I belong. I manage a quick goodbye to Julia, who is still squealing when I tell her I have to hang up. My stomach drops, and my pulse begins to race when I get out of the car with a renewed sense of purpose.

The sidewalk is somewhat crowded as I make my way to stand right across the street of his restaurant, unsure of what to do next. I've made it this far, amazingly enough, but I don't think busting in there out of the blue is going to work.

Why didn't I think this whole thing out more clearly? In the movies they make this crap seem so much easier than it actually is. Stupid romance movies. I swear, I'm never going to watch one of those again.

Frustrated and irritated, an idea forms in my head. I hastily reach into my purse and take out my cell phone. Before I can chicken out, I scroll through my contacts list to find Tyler's name and call him. My heart is in my throat, and I'm pretty sure I'm going to throw up while I wait for him to answer.

"Sabrina."

The sound of my name rolling off his tongue so easily makes me smile like an idiot, and that's how I know I've made the right decision. Just that one word, my name and the way he says it, confirms what my heart is feeling. I love him. Like a blindfold being ripped from my eyes, I see that I have already forgiven him, and now I'm ready to take another chance with him. It's like he said, every part of him has always belonged to me, and it was just a matter of time before I came here.

"Sabrina, are you there?" he asks.

"I'm here," hoping he can see through my answer.

Tyler lets out a small chuckle, then asks, "Are you sure this time?"

"Absolutely positive." I start to pace a bit on the sidewalk as he absorbs my answer.

"So," I say trying to contain my happiness, "I thought you'd like to know I got a new job."

I can hear the commotion in the background when he says, "Congratulations."

"Thanks."

"I thought you loved your job, though."

"I did," I say quickly, "but I couldn't turn this one down."

"Why's that?"

Here it is, the moment of truth. "Well, I couldn't very well say no to the Philadelphia Museum of Art."

Tyler stays silent for a beat. I can tell he's smiling when he says, "No, I guess you couldn't."

"Yeah, it's been pretty amazing so far."

As soon as the word "far" leaves my lips, Tyler speaks up as if he just connected the dots. "What do you mean, 'so far'? Where are you right now?"

"Here."

"Where, here? In Philadelphia?"

"Yes. I've been here for a week."

The commotion that I heard in the background a second ago is gone. I imagine that he must have ducked into his office or to a quiet corner so he can have some privacy, because I can only hear his confused voice over the line and nothing else.

"Let me get this straight. You got a new job, here, in Philadelphia, *and* you've been living here for the past week?"

"Yes."

He takes a breath then exhales before he asks, "Why didn't you tell me sooner?"

Because I'm an idiot, stupidly blind, incredibly stubborn, and stuck on a past that I needed to let go of. I can't tell him all that, so I give him the abbreviated version.

"I don't know, Tyler. I *can* tell you that I wish that I would have come sooner."

"I wish you would have too, Sabrina," he says solemnly.

My heart drops so far that it's dragging behind me on the sidewalk while I pace, thinking my worst fear of him having moved on already is starting to come true. Looking upon the front door of the restaurant, I missed my chance and screwed up by putting him off for too long.

"O-okay," I shakily say, "I'm sorry. I should leave."

"Stop, Sabrina. Do. Not. Hang. Up."

"No, really, Tyler... I get it... I—"

"No, you don't get it, *at all.* I wish you would have told me sooner because I miss you like crazy, and I'm dying to see your beautiful face again. Don't get any crazy ideas in that pretty little head of yours. I told you I'd wait, and I've been doing nothing but waiting. And I'll wait even longer if you need me to."

His calm, deep voice reverberates through every fiber of my being, and now it's just a question of how much longer I can continue this conversation on the phone versus seeing him in person.

"I don't want you to wait anymore, Tyler," I say speaking softly, "I've always been here; it's just taken me a long time to find out where here is."

"Define here," he says in a playful tone.

"Here... as in outside."

"You're outside my restaurant?" he asks in disbelief.

"Well," I continue, trying to contain a laugh, "to be specific, I'm across the street from the restaurant."

Turning my body so I'm facing the restaurant, I impatiently wait for the door to swing open and see him. It might as well have been an hour, because the few seconds I wait feel excruciatingly long. The door finally opens and there he is, as gorgeous as ever, with a ridiculously sexy grin and still cradling the phone to his ear.

Tyler goes to step off the curb when I yell into the phone and at him, since he's kind of right there in front of me now. "Wait!"

He stops in mid-step.

"I want to tell you something first," I say.

Switching the phone to the other ear, he runs his free hand through his thick, already tousled brown hair and sighs. From where I'm standing, I can see he's still grinning when he says, "Make it quick because you're killing me right now."

"I need to tell you that I'm sorry for making you wait and for being a complete idiot after it was more than obvious how you felt about me. That I'm sorry I kept this—the new job, the move, all of it—away from you for so long. More than anything, I'm sorry that it took me all this time to get back here to you."

Tyler's face changes, and he appears to be upset by what I'm saying.

"Is that it?" he asks.

"No," I say forcefully. "I also want to say that I'm really not that sorry for making you wait because you were the one that hurt me. And just so you know, if you ever do that again I'm never coming back for you."

He looks even more upset before he asks, "Is that all of it?"

"Um, I think so, yeah."

"Good. I'm hanging up now."

He steps off the curb as I hit the end button on my phone. Not tearing his eyes away from me, he strides briskly across the empty street. Tyler hesitates for a second, as if he's not completely sure whether I'll walk away, so I take a step closer, followed by him taking another one closer, until the space between us closes.

Cupping my face with both his hands, a smile begins to curl up on the corners of his mouth and he tilts my face up. I stare into those beautiful chocolate eyes that I lost myself in so many years ago and smile back as I bring my hands to rest on his hips.

"Promise me something," he says in a low voice.

My gaze drops to his mouth, and I lick my lips in anticipation of feeling them against mine when I nod. "Anything."

Tyler drops his lips so close to my cheek that his warm breath tickles me and a shiver runs up and down my spine. He kisses me there then drags his lips to my ear when I close my eyes and I let his words wash over me.

"Promise me that you'll never make me wait that long to kiss you again."

Tyler brings his lips back to brush against mine and I smile at him. Keeping my eyes closed, his mouth begins to move slowly over mine, coaxing my lips open to him and making me feel like everything around us disappears. It's not until we garner whistles and cat calls from strangers walking by that we break the kiss reluctantly.

"Can I ask you a question?" he asks in a quiet voice, rubbing his thumbs across my cheeks.

God, I *love* it when he does that.

"Yes," my voice equally quiet.

His mouth curves up into a dazzling smile when he asks, "Do you have any idea how much I love you, Sabrina?"

I run through a few of the catalogued memories in my mind that we've created together, starting as far back as that night when he stole my heart with his few words and comforting embrace. My mind then fast-forwards to the gazebo at the reunion where he made my pulse race and admitted that he was hoping I'd be there. Then to the first time we made love. Still racing, it settles on the memory of the tattoo on his chest that he got just for me. Every memory serving as more proof than the last that his love for me is as strong as mine is for him.

Smiling, I grip onto his wrists and answer him. "I think I have a very good idea."

"Is that so?" he asks in a lighthearted tone, still stroking my cheeks. "How do you know?"

"I know because it's exactly how much I love you."

Tyler dips his head so that his lips are hovering over mine, still smiling but his voice drops to a heart-stopping raspy tone when he asks me one more question.

"And how much is that, baby?"

My head feels like it's spinning, my stomach flip-flopping, my heart soaring...all happening at the same time, reacting to him on every single level that is possible. I don't dare waste another minute of precious time to say what my heart has been wanting. The answer is so simple. It has been right in front of me all along and it feels so good to tell him.

"Tyler James," I watch his eyes light up before saying what has been in my heart for so long. "I love you with all that I am."

EPILOGUE

Tyler James, I love you with all that I am...
 Those words turn over in my head when I look down at Sabrina, resting her head on my lap, wearing her too-cute-for-my-own-sanity pajamas. We're trying to finish *The Godfather* trilogy tonight, but she's too tired to make it to the end. A few minutes later, her breathing evens out and I see that she's fast asleep and looks so fucking beautiful that it hurts. I gently smooth away the stray hairs from her face, and she shifts slightly to get more comfortable. Looking at her this way, I'm reminded again of what I almost threw away and how I'm the luckiest son of a bitch.

As soon as Sabrina said those words on the street a couple of weeks ago, I felt relief wash over me unlike anything I've ever experienced before. It took every ounce of strength not to ravish her immediately. Instead, I slowly kissed those delectable lips of hers until she was a little breathless. When she opened her eyes, I still could see traces of the raw hurt that I caused her, and it killed me to know that I was the one to blame for it. But I deserved that and a hell of a lot more. I'm more than aware of how fucking lucky I am that she's willing to give me a second chance, and I'm going to do everything in my power to make sure she knows how much

I love her. I want to see those gorgeous green eyes of hers light up, make her smile, and more than anything, trust me again.

"Baby, do not apologize for making me wait," I'd said to her on the street, while still gripping her, afraid that she'd come to her senses and disappear like she did before. "I'm the one who fucked up, not you. Ever."

She'd tilted her head before she spoke again in a soft voice that just about ripped my heart out. "Well, I am sorry, and I know that sounds crazy, but it's true."

Before I could say anything, she'd placed her finger on my lips and I couldn't help but grin at her determination. "Here's the thing...I know that whatever it is between us was meant to be. I mean, you'd have to be crazy not to see it or feel it. But I'm not going to lie to you and tell you that I'm not afraid you'll hurt me again, because I am...very much so. I don't know how we'll fix this, Tyler, but I'm willing to try."

There it was, my second chance at redemption...and I wasn't going to fuck it up this time.

In the time we were apart, I was a goddamn mess, especially those first couple of days. I must have gone through two gallons of Jameson whiskey, straight. My liver probably hated me for it, but I didn't give a flying fuck. I wanted to drown out all the emptiness until I couldn't remember jack shit. Jimmy showed up at my apartment after not being able to reach me on the phone for two days, and he was pissed off. Even worse, he was disappointed in me. After I got my ass handed to me on a platter by him, he tried to talk me off the ledge and told me what I already knew, but didn't think I could pull off.

"If you love her and you want her, then you better get your ass in gear and fight for her."

See, Jimmy didn't know too much about me and Sabrina's past. That ten years ago, I was the one that comforted her when she caught her boyfriend and best friend about to fuck each other's brains out. How it took everything in me to walk away from her that night when she looked up at me with those sad eyes of hers. I know that if I had tried, I could have kissed her and probably more...and God, I wanted to. So fucking bad. I had wanted to get close to Sabrina Chandler for a long time, but I was never good enough for her, or at least that's what I'd been telling myself. Now I'd gone and proved all of that with this latest epic fuck-up. And all these years later, I can still hear my dad's voice in my head, clear as a goddamn whistle, as I told Jimmy about my history with Sabrina up until now... *You stupid, worthless piece of shit! You'll never amount to anything!*

When I believed Ava's bullshit lies, I proved my dad right. I don't even have an excuse. Drunk or not, I fucking failed Sabrina. She trusted me, and I turned around and doubted her at the first moment of uncertainty.

I got my shit somewhat together and put my sorry ass on the flight to Miami I was supposed to take that same weekend. She had no idea I was coming. But, Jimmy was right— I had to show her that I was going to fight for her. I had to do something. I couldn't sit around and feel sorry for myself when I knew she was hurting because of something I did. Somewhere in the back of my mind, I almost believed it would work, that she'd see it as some grand gesture and come back to me. God, I'm such an asshole to delude myself for even one fucking second with that crazy thought. But,

Sabrina did exactly what I would do if I was in her shoes. She walked away. It broke me to watch her do that, but I had to give her the time she needed. And honestly, I never in a million years thought she'd come back, so when she did....

Fuck, when I saw her standing there, it nearly gave me a heart attack. She looked so achingly beautiful and nervous that I wanted to sprint across the street and never let her go. But then she apologized, and that made me even more disgusted with myself. Because if there is one thing I'm certain of, it's that Sabrina has nothing to be sorry for other than falling in love with an asshole like me. I'm the one who doesn't deserve her...and it's not lost on me that I told her the exact same thing when that dickhead cheated on her ten years ago. So whatever miracle happened to lead her back to me, I was going to make damn sure she knew how much I cherished her.

After the initial shock from finding her on my door stop wore off, I've been careful in the last couple of weeks not to move things too fast for her sake. It's been hard as hell trying to restrain myself, because I'm dying to love every part of her body whenever I'm around her. Words feel inadequate; I need to show her somehow. But first, I need her to feel more comfortable at the thought of us being together, emotionally committed, before we take the next step of being physical again. I need her to trust me a little more. Because she is the single-most perfect thing in my life. The one thing that makes sense and makes me want to be a better man.

The sound of gunshots blares out from the television, startling Sabrina from her nap. She moves off of me, and I instantly miss the warmth of her body. I nudge her back to me, and she nestles herself into the crook of my arm to place her head on my shoulder. She sits tucked closely to my side and attempts not to doze off during the movie again; it's fucking cute as hell watching her fight it. I bring my head down to place a kiss on her forehead, and she pops her head up with a small smile playing on the corners of her mouth that is both adorable and sexy as fuck. I lightly run my thumb across her lips, before watching her take my wrist and turning my hand, palm up, to place a soft kiss in the center. My dick twitches in my jeans at the sight, but I'm trying to play it cool. Then she goes and tucks her hair behind her ear, which makes me want to keep her close and protect her. I stop short and instead start rubbing small circles on her back with my hand. Sabrina molds her body to my side, closer than before, so that I feel every soft and feminine curve of hers. With that, I find myself struggling to keep from taking her right here on this couch.

"Are you tired, baby?" I ask softly, while gathering her hair in my hand to sweep off of her shoulder. I tilt her chin up a little and brush my lips against hers before I ask, "Do you want to call it a night?"

She once told me that she could drown in my eyes, but I'm the one who's drowning when she lifts her heavy-lidded emerald eyes to mine and parts her lips to answer. "I guess I'm a little tired."

Her hand grazes the side of my face, and I turn my cheek to place a kiss in her palm. She smiles sweetly, and my heart hammers in my chest watching her as she lazily stretches out and eventually lays her head back down on my lap. I hear a low moan of contentment escape her throat right before she relaxes further into the motion of my hand sifting through her hair. Not even ten minutes later, she's fast asleep.

A quick glance of the time says it's just past midnight. I feel guilty having to move her, but I can't let her stay on this couch, even though it's comfortable as all hell. Carefully, I scoop her up in my arms and she lets out a small sigh. I swear to Christ, she's going to kill me with those little sounds she makes. If that wasn't enough torture, she burrows herself into my neck while wrapping her arms around my neck. In turn, I hold her tighter to me and place a kiss on her cheek before finally crossing the threshold into her bedroom, which is in complete darkness.

I lay her down on the bed, and she immediately crawls under the covers with her eyes still shut as if on autopilot. I bend over to tuck her in and go to give her a kiss good night before letting myself out. She smiles when my lips lightly touch hers and her eyes flutter open.

"I don't want you to leave. Stay with me," she says dreamily.

Fuck me... I don't want to leave her either.

"Baby, I don't think that's such a good idea."

She shakes her head. "Sleep here with me. I want to wake up in your arms."

How can I say no to that? I can't. Whatever she asks for, I want to be the one to give it to her. I want to make it all better.

"Okay, I'll stay... but no funny business."

She giggles and moves over to make room while I start to get undressed. Keeping only my boxer briefs on, I lift the comforter and climb in beside her, enjoying the warmth of the spot that her body left behind. Pulling her tight to my chest, I turn her onto her side so that I can spoon her, and my arm wraps possessively around her waist. I close my eyes and know that I am never going to let her go. I want to be right here with this woman who stole my heart so long ago.

"Tyler?" she asks so quietly into the darkness that I can barely hear her.

"Right here, baby."

"I love you."

"I love you, too."

I don't know how I manage it, but I pull her even closer, molding her body to every part of mine perfectly. The cadence of her breathing signals that she's starting to doze off again, until I hear her dreamy voice.

"You promise?" she asks.

"I promise."

ACKNOWLEDGEMENTS

Belinda and Christian, thank you for putting up with me all those nights that I stared at my laptop and ordered take-out just so I could finish this book. Your beautiful smiles are the reason I did this to begin with. I love both of you, more than you will ever know...Infinity X2. And I owe you guys a vacation or a few days at the beach.

Kyle, thank you for putting up with me for the past few months. I love you, baby, always. I wish that I could have granted your request of having a hot dog cart scene included within the actual book, but here's the best I could do: Tyler runs away to NYC and leaves Sabrina in the dust to live out his dream of being a hot dog cart vendor, THE END.

Luisa Hansen, "editor" is such a formal term for someone who has come to mean so much more to me. I consider you a close friend, confidante, and a generally awesome person. Thank you for your encouraging words and faith in me from the beginning and convincing me that I am a writer. Thank you for your honesty, which has always made me want to push myself to work harder and make you proud.

Lisa Chamberlin, who knew that our mutual love of one little curse word would bring us so closely together? Thank you from the very bottom of my heart for every single chapter read, every suggestion, every time you made me laugh, every time I went a little crazy, every little single thing. I love you like the lost sister you are to me. You are the cream of the crop...the best book buddy a girl could ever ask for. (Cue up the Bette Midler.)

Dionne Simmons, my best friend of almost 30 years. I love you, woman. Thank you for reading each chapter as I handed them to you and providing the encouragement that you have for pretty much my entire life.

Sandra Cortez and Sara Queen, my fellow voxy ladies/ besties. Thank you guys for putting up with me while I lost it every so often. For offering all kinds of encouraging words and support. For goofing off with me. For making me laugh so hard that I needed Depends. Thank you more than anything for being the amazing lifelong friends that you are to me. I love you guys!

Claribel Contreras, thank you for all your support and encouragement over the last few months. Thank you for letting me ask all kinds of questions and never ever once saying that you were too busy to answer. In the words of our favorite band, "I get by with a little help from my friends." Love ya and Strawberry Fields, here we come!

Jessica Carnes, thank you, well for just being amazing! Thank you for taking time out of your days and nights to read my little book and providing such great feedback. Every single note and comment you made has brought me closer to realizing my dream. You, my sister friend, are the best!

Angie McKeon, there are not enough words to say thank you for everything you have done for me. Your support astounds me on a daily basis. You stepped in and stepped up and have always had such faith in me. I love ya, chickie!

Crysti Perry, without you this would have never happened, so thank you for making my dreams come true. Between you and LaStephanie Kannady-Foster telling me that I should keep going from that very first submission of my prologue to the Kindle Buddies contest, you will never be forgotten.

Angela McLaurin at Fictional Formats, thank you for the beautiful work you've done with my words and for putting up with every single question I've thrown your way. You are awesome!

Thank you to every blogger, big and small, who helped in spreading the word on *Promise Me.*

Sarah Lowe, thank you, my young Padawan, for being Team Tyler from the very beginning and checking in with me to see where I was in the writing. You always put a smile on my face.

Fred LeBaron, thank you for believing in me. Your encouraging words have helped more than you know.

Michelle Finkle, Ciara Martinez, Dyann Tufts, Missy Malachin, Daisy Medina Esquenazi, Becky Lowe (Sarah's mom LOL), Yvette Huerta, Elle Smith, Lizzy Henriquez, and Natasha Conde, thank you ALL for making me smile over the last few months; know that there are no better book buddies in the world!

To all my close friends and family...I love you ALL and thank you ALL for your support over the years and hopefully many to come.

To all my author friends in ANGTFD, thank you ALL for making me feel more than welcome and always providing great advice, support, and encouragement. You guys rock hard!

And finally...a big thank you to all the authors who have inspired me over the years with their words.

ABOUT THE AUTHOR

 Barbie Bohrman was born and raised in Miami, Florida. She moved to New Jersey after earning her associate's degree in liberal arts at Miami-Dade Community College. She currently resides in the Garden State with her two children. Her hobbies include movies, great TV shows, reading, reading, and even more reading.

She is currently working on her second novel.

Connect with the author at:

Facebook: https://www.facebook.com/pages/Barbie-Bohrman-Author/170019943145037?ref=hl
Goodreads: https://www.goodreads.com/author/show/6875784.Barbie_Bohrman
Twitter: @barbie_bohrman